Kelly McCullough

Magic, Madness, and Mischief

SQUARE
FISH

FEIWEL AND FRIENDS

NEW YORK

W9-BRW-775

SQUARE
FISH

An imprint of Macmillan Publishing Group, LLC
175 Fifth Avenue, New York, NY 10010
mackids.com

Our books may be purchased in bulk for promotional, educational, or business
use. Please contact your local bookseller or the Macmillan Corporate and
Premium Sales Department at (800) 221-7945 ext. 5442 or by email at
MacmillanSpecialMarkets@macmillan.com.

Library of Congress Cataloging-in-Publication Data
Names: McCullough, Kelly, author.
Title: Magic, madness, and mischief / Kelly McCullough.
Description: New York : Feiwel & Friends, 2018. | Summary:
"A 12-year-old boy uses his new magical powers and the help of a snarky
fire hare to defeat his evil stepfather in a magical version of St. Paul"—
Provided by publisher.
Identifiers: LCCN 2016037929 (print) | LCCN 2016050558 (ebook)
ISBN 978-1-250-29420-3 (paperback) | ISBN 978-1-250-10782-4 (ebook)
Subjects: | CYAC: Magic—Fiction. | Ability—Fiction. | Stepfathers—Fiction. |
BISAC: JUVENILE FICTION / Social Issues / Depression & Mental Illness.
Classification: LCC PZ7.M4784149573 Mag 2017 (print) | LCC PZ7.M4784149573
(ebook) | DDC [Fic]—dc23
LC record available at https://lccn.loc.gov/2016037929

Originally published in the United States by Feiwel and Friends
First Square Fish edition, 2019
Book designed by Liz Dresner
Square Fish logo designed by Filomena Tuosto

10 9 8 7 6 5 4 3 2 1

LEXILE: 830L

This book is for Laura, as always.
It's also for my mother, Carol, who worked so hard to make sure
I got into the Saint Paul Open School. I can't even imagine how
different my life would have turned out without that.

1

Fire's Child

FIRE RAN THROUGH all my dreams and I ran after it, the blackened ground crackling beneath my feet. It wasn't the first time I'd dreamed of chasing the fire. I dreamed the flames whenever we moved—eight times in my thirteen years on the planet—and when I'd started at my new school, and right before my mom married Oscar . . .

And that was it; I was awake. I glanced at the clock—my mom was old-fashioned, like, still-reads-the-newspaper old-fashioned, and wasn't going to let me have a cell phone until I turned fifteen—3:08 a.m., sigh. Might as well get a glass of milk and read for a while. I flipped back the covers and started to get out of bed.

That's when I discovered that the sound of the world starting to change is a sort of scratchy, scuffing rasp. It felt like there was sand on the floorboards.

What the heck?

I leaned over and flicked on my lamp. The soles of my feet were covered in gritty black powder. I ran a fingertip along my heel—soot, or something very like it. And more on my sheets. I started to freak out a little at that point, because I couldn't think of any reasonable explanation, and if there wasn't a reasonable explanation, then I might be going . . .

I suddenly felt sick to my stomach. Leaping out of bed, I bolted for the bathroom. I made it as far as the kitchen before I almost tripped over my mother. She was sitting cross-legged in the middle of the kitchen, wearing a full-skirted red dress. All the houseplants were lined up in front of her, and she had a small trowel in one hand. She was singing:

"Daisy, Daisy, give me your answer true. I'm half—" She broke off as she noticed me.

"Oh, hello, Kalvan, what are you doing out of bed? I'm repotting the plants."

At three in the morning? I wanted to ask. But I didn't. It was a long way from the strangest thing she'd ever done. My stomach lurched again, and I forced myself to ignore it for the moment. Being gentle with Mom was much more important than my problems.

"What was that you were singing?" I asked.

"'Daisy Bell,' or 'On A Bicycle Built for Two' . . . Well, one variation on it, anyway. I like to sing to the plants. They listen so well, and it helps them grow." She smiled her lopsided smile and rose to her feet, coming to put her hands on my shoulders and look down into my eyes. "Perhaps I should sing to you more often."

I snorted. Genevieve Monroe *was* a tall woman—much taller than me, her only child, though I hoped to catch up to her not quite six feet in the next year or two. She was also pale, almost shockingly so in contrast to the thick, soot-black hair that hung nearly to her waist. I was much darker—like my dad, she always said. But I had my mother's strange amber-brown eyes.

Strange. That was a good word for my mother. It covered everything from finding her repotting plants at three a.m. in what appeared to be a formal gown to her insistence on sending me to a series of weird schools that had culminated in the five years I'd now spent at the Free School of Saint Paul—a magnet program for the children of people who believed that traditional education stifled creativity. Most of all, *strange* was a kinder word than some I'd heard used to describe her.

My mother looked over my shoulder. "What on earth?"

I turned to follow her gaze and saw the trail of smudged black footprints leading back to my room. "Um . . ."

She let go of my shoulders and stepped around me, squatting so that her red skirt pooled around her feet like a circle of fire. She ran a fingertip across one of the prints and lifted it to her nose, sniffing.

"Ash and char." She spoke as though she were remembering something from long ago and far away. She tilted her head to one side and half sang, "Ash and char, sun and star, wind and smoke, ash and oak . . . No, that's not quite right. How did it go?"

"Mom?"

She jerked as though startled. "Sorry, Kalvan, I got lost there for a moment."

"What was that you were saying?"

"Nothing, a couple of old rhymes your grandmother Elise used to sing to me at night. There was another one that felt the same even if it didn't sound it, but she only sang it on the solstice and the equinox and the turn of the seasons. She said it was important to keep an eye on the North's changing Crown, whatever that meant. Now, what was that other verse . . . Summer's King, brings the birds a-wing, Winter's Queen, draws wolves so lean, Queen of sun, harvest done, King in ice, death's the price . . . something like that, anyway.

"But there I go meandering again." She smiled and shook her head before rising to look down at me. "*You* had better go wash your feet while I clean up here. I don't think your stepfather would be very understanding about the ashes of burned dreams." She made a shooing motion. "Hop to it—tomorrow's a school day."

It wasn't until I was back in bed and half-asleep that I thought to wonder how my mother had known the soot came from my dreams, or to remember how freaked out I'd been about the whole thing before I talked to her. But then, my mother had that effect on me—making the odd feel normal, and the truly bizarre no more than passing strange. It could be scary.

Sometimes it seemed like she wasn't entirely of this world, like she'd wandered in from one of my books about wizards and elves and the misty lands of faerie. It made her a weird mix of fragile and frustrating. I spent half my time wishing I was something out of stories, too, so I could protect her, and half of it wanting to just be part of a normal family with normal problems. I tried to follow that thought further, but sleep had too strong a grip, and before I could chase it very far, I fell once more into dreams and darkness.

The harsh beeping of the alarm felt like someone poking me in the bridge of the nose with a fork, and I half fell out of bed in my rush to shut it off. Saying that morning is not my best time is like saying our Minnesota winters are not the warmest. Forty Below, meet Kalvan when he wakes up: you have a lot in common in the misery department.

That's why the clock was on top of my bookshelf on the far side of the room from my bed. If I can reach the snooze button without getting out from under the covers, I will keep hitting it over and over without ever actually waking up. I blinked at the clock now as I smacked it repeatedly in an effort to get it to shut up—6:15 a.m.!

I felt a brief stab of panic. The bus came at 6:20, and there was no way I could even walk the five blocks to the stop in— *Wait, Kalvan, think it through. The alarm went off at 6:15. That must mean I set it for 6:15, right? So, what was I thinking . . .* I shook my head and tried to clear out the worst of the cobwebs. *Nope, nothing.* I was going to miss my bus.

Just then, my stepdad, Oscar, stuck his head into my room. "Get a move on, Kalvan. Your mom's already gone, so I've got breakfast waiting on the table. We need to be out the door by six forty-five."

I blinked at him stupidly. "What?"

"Move!" he growled. Oscar spent a lot of his time growling. Well, when he wasn't snapping, snarling, or shouting, that is.

My stepfather had a temper on him, and zero patience. Add in that he was a big, burly man, and there was something very troll-like about him. That illusion seemed even stronger than usual this morning, as some trick of the light made his face look as if it were carved from granite and his eyes were as hard and cold as a pair of blue glass marbles. I blinked and rubbed my own eyes then. Red light flared across my vision like dancing flames, and I thought for a moment that I smelled smoke. When I looked at Oscar a second time, he looked even more like a man of stone.

He frowned, and it seemed a miracle that granite could move like that. "Come on, speed it up." Then he was gone from my doorway.

His words came out as a command, and I found myself moving to obey without really thinking about it. Grabbing a pair of socks, some jeans, and a T-shirt from the pile of clean clothes my mother had left on my dresser, I bolted for the shower. I snagged my egg-and-bagel sandwich off the kitchen table as I went by and wolfed it down while I waited for the water to get warm.

After a few minutes, the fact that I had simply done as told like some kind of zombie finally registered and I shook my head angrily. I didn't like that one bit, but I still hadn't sorted out what was going on, and I tried not to fight with Oscar unless I had a very good reason. Especially in the morning when I'm stupid and slow. I *can* win an argument with him, but I have to think fast and make a good case . . . And even when I do win, the end result can look a lot like losing.

Five minutes later I was hopping around as I tried to get my still-damp foot to go the right way into my pants leg. Shirt was next, and then socks. Brushing my teeth ate up a few more precious minutes. When I came out of the bathroom, Oscar was waiting impatiently in the back hall, though he looked human again. Oscar works for a civil engineering firm specializing in highway projects, and he had on the retroreflective vest he always wore for on-site stuff.

That's when I finally woke up enough to remember what the late start was all about—Oscar's current project was in the same direction as my school, which meant he could drop me off along the way. That saved me an hour and change on the bus and bought me an extra twenty minutes in the sack.

"About time!" He tossed me my backpack, which I quickly slung over one shoulder. "Why your mother lets you sleep that close to when you have to leave, I'll never understand."

Because she's got even stranger sleep habits than I do? Because she knows that even fifteen more minutes on the morning side of things makes a huge difference in how well I deal with the rest of the day? Because she's a better person than you are? Of course, I said none of that.

It would only have made Oscar grumpier than he already was, which he would take out on me now and Mom later. Instead, I grabbed a jacket off the coat tree and opened the door for my stepfather. We didn't get along very well, and I had no idea what my mom saw in him, but she needed stability in her life. Oscar was nothing if not stable and predictable, kind of like that geyser at Yellowstone, Old Faithful—right down to the eruptions you could set your watch by.

Oscar and I didn't talk on the way to school—we'd both figured out long ago that us talking in the morning always ended badly. I just slipped into the passenger seat of his big gray Crown Victoria and pulled out a book. Mercifully, it was a brief ride—ten minutes to my downtown school. The janitor was just unlocking the doors as I got there, and he smiled at my sleepy wave.

Score one for weird schools. At a normal school, I'd have had to wait in the office or something until more of the teachers got there, but freedom and personal responsibility are what the Free School is all about. So, I was able to head up to my advisor's homeroom—which was also the school's black box theater—and crash out on a beanbag chair for another forty minutes of catnapping.

At lunch I couldn't bear the thought of spending any more time inside than I had to. So, I headed for the playground in back of the old high school building, which the Free School had taken over. There were probably a dozen other kids heading the same way. Most of them had bag lunches and wanted a chance to hang out in the sun instead of the cafeteria. Others were skipping lunch, or trying to catch a quick game of pickup basketball before heading back in.

At the Free School, lunch is an open period for everybody and you can do pretty much whatever you want, though eating is strongly encouraged. Hmm . . . maybe I should explain open periods for those of you who went to regular schools. At Free we put together our own schedule in consultation with our parents and advisors.

You have to learn all the stuff you would at a regular school, but not necessarily in the same order, or in class. So, if you're reading above your grade level, they won't make you take a class with other kids your age. They'll let you test out of it and offer you the chance to take a literature or drama class a couple of grades ahead so you stay challenged.

They're also super into "unstructured time," or open periods. Everybody has at least one class hour a day that's not scheduled. Some kids use it to play games, or read a book, or write software— whatever you're into. In addition, everybody gets to run a bit wild at lunch.

When I got outside, I saw my best friend, Dave, already sitting on the broad concrete railing that surrounded the playground, a science fiction novel in one hand—books were one of the things we had in common. He waved and smiled as I got closer, and I couldn't help but grin back at him. We'd been tight for about three years now, and he's the sunniest person I know. I'd never understood the idea of an infectious smile until I met Dave. He's got these ridiculously white teeth and skin a couple of shades darker than mine that really makes them shine, and you just can't help but smile with him.

"Hey, Kalvan. Is it Monday enough for you?"

I shook my head ruefully. "I am soooo not ready for it to be the second week of school. What happened to summer?"

"Poof!" He made a popping gesture with his fingers. "But I bet we could grab a bit of it back, if we wanted to . . ." He jerked his chin toward the big wooded hill to the north of the school.

I knew immediately what he was thinking. The hill was the perfect place to sit and read or talk on a sunny afternoon. We'd discovered that the previous school year. And, to be honest, the idea of slipping off for a bit had been in the back of my mind from the moment I'd decided to head for the playground. Things always go chaotic around noon because of lunch and the fact that it's the time of day when a lot of the older kids go off to internships or classes at the local college. People are coming and going like crazy, with kids everywhere doing all kinds of things. It's hard for the teachers to keep track of everybody, which makes it the perfect time to skip out of school for a bit. And this was one of the best places to make the break.

I hopped up onto the concrete beside Dave and pulled a book out of my backpack. We chatted and pretended to read while keeping an eye on Pete—the teacher monitoring the playground. When he went to break up an argument among the basketball players, I rolled off the low railing, hooked my backpack over one shoulder, and dashed across a bit of open lawn to drop into the ditch that ran behind the gym. Dave was right behind me.

The school is built on a steep slope and the ditch keeps the building from flooding. It also makes a great escape route. There aren't many windows on the gym side of the school, and you're much less likely to be spotted going out that way. Now, all we needed to do to make it clean away was duck around the corner and into the hedges that separated the school from the government buildings around the capitol and . . .

"Hello, Kalvan, Dave." I froze as, turning the corner, we nearly ran smack into our principal, Aaron Washington—a tall, black, balding man, though still fit for his age. "Where are you headed on this lovely day?" He smiled as he asked the question, but I knew we'd be in trouble if we couldn't come up with a good answer.

I quickly held up the book I hadn't yet put away. "We were just trying to find a quiet spot to read." As I spoke, I felt a strange heat at the back of my throat, like cocoa on a cold night, or a campfire in the darkness.

"Not planning on sneaking off school grounds, I hope."

I wanted to say no and look innocent, but my mouth didn't want to listen to me. "Thinking about it," I replied with a broad smile as the heat spread from my throat to my lips and tongue. Out of the corner of my eye I saw Dave giving me a *what-are-you-doing!* look—I ignored it. "But we weren't going to sneak off very far, Aaron."

Calling all our teachers and even the principal by their first names was among the hardest things I'd had to learn when I first started at the Free School, but that was one of many tricks the school used to "break down habits of authority." Aaron raised an eyebrow at that, but didn't say anything.

I lowered my voice conspiratorially. "If you follow this hedge back up the slope, you can get to the stoplight behind the court building—which is the safest place to cross over to the big hill." I pointed at the top of a steeply wooded slope visible above the building behind the school. "There's a spot just below the brow of the hill where the afternoon sun is perfect for reading." I shook my book gently.

Aaron's other eyebrow went up, and Dave looked positively gobsmacked. "That's very . . . honest of you. I take it you two've been there before."

I smiled fire and nodded. "It's one of the places Evelyn"—our drama teacher—"takes her roving theater class to work outside. She says the natural setting helps put our minds in a different place from the school environment. She also has us pick up trash as part of our service-to-community requirements."

The Free School was big on service learning, and on taking responsibility for things that had to get done. Anyone who spent any length of time at the school quickly learned that the answer to the question "If not me, then who?" was almost always "*me*." It was another aspect of our whole Freedom Is Responsibility motto.

"We figured we could do a bit of cleanup before we started reading, right, Dave?" Dave nodded rather bemusedly as I reached into my half-open backpack and pulled out a plastic bag from the convenience store. "You know, *if* we were sneaking off school grounds to read a book during the open period at lunchtime, which, of course, we're not going to do . . . and not just because we got caught." I grinned another fiery grin. "No, because it would be *wrong*." I made the puppy eyes of innocence.

Aaron actually chuckled now. "That's probably the most charming lie I've heard from a student in the last ten years— Evelyn is an excellent acting teacher, and I can see why you're one of her favorite students." He turned his gaze on Dave. "Did you have anything you wanted to add?"

Dave just smiled that big smile of his and shook his head. "Not right at this moment, no. I think Kalvan's got it covered."

"Wise move." Aaron assumed a stern expression as he shifted his attention back to me. "However, I can't countenance your leaving school grounds. While the Free School might encourage you to make use of open periods to do whatever most appeals to you in hopes of producing a more well-rounded human being, the State of Minnesota frowns on students leaving the grounds during school hours without a specific educational purpose in mind and written permission."

"I understand that, Aaron." I felt as though I were filled with a fire that warmed without consuming.

"Good." Aaron nodded. "So, I'm going to continue my walk

around the building now, and I would like you two to tell me that you are not going to be off to the hedge as soon as my back is turned. I would also like you *not* to drop off that bag filled with trash from the slope in the trash bin out in front of my office no later than the end of sixth period. Do you understand me, Kalvan, Dave?" He didn't smile, but there was a certain light of mischief in his eyes as he spoke.

"I believe that we do." I nodded. "It's been nice talking with you, Aaron. Thank you for helping keep us out of trouble, and we are absolutely *not* going to sneak away once you're out of sight and carefully cross the street behind the school with the walk signal and go read on the slope, are we?"

"Not a chance," agreed Dave.

"And not pick up trash," added Aaron.

"Definitely not."

"Excellent, then we all understand one another."

"Perfectly." I nodded, and Dave echoed me.

Without another word, Aaron walked around the corner of the school, leaving us alone.

"What just happened there?" demanded Dave.

"No idea." I wasn't ready to share the sense of being filled with fire. Dave looked like he wanted to argue, but I shook my head. "Let's at least get clear before we talk about it."

As we ducked into the hedge, I tried to sort it out for myself. I'm pretty good at talking my way out of trouble with adults, but I'm not *that* good. It felt almost like magic. I was confused, but I didn't let the wonder I was feeling or the fire roaring away in my soul prevent me from quickly heading for the hill, with Dave trailing closely behind.

As soon as we got to the base of the slope, we ducked into the undergrowth. There was a narrow slot of a path that we followed upward. Maybe twenty feet along, Dave bent and picked up a plastic soda bottle and handed it to me. "Get the bag out."

I nodded. "I should have thought of that."

"I don't know what happened back there with Aaron, but if we don't drop off that bag of trash, we'll be in deep weeds." His words came out a bit wheezy from the climb, and he pulled out his asthma inhaler to take a brief hit.

As we finished filling the bag and settled into the little dell below the brow of the hill, Dave gave me a curious look. "Speaking of which, what *did* happen back there?"

I paused for a long time before answering that because I didn't want to lie to Dave, but the truth was going to sound pretty crazy, and crazy was not a thing to talk about lightly between Dave and me.

Finally, I just plunged in. "You know about my mom."

It wasn't a question. It was one of the things that had drawn Dave and me together after we got to know each other. I don't like to use the word *crazy* about my mom, but it saves a lot of time. My mother is more than half-crazy. Or mentally ill, if you prefer the technical term. Dave gets this in ways that most people simply can't because his dad is bipolar and pretty intermittent in taking his meds.

Dave's mom had kicked his dad out because she was afraid he might hurt one of the kids, but he still tried to be a part of their lives when he could. My mom might not have a formal diagnosis, but Dave had eaten a number of meals at my place, and he knew the score. There were conversations we could have together that neither one of us could have with someone who hadn't been in the same place.

Dave nodded. "And . . ."

"When Aaron caught us, I suddenly felt . . . like, well, I could talk my way out of *anything*. It was like I was full of fire and I just knew that whatever I said was going to be the right thing to say and that it would work. Does that sound crazy to you?"

Dave looked a little sick. "Yeah, I'm sorry, Kalvan, but actually it does. My dad can get like that when he's in one of his up phases."

I felt like he'd kicked my stomach, and I must have looked it, too, because Dave quickly held up both hands, like he wanted to soothe me. "On the other hand, when my dad's up and starts spinning lines, he isn't half as smooth as you were back there. Heck, I've heard you spin a few in my time, and *you're* not usually that good. Also . . ." He frowned and trailed off.

"Also what?" I demanded. That was part of our deal. If either one of us started to go the way our parents had, the other was supposed to play the voice of reality.

"Well, what you did *was* weird. I could kind of feel it in my guts. That patter wasn't aimed my way, but it felt like you were . . . I don't know, *projecting* convincing more than being convincing. I could see it affecting Aaron and felt the edges of it, but I didn't feel the need to buy into it."

He shook his head. "I don't know, Kal, the whole thing was hinky." He sighed. "Why don't we talk about something else?"

"All right, but you'd tell me if you thought I was going like my mom, right?"

"That's the deal we shook on." He nodded solemnly.

"Thanks, Dave. I need that."

"Hey," said Dave, "you getting pressure from Evelyn to start thinking about what you want to do with your life? She bugged me about it this morning."

It was an awkward change of subject, but I was happy to move away from the shaky ground of the previous topic. "Yeah, what's up with that? We're barely thirteen."

Dave laughed. "But this is the *Free School*, land of making your own path in life, and it's never too early to start exploring the possibilities. Am I right?"

I had to laugh then, too, and nod, because yeah. All the choose-your-own-adventure stuff could get a little old. "I told her I was mostly thinking about lunch at that point in the day, and she gave me that look."

And here Dave mimed looking at me over a pair of imaginary glasses. "Yeah, I bet she loved that. I told her I'd gotten as far as thinking that maybe I wanted to be an actor, and since that's her thing, I was totally off the hook for a while."

"I could see doing that." Acting *was* my favorite class.

On the other hand, and especially given my morning, what I most wanted in life at the moment was to grow up to not be like my mom. Acting was cool, but it wasn't exactly a normal kind of career, and sometimes what I really wanted from life was a little bit of normal.

Only, that wasn't really true, either, because every time I tried to do normal I got bored, and I didn't do well with bored. Not at all. It gave me too much time to think, and then my brain went weird places and . . . I shied away from that thought. When

I had too much time to think, I started to think too much like my mother.

That's a lot of why I skip so much. Free was better than any of my old schools because I got to take at least some of my classes with the older students, and that pushed me a lot harder. But not all the time, and not all my classes. Reading helps, and exploring or doing something physical helps. But even at Free they expect you to pay attention and participate when you're actually in class. It's just easier to get out of my own head when I'm alone or hanging out with one or two people.

Neither Dave nor I mentioned it again over the next half hour, but the fact that he'd said I was sounding a bit like his dad lay heavily between us until his phone beeped from the depths of his pack.

"Ooh, I gotta go. I can't miss this next class." He hopped to his feet. "Are you coming?"

"Nah, I think I'm gonna stay here. I aced the entry test; I can afford to miss a few science classes."

"All right, catch you later."

"Back atcha."

Dave had been gone for ten minutes when I looked up from my book and saw a bright flash of red at the base of the lilac thicket that walled us off from the crest of the hill. My first thought was that I had spied a fox—I'd seen them in the city once or twice before. But a moment later I got a better look, and no fox ever born had ears *that* long or such a stubby little tail. A rabbit . . . no, it was far too big and rangy for that. A hare, then, but one of very unusual color.

"Aren't you fancy?" I whispered, not wanting to startle it into bolting. "I don't think I've ever seen such a beautiful hare before. Would you like some of my muffin?" I'd decided to save it for later, and now I reached cautiously into my backpack.

The hare cocked its head to one side. "Depends. What kind is it?"

"Banana nut," I replied, then froze. "Wait, did you really ask me what kind of muffin this is?"

"Of course not," the hare said in a masculine voice dripping with sarcasm. "You know as well as I do that rabbits can't talk. Now, cough up the muffin."

2

Burning Hare
and Other Worries

THE HARE WAS absolutely right. Rabbits can't talk. Silently, I split the muffin and offered him half. I figured if we both pretended he couldn't talk, we might both believe it, and then I wouldn't have to panic about ending up like my mom.

The hare took the muffin in both paws and bobbed his head. "Thank you, cousin. May the turning seasons bring you fair fortune."

Then he flared like a fresh-struck match, bursting into flames so bright I had to shut my eyes. When I blinked them open again, the hare was gone, leaving behind a blackened piece of muffin that crumbled to ash when I poked it with the toe of my shoe.

Suddenly, hanging out on the hill didn't seem like such a good idea anymore. I quickly tossed my stuff into my bag and went down the slope at something just shy of a run. I half wanted to head back to school and pretend that most of today had never happened, but we were well past class change and that meant sneaking in would be *much* harder.

Besides, I'd long since learned that class was not a good place for me to be when I was flipping out. Unless it was an active class or a topic I really loved, there simply wasn't enough going on to keep me distracted. Without that, I'd just keep going round and round on the thing that was worrying me until I felt like my brain was eating itself, and that was no good. So, where to go that would give me something else to think about?

I considered crossing one of the freeway bridges and heading down to the science museum, but that felt like too much work. It was most of a mile from my school to the Mississippi and the museum. I had a couple of bucks, which meant I could go down to the Doughboy bakery outlet and get about a bajillion week-old snack cakes and chocolate rolls. Yeah, that was *exactly* what I needed. A sugar buzz to amp up every mental twitch. Well, and . . . I looked at the half a muffin again and shook my head. I'd had enough problems with baked goods for one day.

Then I had it: the capitol tunnels! Because of the Minnesota winters, most of the state government buildings were linked together by underground tunnels. No one would be down there on a sunny fall day, so I'd have the run of the place. And sometimes they left access doors open and you could get into some pretty cool spaces. It was the perfect distraction.

I headed over to the court building. The security there actually made it easier to get in. Well, for a kid anyway. I marched in with my notebook out and started scribbling away as I wandered toward the metal detector, like I was doing some sort of class project.

When I slipped my backpack off my right shoulder and dropped it onto the X-ray machine belt, the security guard cleared his throat and said, "Notebook, too."

"Oh, I'm really sorry. My teacher didn't mention that." I waved vaguely in the direction of the Free School—capitol security was used to Free School students wandering all over the place.

Being this close to the state government apparatus meant we had a lot of kids doing internships or coming over to watch hearings and other "real world" learning experiences. Apologizing again, I stuck my notebook in the bag and went through the metal detector like I belonged there. A few seconds later, I took a flight of stairs down to the tunnels and I was home free. Well, more or less. There were still cameras and a few capitol police, but if you didn't act guilty they'd usually leave you alone.

I wandered aimlessly for twenty minutes or so before passing a half-size door in a passage under the capitol. I'd noticed it on previous trips and always wondered where it went, but whenever I'd checked the knob it was locked. This time, it was slightly ajar. Glancing around to make sure there weren't any adults looking my way, I quickly tugged it open and ducked through.

The low-ceilinged tunnel beyond was half full of thick cables and conduits and only dimly lit by a series of bare red bulbs mounted in little cages on the wall. It was surprisingly clean and *very* warm, and the walls and floor were covered with a thick coat of slick gray paint. I had to practically bend double to keep from banging my head on the pipes that crossed the ceiling every twenty feet or so, and I put my backpack on both shoulders to keep it from slipping off. But that was fine. I actually really like tight spaces. *This* was going to be a great adventure!

I followed the low tunnel for what felt like blocks, periodically passing doors in the walls or hatches in the ceiling before coming to a downward bend where I had to descend a narrow metal ladder to continue. Beyond, the construction went from cement to huge limestone blocks, which didn't hold the gray paint very well.

The passage opened up below, and I could almost walk upright, though I still had to watch for low-hanging pipes. It widened out as well, though part of the space was taken up by stacks of waxed boxes along the left side. Each was marked with a big red stencil that said CIVIL DEFENSE SUPPLIES.

Maybe fifty feet on from there, I came to a huge steel hatch in the floor, like something you'd see on a navy ship in a movie. It opened onto a ladder descending into darkness. I wished I'd thought to bring a flashlight along, because it looked interesting and there was no way I could climb down there without one.

I pulled an empty soda bottle out of my trash sack and dropped it into the hole. I counted as I waited for it to hit bottom, but after hitting thirty without a sound, I figured it must have landed in something soft. *Oh well*. I started to move past the hatch, then froze about ten feet later when I felt a sudden and overwhelming sense of presence, as though something enormous had just awakened and noticed my existence. I pressed my back against the nearest wall and froze.

My heart started to pound like it wanted out of my chest, and my mouth prickled like I'd stuffed a whole handful of Pop Rocks in there. I had never wanted to be someplace else more in my entire life, but the only way that I *knew* led out went right past the hatch and the hole it covered—the hole that centered that feeling of *presence*.

My feet were all for running down the tunnel away from the hole. And, frankly, I was with my feet on that. There was nothing in the world I wanted more than to get away from that hole, but a little voice in the back of my head kept saying *What if*.

What if it's a dead end? What if you still have to come back this way, but with a lot more time to think about it? What if what's ahead is worse? What if IT wants you to run that way?

I didn't know what IT was, and I didn't want to find out, but the surest way out was the way I'd come in. Slowly, I inched my left foot closer to the hole in the floor. It took all my will to move my body after it and get the other foot to follow, but I did it. One dragging step at a time I edged closer and closer to the hole.

When I was finally passing the hatch, I didn't dare look in for fear of seeing something looking back at me. Maybe a gigantic dragon eyeball peering through the hole like a person at a keyhole, or one of those horrible, twisted faces you see in dreams, or something so much worse I couldn't even imagine it. I fixed my gaze on the ladder up to the newer tunnel section and forced myself to keep moving.

Maybe five feet farther on, I broke and bolted for the ladder. That was when I heard the laugh, a harsh chuckle that rumbled like an avalanche. It came from deep within the earth. Or perhaps deep within my head. I couldn't tell the difference in the moment. All I knew was that it belonged to something that hated me.

Run, child of fire. Run far and fast, but never free. No. I know you now, and you are marked. Then the chuckle broke into a full, rolling laugh I half expected to bring the stones down around my ears.

I banged a knee and skinned a knuckle climbing the rusty old ladder to the upper tunnel, but that didn't slow me down. I took the rest of the low hall in a hunched-over run and burst through the door at the end as though I had a whole tribe of demons on my heels.

Fortunately, there were no guards around as I crashed out into the main tunnel, because I'd probably have flipped out completely if someone tried to stop me from getting as far from that little door as possible.

My luck held all the way to the nearest set of steps up into the capitol proper, where I finally remembered that I needed to act like I belonged if I didn't want to spend the rest of the afternoon in Aaron's office answering hard questions or worse. I didn't think my mom or Oscar would be at all happy to have to come downtown and have a chat with the capitol police. I'd spent enough time in the capitol on my various visits, authorized and un-, that I knew the quickest way out to the front doors and sunlight.

Once I got out there, I kept right on going until I was back on school grounds and down in the little drainage ditch behind the gym. By my watch I'd missed the class change and American Government, which meant I had forty-five minutes till the next bell rang and I could get in without arousing suspicion, so I found a sunny spot out of the wind and settled down with my book.

It was a fantasy novel with really creepy elf-like creatures that lived underground and had skin like stone, and I found my heart battering the walls of my chest once again as I read about them. After a few minutes, though, it occurred to me that this was probably where the whole sequence in the tunnel had come from—a book with a similar setting, and my own *very* active imagination. I'd scared myself often enough over the years that I'd pretty much convinced myself that was the answer by the time I dropped my trash bag in the can by Aaron's office.

That answer was soooo much better than the one that included thinking about a talking hare or the weird feeling that had come over me when I talked to the principal. Because that answer meant I wasn't going the way of my mother.

A thought occurred to me then that had never crossed my mind before: If I went mad, who would take care of her? I sure couldn't trust Oscar to do it. It hit me like a rock in the teeth.

Please don't let me be going the way of my mother . . .

"Rise and shine, Kalvan!" A woman's voice, big, musical, and full of bombast—Evelyn Hulsing, the Free School's drama teacher and my advisor.

Wait, what? I blinked my eyes open and it took me a moment to realize that I must have gone down super hard when I tucked myself into a beanbag chair in my homeroom after Oscar dropped me off this morning. Normally I just kind of dozed, but the clock said it was time for classes to start. Hopefully this Monday wouldn't go as weirdly as the last one had.

Finally, I remembered my manners. "Hello, Evelyn. How are you?"

"It's a beautiful September morning with the sun rising like Juliet in the east and the birds singing away as the seasons turn. How could I be anything other than delighted to be alive?" She spread her hands expansively, then swept past me on the way to her desk.

And that was Evelyn to a tee, always sweeping or rolling majestically, or stomping. She never just walked anywhere, and she never missed an opportunity for a grand gesture. She was five foot nothing and couldn't have weighed more than a hundred pounds, but she didn't just teach drama, she lived it. I adored her for that, and it probably saved my life.

Because my mother. Okay, maybe I should back up just a touch, so that makes sense. I'm a dreamer, day and otherwise. My imagination is always running away from me. Sometimes so much so that I can get a little vague on the here and now. That would probably be okay if it weren't for my mom. She's not just *vague* on the here and now, she's only an occasional visitor—a situation I really didn't understand until I was around ten. Once it sank in, though, my own mental flights of fancy took on a much darker tone. What if I was the same way?

I don't think I can possibly express what that means to anyone who hasn't grown up with someone like my mom in their life, but it's not good. Not even a little bit. It's completely terrifying, and I'm not at all sure what would have happened to me back then without Evelyn. I ended up in one of her theater classes at about the same time the whole mental illness thing was sinking in and I started really freaking out.

It was an improvisation exercise about three years ago . . .

Evelyn stood at the front of the room by the stage.

"All right, boys and girls, this next exercise is all about creativity and learning how to let it take you places you didn't know existed before you got there. I'm going to start the music playing and I want you to let it create a scene in your head. Once you've got a place to start, I'd like one of you to get up on the stage and start acting out that scene. We'll do this a lot over the term, so everyone will get a chance to open a scene. This time we'll just go with whoever comes up with an idea first."

She smiled at us all. "But acting is as much about sharing as it is creating. So, next I want someone to get up there and join in whatever scene is going on. I'd like the person who started it to go with what the second person does and let them move the scene forward. As the scene goes on, I want more people to go up. If you run out of things to do, come down off the stage and make room for someone else. Ready?"

We all nodded, and Evelyn left the stage to start the music. I've always been a little shy, and I was petrified by the idea, but even before the music started, Dave poked me in the ribs.

"What?" I whispered.

He grinned at me, white teeth shining bright in the dimly lit space below the stage. "You're always coming up with cool games for us to play, knights and dragons, or spacemen, or whatever. You should be great at this."

I didn't think so. I didn't think so at all. But the second the music started, a picture started painting itself in my head. It was dramatic sneaky music, and I couldn't help thinking of one of the video games I'd been playing the most lately, where you're this super thief in a medieval setting. Half against my will, I found myself getting up off the floor where I'd been sitting and heading for the stage.

When I got there, I pretended to sneak in from the side and started trying to open the shutters on a window. It didn't really exist, of course, but I could see it sooo clearly in my head. It was real to me. A minute or two later, this older girl—the Free School emphasizes working across ages, and you might have students in four grades in an average class—named Millie came up and started walking a beat like a castle guard.

After that, more kids joined in and it changed into something modern with a chase and a shoot-out, and I got shot and fell off the stage. It was a ton of fun and I forgot all about how real the unreal parts of my life felt for a while. But then, when the class was over and it was time to leave, Dave told me how cool my idea was, and I realized how much I'd believed it in the moment, and that scared the bejeebers out of me.

That's when Evelyn came over and asked me to stay a minute after class. She wasn't my advisor then, and I absolutely *knew* she'd seen how much trouble I had separating my daydreams from reality and that's why she wanted to talk to me. I started sweating like crazy over going crazy, and it was all bad.

"Kalvan?"

"Y-yes, Evelyn." Here it comes . . .

"You did really well up there today. I don't think I've ever had a student your age leap into their first improv like that before. More than that, it was a good scene. You convinced me you were really trying to break into a building and really got the scene off to a great start. You have a talent for acting and a truly creative mind. That's a rare gift, and I'd like to see you develop it. Tryouts for the school play will be coming up soon, and I want you to promise me you'll come out for the auditions. Will you do that?"

I nodded mutely, and she smiled that huge, dramatic smile of hers. "Excellent! I look forward to it."

I started to turn away, then stopped and turned back. "You really think what I did up there was good?"

She nodded.

"Because usually people are trying to get me not to . . ."

"Not to what? Indulge your imagination? Live inside your head instead of the *real world*? Spend so much time wool-gathering?"

"Yeah." *Woolgathering* was practically Oscar's favorite word for me.

"They're wrong." It was a flat declarative statement with no room for argument. She went to one knee, putting her face more on a level with mine. "Creativity is one of the things that makes us human. Some people have less. You have more, and that's magnificent! I don't know whether you'll settle in theater or move on to some other art, but it's clear to me that you were born to create, and the world needs that. Don't ever let *anyone* tell you different."

The next day we did more improv, and I was a bit less terri-fied to try it and a little more willing to let my imagination carry me away. And again, Evelyn encouraged me. By the end of the semester, I'd started to see my dreams as a gift instead of the first signs I might be going crazy, and I'd asked to transfer into Evelyn's homeroom.

I still had days where I was afraid I might go the way my mother had, but I no longer lived in fear of my own imagination, and that was thanks to Evelyn. Lately, though, I was starting to worry again. Because if I wasn't cracking up, then I seemed to be wandering headfirst into a Harry Potter novel or *The Lion, the Witch, and the Wardrobe.*

It's a weird sort of problem. I read a lot of books with magic in them, and it always irritates me when the lead character spends a ton of time dithering about whether the magic is real or not. On the other hand, I *wasn't* in a book . . . or at least I didn't think I was. In my life so far, I'd run into zero magic and a fair number of delusions, so you'll have to forgive me if I'm more likely to believe in the latter.

The rest of my advisory group started trailing in after Evelyn arrived. There were fourteen of us in Evelyn's group, which kept it small enough to feel like a family. Free is a tiny school with three hundred students scattered from kindergarten through twelfth grade. Dave and I are the youngest in Evelyn's group, though we've only got one actual senior. Morning advisory group was just a fifteen-minute check-in. Afternoons run half an hour, and once a week we had a two-hour advisory meeting, as well as monthly whole-school get-togethers. I knew everybody within a few years of me, and even if I didn't like some of them, it was generally more like not liking a cousin than the bullying and stuff that used to happen at my old school.

After check-in we all headed down to the cafeteria for breakfast, where I saw Aleta on the way to eat with her girlfriend. She waved and paused, but I just waved back and shook my head.

Aleta's seventeen and my student mentor, but we don't other-wise run in the same circles, so I try not to bother her if I don't really need it. Every new kid gets assigned an older student to help them figure out how to make it in the Free School. It's a good system.

Mind you, it does lead to sharing tips and tricks for ducking out of classes and other things the adults would prefer we not do. Take, for example, hiding out in the gym wing of the school . . .

After stuffing a banana, some Froot Loops, and a carton of milk into my pack—I wasn't hungry enough for a second breakfast quite yet—I ducked out of the caf and headed straight for the gym. I needed some time alone to get my head straight.

The gym's basically a separate building with an enclosed hallway and some low stairs that connect it to the main school. It also doesn't get used much. Free's only phys-ed teacher also teaches math, so there's only three hours of gym a day, all after lunch. That makes it a great place to hide out in the morning if you've got an open period and know the tricks for getting in—all of which Aleta taught me in my second year, once she'd decided I wouldn't rat her out.

Trick number one is the lights. There are very few windows in the gym building, so it's really dark and that can be kinda scary, especially at the back of the hall that runs along the side of the gym. To make things worse, it doesn't have real light switches, just these slot thingies for light keys, but Aleta taught me how to use a nail to flip the switches.

The first switch was just inside the big steel fire door between the main building and the little hallway. As soon as I was through and into the darkness beyond, I bent down and felt around behind the radiator till I found the finishing nail we always left there. Once I had it, it was the work of a moment to slip the tip of the nail into the slot in the switch plate and . . .

FWAZAAM!!!

Blinding light, an impact like someone had hit my hand with a hammer, a sharp fizzy taste in my mouth, and fire burning in my head.

3

Hare, There, and Everywhere

THERE'S THIS MOMENT when something very fast and very bad has happened where you're kind of sitting there full of nothing but blankness, trying to figure out if you're still alive or not. That's where I was now as I attempted to blink the stars out of my eyes and the fizzing copper taste out of my mouth. I honestly didn't know where I was or how I'd gotten there.

"What the . . ." I mumbled, then jerked as I saw the words fly out of my mouth and take wing like little firebirds before each vanished into a puff of smoke when they hit the ceiling.

POOF, POOF . . .

It took me another long moment to realize the ceiling was directly in front of me . . . which meant I must be flat on my back. In turn, that meant the short flight of stairs that looked like I was about to walk down them were really above me and I was lying at the bottom.

I blinked some more and tried to reconstruct what had happened. The last thing I remembered was waving at Aleta, which reminded me of the gym, and . . . oh. I sat up and looked around. I was at the base of the stairs in the little hallway, about ten feet from the light switch, which . . . oh again.

The long black scorch mark on the wall was impressive enough in an I-am-in-sooo-much-trouble-if-I-get-caught kind of way, but that wasn't what really grabbed my attention. No, that was the bright-red rabbit hanging by its ears from the switch plate. Its front legs were crossed in front of its chest in the classic disappointed-parent pose, and the look on its face made me want to melt into a puddle and drain quietly away.

"Um, hello?" I waved a hand vaguely at the rabbit—no, hare; I was pretty sure it was the same one.

"Jerk," replied the hare, confirming my guess.

"What?"

"You heard me, jerk."

"I . . . uh, do you need some help?"

"No, of course not. I love hanging by my ears where any mortal with half a hint of the sight could spot me at a minute's notice. Or worse, one of the delvers might come by and decide to skin me. It's my favorite thing in the whole wide world!"

"Oh, good, I'm glad you're not . . ." I trailed off as the hare's rolling eyes belatedly twigged me in to his sarcasm. Normally, I'm better with that stuff—it's Oscar's favorite parenting mode—but I'd had quite a shock. Both literally and figuratively.

"I'm sorry. Let me see what I can do." When I stood, the whole world went purple and wobbly and I had to grab the handrail, but I managed to stay on my feet and drag myself up the stairs.

As I got closer to where the hare was hanging, I saw that the nail I'd used on the light switch had half melted, curving into a downward-pointing hook. Somehow, that had pinned the hare's ears to the wall, though I couldn't think of any natural explanation for that. Or, well, *anything* about this situation, really.

Closer still, I saw that the hare had a pair of tiny red stone hoops through his ears about halfway down, and the nail was bent through those. "I don't suppose you know how I can get that loose?"

The hare's eyes rolled again. "Conjure and abjure me, of course. I don't know what they're teaching you children these days."

"Huh?" I realized my mouth was hanging open and snapped it shut.

"Do you have wax in your ears, boy? Or are you simply too dumb to know the meaning of words?"

"N-neither. I heard you, and I know what conjure and abjure mean." I ought to; I'd read enough fantasy novels where someone summoned a genie or demon or something.

"Well, then, get it over with. It's your summoning. But you'd better believe I'm going to make you pay for it when I get my freedom back."

"Freedom?"

"Are you sure you're not an idiot?" asked the hare. "Because from where I'm sitting you're really starting to sound like one."

"But I didn't summon anyone!" Which sounded whiny even to me.

"Then how exactly did I get here, do you suppose?"

"I don't know. How did you get to the hill last week?"

"What the . . . wait. You're serious." The hare swore venomously. At least, I presumed he was swearing—I recognized the tone if not the language, which sounded very hot and crackly. Finally, he slowed down and gave me a hard look. "Tell me exactly what you were doing before I wound up here hanging by my ears and you ended up down on the floor staring at the ceiling."

"I don't know. The last thing I remember clearly is the cafeteria."

The hare clenched his jaw for three long beats, opened his mouth, closed it again, then sighed. "Speculate. I presume you've been here before. How did you get here, then?" He waved a foreleg around vaguely.

I explained about the gym and the nail and the light switch, realizing for the first time that the lights were on—so that much had worked, anyway. "Do you know anything about how you got here?"

"There was a great burst of fire, and someone called my true name in the summoning mode. Come here and let me examine you more closely." He looked me up and down. "Right hand."

It was only as I extended it toward him that I noticed char on the tips of my finger and thumb, though I didn't feel any pain. He sniffed at my hand and humphed.

Then, "Open your mouth and say *ahh*." He practically stuck his head in there as I leaned in close. "Yep. That's it, then. It's all over you."

"What is?"

"Words of fire, words of smoke, words of ash, and words of oak."

"Excuse me?"

But the hare didn't answer. Instead, he shook his head and sighed. "What are the freaking odds, man? What are the odds?"

I leaned against the nearest wall and slid to the floor, putting my chin on my knees rather numbly. "I don't understand this at all." This was it—I was going crazy.

"Clearly!" Then he sighed again and his expression softened. "Here's what I think happened. I think you came in here like an idiot and stuck a nail in an electrical fixture like a complete moron and then you got electrocuted, as any sane person would know to expect."

"So, this is all just a hallucination?" I asked rather hopefully— it shouldn't count as going crazy if you'd just electrocuted yourself, right?

"Sadly for both of us, no. If you were an everyday sort of human they'd probably be packing you off to the emergency room about now . . . well, assuming you survived the experience, and that you had the sense to make your way out to someplace they'd notice you before you passed out. Which, I might add, I wouldn't bet a flash or a flicker on."

"I don't understand again."

"Well, of course not. I'm a long way from finished, and I'll never get there if you keep interrupting me."

"Sorry."

"You should be, and not just for that. This predicament I'm in is all your fault. Now, as I was saying. Idiot, complete moron, insanity, and Luck's fool."

"Luck's fool . . ." The hare gave me a sharp look and I snapped my mouth closed.

"Electricity is fire's tricksy sibling. You might be a young fire lord in the making, cousin, but you've no business messing with the lightning even if you've a limited sort of affinity. And that's exactly what you've done. When you took that shock it not only threw you down the stairs, it also must have caused you to convulse pretty badly. I'm guessing you shouted mid-convulsion and by the hand of Luck or Fate you blurted out my true name in the shout."

"I . . . okay. But how? And why?"

"Well, if it was Luck, I'm guessing I've irritated her somehow and you're my punishment. Wouldn't be the first time. And if it's Fate, well, I don't like to think about that at all. Not here in the deeps of the fall fallow. In either case, I'm stuck here on your word, and it's you who'll need to get me loose."

"How?"

"This again? What's wrong with you? I'm the one who's pinned up here by my ears with a blinding headache. Conjure and abjure me, of course. Then you can free me."

"All right, how?"

"Am I really going to have to hold your hand through the whole thing? No, don't answer that. It's obvious." He sighed heavily. "Say, 'I conjure and abjure thee, insert my true name here, and—'"

I held up a hand. "Wait a second, I don't know your true name. You'll have to tell me what it is if you want me to do that."

He looked positively scandalized. "I am NOT telling you anything of the kind. If I did, you could command me to serve you for the rest of your life."

"I wouldn't do that."

"Sure, you say that now, but once you had the power in your hands? I do not trust you half so far as I could fling you."

"All right, then, how do I get you loose?"

"Conjure and . . . oh. Drat. That is a conundrum. And it's ALL YOUR FAULT." The hare crossed his forelegs angrily again and clenched his jaw tightly shut.

My stomach growled then and I remembered the food in my pack, which was . . . ah, there, at the bottom of the stairs.

"Where are you going?" demanded the hare.

"To grab my snack."

"Without getting me loose?"

"I haven't any idea how to, and even if I did, I'm not entirely certain you're real. If you come up with something, let me know. Until then . . ." I shrugged. I was hungry. Besides, food was good. Food was normal. Food didn't tell you that you were some kind of child of fire.

A few moments later I settled down against the wall again. "Banana?"

The hare sighed. "No, but thank you. . . . Wait. Yes." As I proffered the banana, the hare suddenly froze mid-reach. "Noooo, that'd never work. Would it? It wouldn't obviate the summoning or cut me loose of you, that's sure. But it might get me down off this wall, which solves the immediate problem. What do you know about use names?"

"Not a single thing."

"Good. You're about to learn the bits I think you need to know. Given the way this all started . . . hmm. Yes, that will do nicely. Call me Sparx."

"Sparx?" I nodded. "All right."

There was a long silence before the hare put his face in his paws and shook his head as well as his pinned ears would allow. Finally, he said, "Repeat after me: 'I conjure and abjure thee, Sparx. By fire and smoke, by ash and oak, by the flame in the darkness and the powers it awoke.'"

"All right." If it worked, the stupid hare would be out of my life and I could go back to pretending I'd never met him.

So I did. Nothing happened. Before I could speak, though, he angrily held up one paw. "'I conjure and abjure thee, Sparx. Come now and do my bidding.'"

I repeated that as well, and with a flash and a pop the hare vanished from the wall and reappeared on the floor in front of me.

"Oh, hallelujah, it worked." Then he took off like all the hounds of hell were after him, racing headfirst into the nearest wall. He hit with a THUD I could feel through my feet before bouncing off and landing on his back on the floor. He looked so stunned I half expected little cartoon birds to appear and fly around his head.

"Are you all right?" I knelt and reached out toward him, though I didn't quite dare touch him.

"What in the ever-loving fires of blame just happened?"

"You ran face-first into a wall like an idiot and bounced off it like a complete moron, as any sane person would have known to expect."

"That sounds vaguely familiar," replied the hare. "Also, touché. However, and for the record, I'm a spirit of fire and I am not, under normal circumstances, subject to the rules of the material world."

"So, what happened with the wall, then, smart guy?"

"I have no freaking clue."

"Do you need a hand getting up?"

"No!" With a sudden twist the hare was back on his feet.

"Maybe we should go talk this out." I pointed toward the gym.

"Sure, why not? There's nothing in the world I'd like better than to spend more time with someone who conjured and abjured me into magical servitude. We spirits of the elements absolutely adore us some bringers and binders. It's just all love and . . ." He ran down and gave me a bit of a sheepish look. "Over the top?"

"A little, maybe. After all, it *was* an ACCIDENT!"

The hare rocked back onto his hind feet and held his paws up placatingly. "Hey, no reason to get all yelly about it. Yeesh. All right, let's go talk."

There was another eight feet or so of hallway at the bottom of the stairs, ending at the next steel door. I pulled the door open and was just starting to step through when a blur of red went past my ankles and shot away into the hall.

"See ya, suck—URK!" About thirty feet down the hall the hare came to an abrupt halt like a yap dog hitting the end of its leash, as he once again ended up flat on his back.

When I caught up to him he was swearing in that strange crackly language full of hisses and sizzles and sharp popping sounds. After a while he spat out one last fiery word so pungent that it actually flared briefly in the air in front of his face before it puffed into smoke.

"You okay?" I asked.

"No. I am not okay." The hare's voice sounded husky and

harsh, as though he really had been yanked back by a collar around his throat. "Nor am I all right, or any other human inanity. I am, in point of fact, bound to a mortal sorcerer, burn and blight you."

"I'm not, you know."

"Bound?" he growled. "Of course not!"

"No. A sorcerer. Not by any means or measure." Nope, I was just going slowly mad.

"Not even, say, the binding of spirits of fire? Because your binding is what just kept me from making my exit stage right."

"I . . . Well, when you put it that way, I don't know what to say."

He raised a paw like a student in class.

"What?" I asked.

"Say yes. Because, in the only way that matters from my point of view, you are definitely a sorcerer, and not the good kind."

"I'm sorry! I'd release you if you'd just tell me your true name and how to do it."

"Not happening, kid. Look, can we try an experiment? Because this has been a really crappy day for me and I'd like to know exactly how bad it's going to get."

"Sure, what do you want to do?"

"*I'm* going to lie here on the floor and try to get my throat to stop feeling like I swallowed a hedgehog, and *you* are going to walk back up the hall to that door and a little bit past it. But not far past and not very fast. Do you understand?"

"Sure. But—"

"Just go, please."

I shrugged and went. When I got to the door I turned around so I could see Sparx, and then I began slowly backing up. As I passed the edge of the frame I felt a faint tugging sensation in the hand with the char marks from the nail. I also noticed that Sparx seemed to be moving with me, though at this distance it was hard to be sure.

"Stop," called the hare. "Come back." As I got closer I could hear him mumbling to himself. "Right, I'm in hell. And it looks exactly like an American high school. Is anyone surprised? Yeah, didn't think so."

I squatted on the tile beside him. "*Now* do you want to talk about it?"

"Fine. Whatever. I can't see what good it'll do, but we're stuck with each other for the moment, so we might as well chatter away like a couple of airheaded sprites."

"My teachers all say communication can solve a lot of problems if you give it a chance."

"Of course they do," said the hare. "They're liberal, crunchy-granola tree huggers. They probably use words like *dialoguing* and want you to *be in touch with your feelings*. Barf!"

I didn't bother to answer. Instead, I headed to the far end of the hall, where someone had parked an old desk and some big metal shelves in a corner. Climbing them got me up to ceiling height, where I was able to push aside one of the tiles in the drop ceiling and go from there to the top of the wall between the hall and the locker rooms. Sparx followed me up as nimbly as a cat.

Putting the tile back in place left us in complete darkness. I had added a little LED flashlight to my bag after the incident under the capitol, but I didn't bother getting it out. We weren't going to be there long. Past exploration had told me everything I needed to know about the area. It was full of dust and cobwebs, and the top of the wall was the only solid footing. Which was too bad, because the narrow space between the true ceiling and the tiles was pretty cool in other ways. Tight and secret and protected. I'd always loved places like that—closets, the hidden space behind the drawers under my bed, the low tunnels through the underbrush on the hill above the school.

I raised a ceiling tile on the other side and climbed down to the top of the lockers. The first had had its door ripped off by some previous student, and it made a dandy ladder. The gym beyond was dimly lit by a few high and filthy clerestory windows, so I didn't turn the lights on, just climbed to the top of the bleachers, where the windows normally gave me enough light to read.

Going up there also made it dead easy to hide by ducking between the benches if someone did poke a nose into the gym—no teacher ever bothered to climb all the way to the top to check. Setting my jacket on the floor between the top two benches as a pad, I settled in and put my back against the side wall.

Sparx perched himself on a bench a few feet away. "It's your nickel."

"What? I'm confused again."

The hare sighed. "About a million years ago, in the days before cellphones stalked the earth, there used to be these things called pay phones that allowed you to make calls from public places by putting coins into them and . . . Forget it. You're too young for that to even be funny anymore. You wanted to talk. Talk." He settled back on his haunches and crossed his front legs impatiently.

"I . . . uh . . . That is . . ." What *did* you say to a magic hare that you didn't entirely believe in?

"Very enlightening. Do you always make this much sense? Or is it my lucky day? I have lots of those, you know. I've got four lucky rabbit feet. *Ba-dum-tsh!*" When I didn't respond, he shook his head. "Come on, kid, that was a joke—you can tell by the rim-shot noise—work with me. Laugh."

"I'm not really in a laughing mood."

"Why's that? I'm the one who's bound in durance vile, and you're the wicked sorcerer who put me there. Oh, and there's clearly something wrong with my powers since I can't seem to walk through walls to save my fuzzy soul. I'm the one who ought to be down in the dumps, not you."

It was my turn to sigh. "Well, one of two things is true. Either I'm going crazy like my mom"—but then I shook my head—"which, at this point I'm going to put aside, because I'm pretty sure I'm not clever enough to hallucinate something as simultaneously sarcastic and preposterous as you."

"Or?" The hare cocked one ear forward.

"Or, you're for real and magic is for real."

"I'd think you'd be all over that. I mean, you kids love Harry Potter, right? And this makes you a boy wizard."

I snorted. "Those are more my mom's books than mine, though she did make me read them and I like them well enough. It's more that if magic is real, I'm going to have to believe in a

bunch of other stuff besides you, and some of that's pretty scary."
I thought of the presence in the tunnels under the capitol with a shiver.

Sparx nodded. "Oh, sure, there's all kinds of nastiness in the world—delvers and drowners and devourers galore. But they've always been there whether you believed in them or not. At least this way you can see them coming and maybe do something about it—though it's more likely you'll simply have a bit more time to think about what's about to happen to you than the magic-blind get."

"Not helping." Because if magic *was* real, my little "adventure" in the tunnel wasn't anything like my books and movies and games, the ones where the good guys always win in the end. It meant I'd been taking risks far beyond what I could have imagined.

The hare shrugged. "Suit yourself."

"I— Hang on, is that the time?" I shot to my feet as I read the clock on the far wall.

I must have been out for longer than I'd thought after my shock. Class change was going to ring in about five minutes, and it would take most of that to retrace the path I'd taken to get here. I had math next, which was one of the few classes where I was doing badly enough that I didn't dare skip very often, and I needed to hustle to beat the second-hour bell. I didn't want anyone seeing me coming out of the gym right now. Not with that melted nail and the giant scorch mark on the wall to explain.

Snatching up my bag, I bounced down the bleachers with Sparx leaping after me. "Hang on, kid. Weren't we supposed to talk this out? What's the rush?"

"Later. Got to get to class now!"

I slipped and nearly fell as I slithered down the pile of furniture in the hall outside the locker room, but I landed running. When I hit the steps up to the main building I felt a sudden sharp tug on my pants leg.

It was Sparx. "Kid, kid, wait up!"

"I told you, I don't have time right now. I can't afford to make a scene coming out of the gym. Oh, and my name's Kalvan, not kid!"

"All right, chill. But if you don't want to make a scene, what do you think is going to happen when you hit the hall out there with a flaming-red bunny trailing you?"

I stopped halfway up the stairs. "I . . . Wait, what now? Aren't you invisible to most people?" He hadn't ever said it explicitly, but that had pretty clearly been the implication of some of the stuff he'd talked about.

"Normally, yes, mostly. But normally, I can walk through walls, and get more than ten yards away from my summoner. We won't know if I'm visible to mortals now until we test it out. Do you want to do that the hard way?"

"No." Though it would be further proof this was all real . . . "No. Definitely no. Good point." I opened my backpack and set it on the floor. "Get in."

"Are you kidding me?"

"Look, I don't have time to argue. We need to go *now*." I made a shooing motion and he reluctantly poked his head and forepaws into the bag. That was enough for me. Though I suspected he was going to make me regret it later, I put one hand on his butt and shoved him the rest of the way in.

"HEY!" But I was already zipping it closed.

"Hush, you can yell at me all you want once school's over. Until then, if you don't want to find out the hard way if you're visible to everybody, you might want to shut it."

"You're going to pay for this, kid, I promise you that."

"Surprise, surprise, you're—" But the bell rang just then and I bolted up the last few steps and through the door, praying I didn't come out in front of any—

Oh, crap. Josh Reiner, one of Free's few bullies.

4

Elementally Yours

"HEY, KALBELLS, WHATCHA doing in the gym all by your lone-some?" Josh asked. "Figure that's the only way you can win at dodgeball?"

I bit back the impulse to argue about rhyming my name with *bell* instead of *pal*; it wouldn't get me anywhere, and it would let Josh know he'd scored. I *hated* that name, and I *really* didn't want Josh to have any idea how much.

I was *still* trying to think of a suitable comeback when Josh stepped in closer and dropped his voice. "What's in the backpack, Kalbells?"

"Huh?" *Argh,* that'll *show him.* I was sooo not good at the snappy-comeback thing today.

He grabbed at my bag. "The backpack, Chuckles. I saw it move. Whatcha got in there? You bringing your mom to school to protect you?"

At the words *your mom* my vision flashed as red as if the whole world had filled with flame. Without thought or pause I slugged Josh in the nose as hard as I could.

Josh's hands flew to his face. "Son of—"

"Boys, my office, now!" The principal seemed to appear from nowhere.

"Aaron—" I began, still furious, though the fire was fading from my vision.

He pointed. "Office."

I dropped my eyes. "Yes, sir."

Josh didn't say a word, just nodded with his hands still pressed tightly to his nose. I saw blood on his fingers and felt a certain amount of triumph at marking him up. He was two grades ahead of me and probably half again my size. Still, I winced at the sight. I was in sooooo much trouble.

The principal visibly sighed. "It's not *sir*, Kalvan, it's Aaron."

"Even when . . ." *Stop digging and start walking, Kalvan.* "Yes, Aaron."

He nodded as we headed for the principal's office. "Better. And, yes, even when you're in trouble. Maybe *especially* when you're in trouble. It's important to our mission here at Free that you learn to think independently, and that's a lot harder to do when you're under pressure from an authority figure. We want you to build the habits that will let you do that once you've grown up and gone out on your own. Do you understand what I'm saying, boys?"

Josh silently nodded again and a little more blood leaked out. Aaron pulled a handkerchief out of his pocket. "Here, use this." He looked at me expectantly. "Well, do you understand?"

"I think so?" I said uncertainly.

"One of our explicit goals in founding the Free School was to help nurture future generations of artists and thinkers and, well, intellectual rebels. A society needs the people who do the day-to-day jobs and the normal type of leaders, and a lot of schools work to shape those people. But it also needs those who aren't satisfied with 'because we've always done it that way,' people who will stand in the way and say no when the crowd is all heading in the same direction."

The boys' room was on the way to the office, so we stopped outside for a moment while Josh went in and cleaned up his face and got some tissue to stuff in his nose. When he came back out Aaron took a good look at him and said, "Right, my office first, then you're off to the nurse afterward."

"Cad I go dow?" Josh asked, sounding rather pathetic—acting, I thought, and not particularly good acting.

"Not yet." Aaron shook his head. "It doesn't look broken, and I've seen you get and give worse and walk it off. I do want Marsha to take a look at it, but it'll keep for a few minutes."

Josh nodded glumly, then glared icy death at me when Aaron looked away. I felt the look like a gut punch, and his muddy green eyes seemed to whirl and swirl like eddies in a swamp. No matter what happened in the next hour or two, things were a long way from over between us. When we entered Aaron's office, he pointed at chairs in front of his desk.

"Sit."

I put my backpack on the floor by my feet.

"Now, tell me what happened; Kalvan first."

My heart suddenly started to beat faster as I faced the eternal dilemma of being in trouble with teachers and parents—how to get the mix of truth, omission, and lies just right to minimize punishment without coming off as unbelievable.

There was no way on earth I was going to tell him about Sparx and the magic stuff. That would probably get me sent for a psych evaluation, so it was completely out. Speaking of which, just then I heard the very slight sound of a zipper and glanced down to see my backpack quietly opening itself. *Oh crap!* I silently and gently kicked the bag, but the zipper kept moving.

Aaron cleared his throat. Right, one thing at a time—I needed to deal with the principal before I could solve my magic rabbit problem. Considering what I'd done to the light switch, I definitely didn't *want* to tell Aaron about the gym, but I had to weigh up whether Josh would rat on me. I didn't think so—Josh was too much of a troublemaker to want to get a reputation as a tattletale as well. That way led to everyone else deciding it was fair game to rat *him* out. But you never know for sure. On the other hand, I couldn't afford to play the angel, either—Aaron had seen me throw that punch. Even if he hadn't, Josh's nose would have given me away.

So, start with a lie that made me look bad but not *too* bad, and hope Sparx didn't blow up my whole life in the next ten seconds. "I was worried about being late to my math class. I'm not doing very well and I can't afford to get on Scott's bad side"— Scott was our math/gym teacher. "Anyway, I was hurrying and not paying enough attention to where I was going, so I ran smack into Josh—my fault entirely."

As I spoke I felt a sensation of warmth in my throat and across my tongue, a sort of gentle heat like you got sitting near the fireplace. It made a weird contrast with the cold, sick feeling I'd had building in my stomach ever since Josh's glare after he came back from the bathroom.

Aaron looked at Josh, who nodded mutely—I could see his eyes flicking back and forth between the top of Aaron's desk and my backpack, but I didn't dare look down right then. Keeping eye contact was a really important part of convincing someone of the truth of what you were saying—another useful thing I'd learned from Evelyn and my acting classes, though I wasn't sure she'd approve of my present application of the lesson.

"Go on," Aaron said to me.

"Then Josh shoved me and told me to watch where I was going and I called him a freaking jerk."

"Do you think that was a smart response, Kalvan?"

"No." I shook my head, taking the opportunity to glance at my backpack, where a pair of long red ears were slowly emerging—*Argh!* "I ran into Josh and I should have apologized. But he shouldn't have pushed me, either!" I was starting to buy into the story I was telling in a way I didn't normally.

"No, certainly not. Josh?"

Josh whipped his gaze up and away from my bag, his eyes looking more than a little wild—I could almost see him reviewing the conversation and figuring out what his answer was *supposed* to be. "I'm sorry I shoved you, Kalvan, but that was no reason to punch me."

"Then you shouldn't have talked about my mother!" I snapped without even thinking.

Aaron leaned forward. "What did you say about Kalvan's mother?"

I didn't dare look at Josh. This was where the story would either hold together or fall apart. I held my breath. Josh had no reason to do me any favors, but right now he was in less trouble than he would be if I'd told the truth.

It would save *me* even more grief, but Josh didn't know about the light switch. What he or the principal would make of the rabbit in my bag, on the other hand . . . I glanced down to see that yes, Sparx *had* stuck his head out and was glaring up at the other boy. No, not just glaring, he was pointing his paw from his eyes to Josh and back again in the classic *I'm watching you* gesture. What he hoped to achieve by that and how Josh would react, I couldn't even guess, and there was nothing at all I could do about it without giving the whole thing away.

Josh took a deep breath and then mumbled, "It wasn't really anything, Aaron. I, uh, just said 'your mother' when he called me a jerk. It was almost a reflex." As he spoke, I felt my stomach start to unclench—I might actually get out of this without getting too deep into the weeds.

"And then Kalvan hit you?" Aaron asked. Josh nodded and I nodded, and much to my surprise so did Sparx.

"All right. Josh, you've lost your open periods for the next week. You'll be spending them here in the office doing whatever copying and errands Jan needs, or quietly writing me an essay on why you need to keep that temper under control—a thousand words on my desk by next Friday. Understood?"

"Yes, Aaron." Josh nodded. "Can I go to the nurse now?"

"All right, go." Josh got up and left and Aaron turned back to me while Sparx, sadly, stayed right where he was, in plain sight of anyone on my side of the desk. I kicked at my backpack again, but he ignored me.

"This isn't the first time you've been in here by any reckoning, Kalvan. But usually it's for leaving school grounds or skipping class, or some other nonconformance. But I've never had you in here for violence, and I'm quite disappointed in you."

"I'm sorry. I behaved badly, and I take full responsibility for my actions." *Taking responsibility* was very big with the staff at Free, practically a magic phrase.

"That's a good start," said Aaron.

I took a deep breath and looked down at the desk. "May I explain? I don't want to make an excuse or try to justify my behavior, and I'm not asking you to change any decision about my punishment, but I would like you to understand." I closed my mouth and waited—going on if he didn't want to hear it wouldn't buy me anything.

"I'm listening." Listening was another thing they were big on at Free.

"I know I shouldn't have punched Josh, but I'm really sensitive about my mother because . . ." And that was all I could get out.

I wanted to say more, to tell someone . . . *anyone*, about my worries about my mother. About how terrified I was of becoming her and about how I felt the need to protect her, and, and, and! But I literally couldn't make my throat work—all the heat had faded away, leaving behind a hard, tight knot. Worse, *far worse*, I could feel tears starting to burn the edges of my eyes. If I tried to say another word I was going to start crying, and that simply wasn't acceptable.

Finally, I just shook my head. "Never mind. I screwed up and why doesn't really matter. I'll try to do better next time."

I heard Aaron's chair move, but I couldn't even bring myself to look up from the desk as he came around to my side. It wasn't until he was standing right next to me that I remembered about Sparx and frantically shifted my attention to my backpack.

Oh, thank God. The hare had ducked back down into the depths.

"Kalvan." Aaron put one hand on my shoulder gently. "It's all right, really. We all have things we're defensive or angry about. I've met your mom, and I like her. She's probably a little . . . fragile, but, then, a lot of people are. I can understand why you'd want to protect her, but you have to know that punching Josh isn't going to do that. Violence isn't a good answer."

"I do know that, Aaron. I just . . . I didn't even think. It was like my fist punched Josh and then let the rest of me in on the deal."

"That happens sometimes when we're really sensitive about a subject, but it's a response we have to learn to control. Here." Aaron set a slender book in front of me: *Remaining Calm: A Guide to Nonviolent Conflict Resolution for the Young.* "I want you to take this home and read it over the next few days. It's short and I know you read very quickly. When you're done, and no later than a week from Friday, I want you to write me a five-hundred-word paper on other things you could have done instead of punching Josh, better responses."

I took the book. "Thank you. Can I ask a question?"

"Why did I give Josh a tougher punishment?"

I nodded. "Uh, yeah. How'd you guess? I mean, I was clearly more in the wrong here."

"I'm glad you're aware of that. The reason is simple: this is the first time I've had a violence problem with you, and I'm very much hoping it'll be the last. Josh . . . is in here for fighting a lot."

That only made me more confused. "All right, then why isn't he in more trouble than he is? Or if he has such a violence problem, why is he still at Free?"

"Because we're all hoping he can turn it around at some point. Under all that bluster and rage he's basically a good kid in a difficult situation. He's smart and he's an extremely talented young artist, and another thing we believe in here at Free is redemption. Now, take this note for Scott and go catch the rest of your math class."

I took the note and dropped the book into my backpack from as high up as I dared—stupid rabbit—and then zipped it up and headed for the door.

As I crossed the threshold into the outer office, Aaron spoke again. "Oh, and Kalvan, I've had two little chats with you in barely a week. Try not to go for third time's the charm, all right? I'm a patient man and you're a good student, but the ice you're treading is getting mighty thin and I'd rather not have to have a chat with your parents."

"Yes, s—Aaron, I'll try to keep out of trouble."

"That would be for the best. Now, close the door, please."

I was barely out into the hall when I felt a sharp thump in the ribs and my backpack bounced wildly.

"Not now," I hissed, but I could already hear the zipper opening again. "All right, but it's got to be quick—and hang on for ten seconds!"

I quickly ducked into the boys' room. It was empty, but I went into a stall anyway. "What is wrong with you?!"

Sparx poked his head out of the bag. "You mean *besides* being bound in durance vile to a complete chucklehead? Because I've got a long list and you're right at the top, buddy."

"I mean back there in the office! What were you thinking? Josh saw you!"

"You bet he did, and if he hadn't you'd be in three times the trouble you're in now—bent over and heaving your guts all over the principal's desk with a charm of sickness on you."

"I'd . . . wait, what now?"

"That boy was halfway to hexing you into next Sunday. If I hadn't intervened you'd probably have barfed all over me as well."

"Josh?" I was completely baffled—though I *had* felt pretty sick to my stomach there for a bit.

"Of course Josh. Did you not see the sign of bitter water all over him?"

"Bitter water? Josh?"

"What are you, a human echo? That one's a child of water and more than half into the swamps already."

"Swamps?" I asked, though I couldn't help but remember the swirling of those muddy green eyes.

"Echo . . . echo . . . echo." The hare somehow managed to make a noise like snapping fingers. "Wake up, child of fire. You have enemies in this world simply for what you are. If you don't learn to recognize them, you'll be in a world of misery before you half know it."

"I don't . . . wait, why would you even care?"

"Remember that list I mentioned, with being bound to you at the top if it, idiot boy? I may be only half-summoned, but that's enough to put me square in the splash zone if you get squashed. Until I'm shut of you, I need to make sure you don't draw anything that lands hard on me as well."

"Josh?"

"Probably not the boy himself, but if he marks you out it might draw the eye of more serious trouble. The Rusalka Her ownself, maybe. She's a mighty power, and strongest now between the Season Crowns."

"I . . . huh? No, you know what? I don't have time for any of this. I don't know anything about rusalkas and I don't care. Josh is just a bully, but he's hardly a—a bitter-water sorcerer or whatever."

"It's pretty much the opposite of what you are, child of fire. Speaking of which, you're going to have get a grip on that silver tongue of yours."

"What are you even talking about?"

"The persuasion you laid on your principal. You've a powerful gift on that front, and you'd best not let it get away from you any more than it already has. When you back words with the fire of your soul, it can go very wrong very quickly."

"I really don't understand."

He put his face in his paws. "Of course you don't. So, simple words. When you speak, you have the power to make people listen to you, and sometimes to make them believe outright lies.

It's the fascination of fire, and until you learn to control it, it will come on any time you try to hold someone's attention. Each time you use it will make the next easier. But like any power of fire, it can run wild. Compel belief too often or too forcefully and you will come to believe your own lies, losing all touch with truth and reality."

And THAT scared me so much I couldn't even bear to think about it. "Look, I'm already practically failing math and we're barely a week into school. That note Aaron wrote has a time on it, and if I don't get to class soon, I'll be in *real world* trouble. So, right now, I'm done with all this magic stuff. We can talk about all of this tonight. Now, I need you to hunker down, hold still, and, most of all, shut up."

Sparx shrugged. "Suit yourself, but when things start falling on you, don't say I didn't warn you."

Homework, why did it have to be homework? Math. Which made it even worse because I really did have to do it. That's another Free School thing. Teachers like it if you do your homework, but it's not absolutely necessary as long as you demonstrate you've learned the material.

Take science. I ignored homework that covered stuff I'd learned in other ways, like reading science fiction or watching documentaries. Since I was doing well on tests, Tanya mostly let me slide. I'd hear about it in my end-of-semester evaluations when I got dinged a bit for not really applying myself, but I could practically recite *that* lecture in my sleep.

Kalvan is a really bright student and I enjoy having him in my classes, but he could accomplish so much more if he really applied *himself. He seems to have a talent for the material and might even make a good—*fill in the teacher's favorite profession here—*but he just isn't making the effort. I hope he will do better in the next class I have him in. Blah, blah, blahity-blah.*

Actually, that sounded a bit like Oscar, too. It really irritated my stepdad when I didn't leap at every opportunity to mow the lawn or shovel the sidewalk. Like he'd never dodged *his* chores as a kid—*I'm sooo sure.* To hear him tell it, he'd practically run home from school every day—uphill, of course—just so he could push the stinky old lawnmower around and pull dandelions.

At least my mom didn't get on my case about the small stuff. I'd hear about it if I failed math, but as long as I kept learning the things I needed to learn she pretty much let me do what interested me. Some of that was because she and the real world operated at about ninety degrees to each other, but I thought in this case it was more about her thinking process being different than her . . . problems.

"Hey, kid, I think you dropped a variable."

Startled, I turned to look at the hare. "What?"

Sparx rolled his eyes. "I'm beginning to think you have plugged-up ears or something. I said I think you dropped a variable on that problem you're working."

"Wait, you can do algebra?"

"Sure, a little. I'm actually better with calculus."

"You're a rabbit."

"Fire hare, if you please."

"Whatever. Either way, you're a bunny. Since when do you know math?"

"I learned a lot of algebra from this Arabic fellow who

summoned me back in . . . well, let's leave that aside for now—it says too much about my age. The key thing was, he was super hot on the subject, said one of his many-times-great-grandfathers invented the stuff. The calculus came later, of course, but it made more sense to me."

I rubbed my forehead. "I can't believe I'm having this conversation."

Sparx snorted. "Well, you wouldn't be if you were doing the problem right."

That's when my mom pushed my door open and stuck her head into the room. "Honey, who are you talking to?"

"Uh . . . deh . . . dur . . . that is, I . . ." I couldn't for the life of me think of what to say, and Sparx simply froze.

Mom looked from me to my desk to the shelf where Sparx was perched and back again. "Well, dear, I'm waiting."

"Uh, Mom, this is . . . Sparx. He's a rabbit—"

"Fire hare, and it's nice to meet you, ma'am."

I rolled my eyes. "Fine, hare, then. He's . . . um . . . he's helping me with my algebra."

"Oh, excellent! Thank you, Sparx, it's lovely to meet you as well." She turned her gaze back to me. "I know you've been having a lot of trouble with it, and all that happens when Oscar tries to help is that you both go around slamming doors for days afterward. Speaking of which, we'd better not tell him about this; he's dead against pets of any sort."

"Pets!" barked Sparx.

My mom shrugged. "Pets, companion animals, familiars, whatever. He doesn't like any of it."

"You're not concerned that I'm hallucinating?" I asked rather distractedly.

"Of course not. I'd never have gotten through my twelfth-grade composition class if I hadn't met that very helpful hedgehog." She smiled vaguely then and ducked back out of my room, closing the door behind her.

Sparx leaned back and rubbed his chin with his paw. "A hedgehog? Really? They're usually awful with grammar, to say nothing of the fact they're rarely aligned with fire."

"I . . . Wait, grammar . . . what?"

"Grammar. Very important for composition. What *are* they teaching you at that hippie school?"

"I *know* what grammar is. It's just, hedgehogs? And what did you mean about them not aligning with fire? What does that have to do with my mother?"

The hare sniffed loudly. "You don't actually listen to anything anyone says, do you? Do you remember all the times I've called you a child of fire?" I nodded and Sparx pointed after my mother. "Child, the fire that bore you just walked out that door, and she burns very bright indeed."

"But she's crazy!" The words just burst out of me, though I'd never dared to say them to anyone before, and I quickly slapped my hands over my mouth as though that would unsay the awful truth.

But Sparx merely nodded as if that were the most ordinary thing in the world. "Some the fire within illuminates. Some it consumes."

5

Rabbit, Aim, Fire!

I FELT LIKE someone had kicked me in the chest. "Wait, are you saying that this fire you claim I have within me might drive me crazy?"

Sparx shrugged. "I don't see any signs of that, and it's not likely at this point, but it's certainly possible."

"That's not very reassuring."

"No worries, then. I'm not here to reassure you. I don't even like you all that much."

"Is there anything I can do?" The fear burned higher than it had in a long time.

"You're starting to own your power and to find outlets for it. That's certainly a step in the right direction on the magic side. On the brain side, you're mostly on your own. That's more a matter of biology and chemistry and luck than it is anything you can control—pretty much like all the other ailments your kind are subject to."

Before I could ask any more questions, my mother called from the kitchen, "Kalvan, dinner!"

Our house was a duplex that Oscar had converted into a single-family home before he even met my mom, so the dining room was right outside my door, but we almost always ate in the family kitchen beyond. There was a second kitchen upstairs, where my mom and Oscar had converted about half the floor into a master suite, but that kitchen only got used during the holiday baking season, when my mom would stay up half the night making cookies in both ovens. Even though Mom knew about Sparx now, I told him to wait in my room. We still didn't know who could or couldn't see him, and I really didn't want Oscar to know about him.

Mom was just dishing out some casserole as I came through the door. "Kalvan, could you take this down to your stepfather? There was some screwup at work he needs to sort out before tomorrow, so he can't eat with us tonight."

Oh drat, I sooo hate that, I didn't say. Instead I went with "Sure, Mom," even though I loathed going down there.

The basement door was closed, as usual, though it was unlocked this time. Beyond the thick oak door, a huge iron spiral staircase spun itself down into the depths. The basement was much older than the house—the last remnant of a brewery that had stood on the site sometime in the late eighteen hundreds. At the bottom of the double-length staircase I stepped out into a huge barrel-vaulted room walled and roofed with rough limestone block. According to Oscar, this was where they'd stored the beer casks while waiting to ship them off to local bars.

It was only then that I thought to wonder if I was getting far enough away from Sparx that it would be a problem. Too late to do anything about it now. The basement had a ten-foot ceiling at the center and no walls to speak of, but it always felt claustrophobic and dead to me. Maybe because it was so much deeper than a normal basement, with the ceiling a full six feet below the earth outside—they'd dug it that way to help maintain a constant temperature in winter and summer—and that made it super quiet and still. Or maybe it was the lack of windows.

Whatever the reason, it gave me the creeps, and none of Oscar's modern touches helped. Two thick tracks bristling with high-intensity LED spotlights ran the length of the ceiling about ten feet apart, and the floor was red concrete molded to look like tile, with built-in heat—Oscar liked things much warmer than the beer had. He'd also sealed the limestone with some sort of clear plastic finish that made it look and feel slick and slippery.

I spotted Oscar halfway down the length of the basement, working on the third largest of the enormous tables he used for three-dimensional models of highway projects. The biggest, which took up a quarter of the whole basement in the exact middle of the space, held a topographic map of downtown Saint Paul and Spaghetti Junction, and had for as long as I could remember. Directly above it, the hatch where they used to haul the kegs out had been replaced with rough oak planks.

Either Oscar didn't see me or he ignored me as I approached with his dinner, but when I got within a few feet, he said, "Put it on the desk." I did, then started to turn away.

That's when he finally looked up. His usually grim expression was about two notches harsher than normal, but he made an effort to smile and said, "Thank you, Kalvan."

"You're welcome, Oscar." I never called him Dad—I couldn't even imagine doing that. Silence fell between us, and I almost turned away, but then, in one of my periodic and mostly desperate efforts to find some common ground, I jerked my chin at the table where he'd been working. "Problems?" I didn't like Oscar, but he was good for my mom, and that meant a lot. If getting along with him gave my mom more of whatever she needed, I owed it to her to try.

Oscar raised one eyebrow slightly and his face soured, but then he took a deep breath and his brow smoothed. "Yeah, big one. We're softening a curve on an old county road out in the southern burbs, which means tearing out a big chunk of hillside. It's mostly sandstone and easy to crack, but my backhoe broke through into a cave this morning and there was a skeleton in there, along with some artifacts that look Native American."

"Cool!" I knew as soon as I spoke that it was the wrong thing to say, but it was already too late.

Oscar's face closed up as hard and fast as any trap. "No, Kalvan, it's not cool. It's six kinds of government regulations and three weeks of site assessments and other crap that's going to put this project seriously behind schedule. It's also a giant headache for me."

He turned and went back to poking at the model on the table without another word, and I knew we were done. I had about a minute to clear the area before things would go from silent to ugly, so I started for the stairs.

On the way, I passed the large model of downtown. As usual, I took a moment to pick out the state capitol and my nearby school. That was always kind of neat. Only this time it wasn't. When my eyes touched the capitol, I found myself looking down at the base of the miniature and remembering the tunnels beneath, as I felt an echo of that terrible sense of presence I'd encountered there. Creepy enough by itself, but infinitely compounded by the feeling that while I was looking into the model, it was, in turn, looking outward . . . looking for me.

In the face of that searching presence I froze completely, unable to move or look away or even release the scream I could feel building in my chest. I don't know how long I stood there before I felt a hand come down on my shoulder and spin me around. Suddenly, I was looking up into Oscar's eyes, dark and cold and, in that moment, utterly inhuman. I opened my mouth, but no sound came out, as the scream I'd expected fell dead beside my suddenly hammering heart. He reminded me once again of the stone monster I'd seen in him the other morning, looking more like a statue pretending to be a man than anything human.

"Kalvan, I need you to go back upstairs now and let me complete my work in peace." It wasn't Oscar's usual angry tone, which always felt raw and red to me. This was quieter, darker, and infinitely more menacing.

It was that same commanding tone he had used on me earlier, and I found that my legs were marching me toward the stairs almost independently of my will. That scared me even more, and I suddenly felt a wild itching heat in the skin of my shins and calves, like someone had rubbed me with nettles. But as soon as I reached the back hall it faded and I bolted for my room.

If I hadn't had to pass through the kitchen on the way, I'd have forgotten dinner entirely. As it was, I mumbled my way through some generic phrases about school when Mom asked me how my day had gone and then subsided into a quiet series of *um*s and *uh-huh*s while she told me about her latest project, getting some nonprofit's books ready for an annual audit. I was only too happy when it was over and I could numbly retreat to my room.

"Dave, meet Sparx. Sparx, Dave. Dave is my best friend, and Sparx is a fire hare." For perhaps the dozenth time I tried to make that sound normal as I rehearsed and re-rehearsed the introduction, but every time it just came out sounding crazier and crazier.

"Relax." Sparx was lying under one of the low bushes that surrounded the dell on the hillside above school. "I got a good look at him in your advisory group thingy this morning. No magic to speak of. He probably won't even be able to see me."

"Oh, *that* helps." I banged my forehead against a small tree. It was first period and just *imagining* having to deal with Sparx through another school day had already driven me off the grounds. Between the problems I usually had focusing in class and knowing there was a magical hare in my bag, I could practically feel my brain trying to eat itself with worries. "Dave's the guy who's supposed to act as a sanity check and tell me if you're a hallucination. If he can't see you . . ." I wanted to punch something.

Twenty-four-hours had passed since I . . . what? I hadn't actually summoned the hare, no matter what *he* said about it. Summoning would have implied that I *wanted* a sarcastic critic who was magically attached to me like some kind of ball and chain. Maybe I ought to start calling him *The Curse of the Bunny*. No, that just made me think of those Egyptian mummy cats, and Sparx covered in flaming bandages was way too much.

I glared at the hare. "You are a SERIOUS problem for me."

"Who summoned whom here?"

"No one summoned anybody!" I leaped to my feet. "I'm not a boy wizard, okay?! I'm just an ordinary kid with an overactive imagination."

"You're not going back to pretending I'm a hallucination, are you? Because that got old really fast."

"No." I kicked the dirt. "But I can't even begin to figure out how to deal with you, and the idea that I'm some kind of child of fire is . . ." I waved my arms in the air. "It's ridiculous."

Sparx shrugged. "A little bit, yes. But it's also what you are. A budding power of fire, that is."

"I am not!"

"Are too."

"Not!"

"Really, you are."

"Then why can't I wave my hands and shoot fireballs? Or breathe flames like a dragon?" I demanded.

"Have you ever tried to breathe flames? Because that fire-powered tongue of yours suggests to me that you probably could."

"What?" I found my heart burning in my chest with a terrible anger at all the stuff that was happening to me, all the things that I couldn't control because of my mother, or Oscar, or simply being thirteen and under everybody else's thumb. "Just open my mouth and blow fire all over? Is that what you're suggesting?"

Sparx rolled his eyes. "No, I think that would be an incredibly stupid thing to do. That's a power of rage and nearly impossible to control."

"It's not even a thing!" I was getting angrier and angrier. "You're just making crap up to sound all smart and stuff!"

"No, I'm not. I'm trying to keep you from doing something dumb."

"It's not even possible. SEE!" I took a deep breath and blew all my rage out in one long exhalation.

And, in complete defiance of my expectations, jets of flame roared out of my mouth, all red and gold and blue and green. The bush Sparx was resting under exploded into fire, like the world's biggest struck match.

Oh. Crap.

Before I could even begin to think about what to do and in defiance of the nonexistent wind, the flames leaped to other bushes and trees, moving more like some raging beast than any fire I'd ever seen. In seconds, the whole top of the hill was burning, though the heat and smoke hardly seemed to bother me.

Sparx leaped clear of the flames. "Idiot boy!"

"How do we fix it?" I whispered.

"We can't."

"What?!? But there are all kinds of buildings around, and . . ." I felt a sort of sick horror at what I had done and the beginnings of fear as the flames began to surround me.

"You released the fires within unfettered by anything but rage and petulance. They cannot be called back or unmade by any power of our element."

"What *can* we do?"

"We? Nothing. You? Contain them, perhaps. Constrain them

until they burn themselves out or your firemen bring the power of water to bear on the problem. Is that what you wish?"

I nodded even as I heard the sound of sirens in the distance. This was my mistake. I had to fix it. "Tell me what to do."

"To control your magic, first you must learn to control your heart."

I felt another pulse of anger at that. What I needed was practical advice I could apply right now, not Yoda-esque claptrap. But in that same instant, the flames grew suddenly bigger and brighter. "Did I do that?"

"Of course you did." Sparx looked like he wanted to slap me, but he kept his voice calm, soothing even, as he pointed at the blaze. "All of that comes from your heartfire. If you can't learn to control yourself, you'll never learn to control fire."

I gritted my teeth and tried to force myself to calm down. Not easy given the circumstances. Maybe not even possible. "Look, we're kind of under some time pressure here. . . ."

"Let that go for a moment and just breathe."

"What about all the smoke?" The sirens were reminding me rather vividly of the lecture the local fire department gave when they did their annual school visit. Smoke can kill you faster than fire.

He ignored my question. "In. Out. Breathe. In. Out."

To be fair, the smoke wasn't even making my eyes water, so I tried doing what he told me.

After perhaps twenty cycles of breathing, Sparx nodded. "Good. Now, reach out to the fire."

"How?"

"With your heart. You love your mother. I've seen it. Keep

breathing. That feeling you have when you look at her, that sense of connection, that you are part of one thing . . . you and the fire are one, too. It came from your heart and your heart can govern it."

"But I don't know how . . ." I felt like crying as I watched the flames devouring one of my favorite places. I had done this.

"Look, we all get mad at people we love, right? Well, this is a bit like that. Keep breathing. In. Out. Surely, you've tried to wish your mom into doing things differently when you're mad at her. This is a bit like that, only the fire *must* listen to the will of your heart. Can you try it now?"

"I . . . maybe." I wasn't sure that I understood him, but thinking about my mom had . . . kind of grounded me. I could feel the fire, if only dimly. I reached out. "I'm touching something . . ."

"Good! You're doing it. I can see the magic. Wish the fire to remain within its current bounds. Tell it that you need it to stay close, to only burn the ground you've already given it."

The idea that I had given the fire anything made me feel sick to my stomach, but I forced myself not to let that interfere with the connection I'd established. *Please.*

Please.

Please.

"It's working," said Sparx. "It's working. Ask it to do no more harm."

No more. Please. No more.

"And that's it! It will remain on this hill and take none of the buildings around us. Now, we need to get out of here. Quickly and quietly."

"Huh?"

"I have some familiarity with your human authorities. I don't think that you would much like the consequences of them finding you here in the heart of the flames." The sound of wailing sirens punctuated his words.

I imagined trying to explain this to the firefighters, and the police, and Aaron, and my mom, and Oscar. Oh God.

And I thought I'd felt sick before . . . It was all too much. I could see nothing but flames, hear only the fire, smell smoke . . . I started to lose control again, to lose myself, and the fire burned brighter in response.

6

Red Haring

I STOOD IN the heart of the fire and the fire burned in my heart. We were one and the same. We would burn together until all the fuel ran out, and then we would burn out. And there was nothing I could do about it.

Or at least that was what I believed in the moment. But then I felt a sharp stinging pain in my lower leg, which snapped me out of the world of flame and returned me to the world of the flesh.

"What . . ." I glanced down and saw blood welling up from a set of short parallel slices across my shin and Sparx drawing back his right front paw in preparation for clawing me again. "Hey!" I leaped away from him.

"Good, you're back."

"What happened?"

"The fascination of fire, but we don't have time to talk about it right now. We have to leave before the firemen get up here."

"But where can we go?" I wailed.

Sparx said, "I don't know. The fire trucks started unloading while you were gone. Is there any other way for a human to get off this hill? The ways I know won't help you."

I wanted to panic again, but I fought it down. *Come on, Kalvan, think! Can't go up . . . can't go down. Left's no good. Right? Right might work.*

"Yeah, maybe; there's this little ravine. Follow me." I started forward, then stopped. We needed to go around the right side of the hill, but the fire had surrounded us completely.

"It's all right. This fire is a part of you. It can only hurt you if you lose control of yourself again, and . . . BREATHE."

Right. In. Out. In. Out. I stepped into the flames . . . and they didn't burn me. Weirdest sensation EVER. I felt like I was walking through liquid light, or love mixed with rage, or . . . it seemed impossible to talk about it in words. I could feel heat, but it didn't burn me. It just kind of let me know that it was there and a part of me . . . the worst impulse of my heart made into something real and almost solid.

All I knew for sure was that I never, ever wanted to feel it again.

We had just reached the edge of the fire when Sparx suddenly pressed himself against the side of my leg. "'Ware, the bitter-water boy is just ahead."

"Huh?" But then I was looking down a steep slope into the little ravine with its tiny trickle of a stream that ran from a small spring near the top. And there was Josh, sitting on a rock with his toes in the water.

Josh looked up at me and smiled in a way that made my bones itch. "Pretty work there." He jerked his chin at the fire behind me.

"I didn't mean to do it!"

He shrugged. "It's still beautiful, and a fancy bit of magic, even if you're too precious a mama's boy to own it."

I bristled at that, but I didn't dare let my temper get out of control there on the edge of the mess I'd made with it already. *Breathe.*

"You like fire?" Sparx asked Josh as we slid down into the ravine.

It was a nasty little drop, but the only way forward. I landed hard and twisted my left ankle, biting my lip to keep from crying out. I wasn't going to let Josh see me that vulnerable.

Josh shook his head at Sparx. "Not really, but I can appreciate what it does, and I like the odds of this getting Kalvan so deep in trouble that they send him off to reform school."

I kept on, silently talking to myself as I limped closer to Josh. *In. Out. Getting pissed off is what put you here in the first place, Kalvan. Don't make things worse. In. Out.* A few moments later we were past him and moving up the ravine, away from the fire trucks.

I was just starting to relax when the streambed seemed to go as slick as black ice. I couldn't adjust fast enough with my bad ankle and I fell again, landing hard on my hands and knees. Behind me, Josh laughed, and I knew without asking that he'd had something to do with my tumble. I forced myself to ignore the laughter as I dragged myself upright and continued on. I was limping badly now, but I kept moving, starting to pick bits of gravel out of my skinned palms as I went.

Sparx gave Josh a hard look but waited until we were out of sight to say anything more. "That one's got a bad streak as wide as any river. I'll be wanting to keep an eye on him when the seasons turn and the Crown with them."

I nodded but didn't say anything because the fire had left me feeling like I didn't have a lot of room to criticize anybody else's bad streaks. Somehow we got out of the ravine and the area, avoiding all the police and firefighters who had come to deal with my mess.

"What happened to you?" Dave had been on the back playground watching the fire with about half the school when I finally managed to work my way back to school. I'd caught his attention from the bushes and he came over as soon as he had a chance to slip past the teachers—easy enough given the distraction of the fire.

He continued now, "You're filthy and you smell like smoke and . . . wait, you weren't caught in the fire, were you? Because you'll be grounded for a million years, and that's *after* they suspend you."

"I, uh, yeah, but it's not like you'd think. Look, it's a long story."

Dave rolled his eyes. "Well, you'll have to tell me later. After we get you cleaned up, that is." He looked thoughtful. "The gym's your best bet. You hide out close to the pass-through and I'll run around and open up one of the windows."

I nodded. "Thank you!"

The windows were huge and heavy, old-fashioned sash windows with the weights long since gone. They should have been replaced years ago, but so should a lot of things in the school. They were hard to lift and prone to slamming on fingers if you tried to get out that way. Not to mention they barely opened wide enough for someone my size to wiggle through.

Climbing over the window ledge with my skinned hands and bad ankle hurt so much I might have started crying if Dave hadn't been there to see it. Sparx stayed quietly hidden in my backpack while Dave helped me climb the furniture to get into the showers, which was a small mercy. I still wasn't quite ready to cross that bridge.

Getting the last of the gravel out of my palms and washing the cuts made me want to scream. When I got out of the shower I found Dave waiting.

"I snagged you a spare tee out of the gym's loaner bin." He handed me a green shirt with the school motto on it above a picture of Icarus—the Greek hero who had flown too close to the sun and melted his wax wings. It was a little ragged around the neckline, but it was clean. "I rinsed out your cargo shorts too. They might be a little uncomfortable while they're drying, but they smelled like smoke something awful. Oh, and I found you some gauze for your palms."

"Thank you." I let Dave wrap my hands, then took the clothes and put them on along with my sandals, which squelched a bit from rinsing—I was super glad it wasn't jeans-and-boots weather yet, because that would have been much more challenging. "I owe you big-time."

"Do you?" I nodded. "Then talk to me, Kalvan."

"What do you mean?"

Dave rolled his eyes. "You vanished right after advisory group this morning after barely saying hello. When I see you next you're covered with soot. You're bleeding and limping. And the whole hill behind the school is on fire. What the heck happened? Were you playing with matches? Because if that fire was your fault . . ."

"No. I . . ." I wanted to say the fire wasn't my fault, but it totally was. "It's complicated."

Dave looked me straight in the eye. "I've got time."

Apparently, rehearsal was over. "All right, come on."

I scooped up my bag and we headed out into the main part of the gym. I figured it would be better if we were both sitting down for this. We climbed up to the top of the bleachers so we could duck between them in case anyone stuck their head into the gym.

But now that the moment had come, it felt even harder to get started than I'd feared. "It's been a strange couple of days for me."

"I'm listening." Dave's expression was closed and tight, completely lacking his usual infectious smile.

I took a deep breath. "I started the semester off thinking I was starting down the road my mom's on."

"Yeah, I saw a little bit of that when we skipped out of class last week, but you haven't mentioned it since. So, are you?"

I started to feel sick again. "I . . . don't think so. But honestly, I don't know if I'd know, you know?"

Dave almost smiled. "It's probably a good thing that you're

worried about it, but why didn't you talk to me right away? You know I've got your back on that stuff."

"It got really weird really fast."

"How so?" Dave tilted his head to one side skeptically.

"It's probably easier to show you." I bent over and unzipped my backpack—hoping desperately that Dave would be able to see the hare. "Hey, Sparx, come on out of there."

There was a long pause and Dave began to look really worried, but then my sort-of familiar poked his head out of the bag.

Dave jerked backward, almost falling off his seat. "Why do you have a giant rabbit in your bag?"

"Fire hare," Sparx corrected. "Why does everybody get that wrong?"

This time, Dave did fall off his seat, sliding into the gap between his bench and the next one up. "Giant talking rabbit!"

"Yeah, that." I leaned forward and offered Dave a hand up. "Welcome to my messed-up world."

After several long moments where I was beginning to worry I'd just lost my best friend, Dave took my hand. "Complicated. Right. Tell me about it."

So, I did, with the occasional interjection from Sparx. Dave mostly kept quiet, though he did ask a few clarifying questions about the thing under the capitol and the summoning.

When I was done, Dave let out a long, low whistle. "You can actually breathe fire?"

"Apparently."

"I'd like to see that sometime."

"No, you wouldn't." Sparx's voice came out flat and hard. "It's incredibly dangerous and it's only luck that someone wasn't seriously hurt. On top of that, he probably couldn't replicate it if he tried, not anything like safely. It's a discipline well beyond his training."

"But I haven't had *any* training," I protested.

"Exactly!" Sparx turned and looked me in the eyes now. "I don't know how long I'm stuck with you, but if it's more than the next fifteen minutes we have *got* to get your powers under control. At the moment you're basically a walking fireworks display waiting only for the wrong match. The next time you lose control, you could burn down your house."

"I . . . oh." I hadn't had a chance to think about what I'd done beyond the immediate consequences until now. "I'm never going to breathe fire again, I promise."

"Oh, good." Sparx relaxed a little. "You're going to be sensible about this. But be careful with your words. It may be that someday it will come to a choice between letting the fire out or letting it devour you from within."

That sounded particularly awful. "All right, what do I need to do?"

"Learn control." Sparx sighed. "And, thanks to Fate or Luck, I'm the one who's going to have to teach you. Go, me."

"Good luck with that," said Dave. "He's kind of a handful. Two or three, really."

I gave him the stink eye. "Gosh, thanks, friend. I'm glad you're here for me."

"I really am," said Dave. "Well, assuming this isn't me having a break with reality, anyway." He laughed, not entirely happily. "I can see why you were reluctant to talk about all this, especially if there was a real chance I wouldn't be able to see Mr. Bunn here."

"Mr. Bunn?!" Sparx reared back onto his hind legs. "Mr. Bunn?!"

"Oh, chill out," I said, then turned back to Dave, leaving Sparx to glare at my back. "Yeah, *that* would have been gangs of fun."

Dave smiled. "But it didn't happen that way, and I'm going to roll with the whole magic thing for now because that's a much happier option than the one where I've cracked up and this is all happening in my head. If it really is the latter, don't tell me about it for at least a few days, okay?"

"Deal, but no worries. It's all real."

Dave chuckled. "Yeah, no offense, but you're not a reliable witness on this one. It's your imagination he's a figment of."

"I am *not* a figment," said Sparx. "No butterfly wings, no antlers, and my ears are way too short. What *are* they teaching you children in school these days?"

"Is he serious?" Dave jerked his chin at Sparx.

"Sometimes, but it's really hard to tell when he is and when he isn't."

Sparx looked puzzled. "Figments? Aligned with air? Look like a flying version of those jackalope things you people invented?" He held up his paws like a pair of antlers. "No? You've really never heard of them?"

"See?" I said. "I can never tell when he's making stuff up to mess with me."

Evelyn stepped to the front of the stage. "All right, today we're going to do something a little more challenging."

I elbowed my bag as it moved on the seat beside me—it had become almost a reflex over the last few days. It was dark in the big theater and nobody was likely to notice a backpack that refused to hold still, but I reeeeeally didn't want to have to explain a magic hare to . . . well, anybody.

Evelyn continued, "We've been focusing on improv while you were all getting comfortable with each other."

It was third period and Evelyn's advanced theater class, which drew students from all six of the upper grades, and you had to have special permission from her to get in. Dave and I were the only seventh graders, and there was just one eighth grader—a girl named Devi who had transferred in from the arts magnet late in the previous year. Josh was in the class as well, and sitting a few rows behind me, which made me feel like I had a target on the back of my neck.

Evelyn clapped her hands, recentering my attention on the stage. "Now that we all know each other, I want to try something hard. At the end of the first week of class, I gave each of you a short piece from a classical play and asked you to read and familiarize yourself with it. I'm sure you've all done the homework, and I'd guess some of you even memorized your pieces."

Beside me, I noticed Dave nodding and I winced. I'd read mine a couple of times, but then Sparx happened and I got distracted. Now I wasn't even sure if I had it with me. As Evelyn continued I surreptitiously leaned over my bag and unzipped the top.

"Today we're going to perform them for the first time," said Evelyn. "These are really hard pieces, and I don't expect you to get them right the first time. This is all about learning to work with tough language and someone else's words. Dave, you're up first. We're going to work our way up through the grades on this go-round, though we'll change that up as the semester goes along."

That meant I was second! Sweat broke out on my forehead as Dave headed for the stage. I was going to bomb this badly. I leaned into my bag and whispered, "I don't suppose you can see a sheet with a speech on it in there anywhere."

"Here." Sparx kept his voice low as well, and a single crumpled piece of paper emerged a moment later, and I was so grateful I barely thought about the issue of someone noticing. "*Henry V,* great play."

"You know it?"

"Oh yeah, I love Shakespeare. Great writer. Nice man, too."

"Can you help me out?"

On the stage, Dave was beginning his speech, something from Oscar Wilde.

"How?"

"I don't know . . ." I'd have said more, but I noticed Evelyn giving me the stink eye and subsided.

A few minutes later, it was my turn. I hadn't heard a word of Dave's piece, or of Evelyn's comments about it, and I felt a little guilty about that. But then she called on me and all I felt was panic. As nonchalantly as possible, I hooked my backpack over one shoulder, leaving the top partially unzipped. Normally, I'd have left it behind for something like this, but A) I couldn't go more than thirty feet from it without bad things happening, and B) I was hoping that Sparx could somehow help me with the speech, even if I couldn't think of any way that would work.

As I passed the seat where my mentor, Aleta, was sitting, she gave me a gentle punch on the shoulder. "You've got this, Kal."

No. I don't got this. I'd never felt sicker getting up on a stage, and my shins started to itch like mad—my normal reaction to stage fright.

Right. I was soooooo doomed.

I uncrumpled the piece of paper and, hands shaking, began to read. "*King Henry V*, Act III, Scene I, France. Before . . . Harfleur . . ." My voice broke, and I heard Josh's nasty little chuckle from the audience. Sweat started rolling down my temples.

> *Once more unto the breach, dear friends, once*
> *more;*

Oh my god, was I going to bomb this. I could barely understand what I was reading, much less get it out with any emphasis.

> *Or close the wall up with our English dead.*
> *In peace there's nothing so becomes a man*
> *As modest stillness and humility:*

I stumbled over *humility* and ground to a halt for a second. Josh snickered and Evelyn shushed him.

From my backpack, Sparx hissed quietly at me. "Punch it up, kid. This is a speech designed to convince an army to fight harder in the face of tough odds. Think Lord of the Rings movies.

Théoden getting the Rohirrim ready to charge the orcs at the battle for Gondor. Aragorn before the walls of Mordor."

I almost said, *Is that what this is about?* Instead, I kept going.

> *But when the blast of war blows in our ears,*
> *Then imitate the action of the tiger;*

I didn't botch it too badly, but my voice sounded weak and wavery in my own ears, and I knew I'd never done a worse reading. I felt like the faith Evelyn had shown in me by letting me be the youngest student in this class was wasted. Like I was betraying *all* the faith she'd shown in me over the years, and I wanted nothing more than to simply walk off that stage and never come back.

I *had* to do better.

> *Stiffen the sinews, summon up the blood,*
> *Disguise fair nature with hard-favour'd rage;*

But I hadn't done my homework and I barely understood what I was saying. It would take a miracle to get me out of this with any grace at all.

A miracle . . . or magic?

Hadn't Sparx said I had the power of silvertongue . . . the fascination of fire. I could make people listen to me if I tried. Heck, wasn't it supposed to be harder for me *not* to use it? Not using my magic was the main thing Sparx and I had been working on for the last few days. He said you have to learn how *not* to do things before you mastered doing them. Maybe if I let my inner fire off the leash just a *little* . . . My throat warmed as I spoke the next line.

Then lend the eye a terrible aspect;

Oh. That's what it was supposed to feel like! The speech was talking about looking fierce here. Looking fierce and feeling fierce and . . .

Let pry through the portage of the head
Like the brass cannon; let the brow o'erwhelm it
As fearfully as doth a galled rock
O'erhang and jutty his confounded base,
Swill'd with the wild and wasteful ocean.

That bit really didn't make any sense to me, but I imagined myself leading an army and trying to rouse them, and my throat grew warmer still. Out in the audience, I could see the other kids sitting up straighter and listening more closely.

Now set the teeth and stretch the nostril wide,
Hold hard the breath and bend up every spirit
To his full height.

Right, this I could work with. I lifted my chin and flared my nostrils, declaiming the lines so I could hear my words ringing out across the theater. Fire roared in my throat, and I saw Dave stand up in the audience, then Aleta.

On, on, you noblest English.

Whose blood is fet from fathers of war-proof!

I could feel their sudden fierce belief in the speech rising with my own and amplifying it as they rose on the floor of the theater to stand with me. This was the most brilliant speech ever. I wasn't just saying it. It was TRUTH. I *was* Henry V, and I would lead my troops onward into battle! The belief flowing from my fellow students buoyed me up and filled me with a power beyond anything I could imagine. In that moment, they made me a king.

I lost track of the exact words I was saying as they roared through me and brought my followers cheering to the brink of battle. We would smash the enemy and burn their cities!

I noticed Josh then leaping from his seat and sprinting toward the door with his hands clapped over his ears. Here was the very enemy himself! I pointed at Josh.

"DESTROY HIM!"

As one, the class turned toward Josh and a great howl went up as of hunting dogs readying themselves for the pursuit. This was my triumph!

7

Muskrat, Packrat, Give
the Hare a Bone

A VOICE SOMEWHERE in the back of my mind was screaming, "No, no, no!" over and over again, but I could barely hear it above the roar of the blood in my ears and the howling hunter in my heart. I glanced at the slip of paper in my hands and saw the last few lines of my speech.

> *I see you stand like greyhounds in the slips,*
> *Straining upon the start. The game's afoot:*
> *Follow your spirit, and upon this charge*
> *Cry "God for Harry, England, and Saint George!"*

As one, my army turned toward my enemy. . . . That's when Sparx kicked me in the back of the head with both feet. My whole world went purple and foggy for a few long seconds and my skull felt like someone had turned it inside out. I landed on my knees, hard, and suddenly reality seemed to snap back into focus with an unnatural clarity.

If I didn't act right now, my schoolmates might chase Josh down and literally tear him apart, but I didn't know how to fix things. "What do I do?" I whispered.

Sparx had leaped down to the stage beside me. "You and Shakespeare started this; you and Shakespeare can stop it. I know just the cantrip, but I need you to repeat everything I say with the full power of that silver tongue, and I need you to repeat it EXACTLY."

I nodded.

He cried then, "Hold enough!" and I repeated it.

That halted the immediate rush toward Josh, and Sparx nodded. He began to speak then, declaiming clearly and cleanly with a full stop at the end of each line to allow me to echo him.

If we shadows have offended,
Think but this, and all is mended,
That you have but slumber'd here
While these visions did appear.

On some level I recognized the words as coming from the closing speech of *A Midsummer Night's Dream*, when Puck tells the audience that they have merely been dreaming and none of the events they've witnessed are real. Evelyn had given it to me to read in her first- through sixth-grade advanced theater class, which I had taken last year. As I spoke I could feel the power I had gathered earlier flowing out of me in great pulses, leaving me measurably weaker with each word.

And this weak and idle theme,
No more yielding but a dream,
Gentles, do not reprehend:
If you pardon, we will mend.

But on a deeper level still, with the belief of my audience driven by the fascination of fire, I *was* Puck, and when I wove my spell to put the events just passed into the frame of a dream, I knew that it would bind them all to that version of reality, and no one who was there would remember it as anything other than a fanciful dream of the theater. I knew it because I was as bound by the power of my silver tongue as any of my listeners.

And, as I am an honest Puck,
If we have unearned luck
Now to 'scape the serpent's tongue,
We will make amends ere long;
Else the Puck a liar call:
So, good night unto you all.
Give me your hands, if we be friends,
And Robin shall restore amends.

I felt my knees go spongy as I finished the speech and noticed the members of my class slowly sagging back into their seats and dropping into sleep one by one. I'd done it. With Sparx's help, I had corrected my terrible mistake. No one would even remem . . . wait. Even as I thought it, I saw Josh, hands still clapped over his ears, duck through the exit and run out of the theater.

"You," said Sparx, his voice flat and angry. "Somewhere we can talk privately, right now."

I scooped up my bag and led us through the rear stage door into the scene shop beyond. Behind us, the class snored blissfully away.

When I closed the door, Sparx leaped up onto a table saw and reared back so that our eyes were nearly on a level. "NEVER, EVER DO THAT AGAIN!"

"I—" But Sparx clapped his paws sharply together and shook his head.

"You shut up. I'm not done yet. You're one of the most powerful young idiots it's ever been my headache to have to babysit, but you have no control whatsoever. ZERO. That's not all right. With my help you've managed to clean up your own messes twice, but only barely. That could get someone killed, and if that's not your plan, you need to get a grip."

"I—" A paw went up again and I stopped.

"I don't want to hear it. What I want to hear is yes or no, and only yes or no. Can you do that?"

I nodded. "Yes."

"It's a start. Do you want to get someone killed?"

"No." I shook my head wildly.

"So, you're going to listen to what I tell you and stop ad-libbing with dangerous magic?"

"Yes."

"All right, then. I'm not going to ask for your word, because either you will do what you say you will or you won't, and promises are thin tissue. Words *can* have great power. You can use rhymes and spells to control the shape of the fires within, but those are lessons you won't be ready to learn anytime soon."

He canted his head to one side. "You look like maybe some of that has gotten through your thick skull, which is a start. Now, we're going to go back out there and gently wake people up. And then you're going to give that speech again without magic, and bomb it badly because you didn't prepare for it and that's what you've earned. Right?"

"Yes." And that's what we did, complete with the worst performance I'd ever given. Evelyn was very disappointed and I had to apologize and promise her that I would be ready to give the speech again on Monday and get it right then.

If that wasn't all awful enough, there was a message from my mom waiting at my afternoon advisory group meeting saying not to take the bus because Oscar was going to pick me up so we could all go out to dinner.

"I can wait with you," said Dave. "My dad's supposed to come by and take me out as well. Not that he's going to show up."

I squeezed his shoulder. "I'm sorry."

"It is what it is. Mom gave me ten bucks to get fast food and catch the light rail when he doesn't show up. I figure if I do the dollar menu I can squeeze a couple of comic books out of that as well."

We settled on the ledge of the playground out back, a much better place to meet parents than the front door with all the bus traffic. After a few minutes I realized there was one more piece of fallout from the incident this morning that I had to deal with, and this one really scared me.

"Dave."

"Yeah." A long silence followed before he raised an eyebrow at me. "Come on, cough it up."

"What do you remember from theater this afternoon?"

"Besides you crashing and burning on your speech?"

"Yeah, besides that."

He grinned. "I remember nailing mine." He looked at me with sudden concern. "Ah, come on. It wasn't that much of a burn, and I'm sure you'll do better on the next go."

"It's not that. It's . . . well, I did some magic and it went all wrong . . . and . . . well, you got caught in that, and I'm really, really sorry."

"Did somebody hit you in the head or something? Because nothing like that happened."

"It did, but you not remembering it is part of the magic. Look, just let me tell you about it. I owe you that, even if it makes you hate me forever." So, I did.

When I was done, Dave gave me a long appraising look. "For true?"

"For true."

"Huh." Dave's eyes went far away.

"Do you hate me?"

He laughed. "Nah. It's kind of creepy and I should probably be honked off, but mostly I'm thinking how handy that silver-tongue thing could be. I wonder if you could teach me how to do it."

"Probably not," said my bag. "But nothing's impossible."

"Cool!"

He might have said more, but Oscar's big gray sedan pulled up at that exact moment. I punched Dave gently in the shoulder and hopped to open the passenger door. Before I could slide in Oscar leaned over, shook his head, and jerked his chin toward the back seat. He was wearing a pair of blue mirror shades and his I've-had-a-bad-day face. *Great.*

I closed the door quickly, grimaced at Dave, and crawled in back. That was always creepy since the car was a police conversion and you couldn't actually open those doors from the inside, though the cage between the seats had been removed so you could get out of there if you had to.

"Did you get that cave thing fixed?" I asked.

"No." His voice came out flat and stony.

"Oh, sorry. Project behind schedule?"

"Yes." He slowed the car then and turned to look at me through those cold blue mirrors. "Look, I've had a hard day and I don't want to talk about it. Not only that, but *you* don't particularly want to talk to *me*, either, and we both know it, so can we skip the chitchat?"

"Uh, sure. I guess. I just . . ."

He shook his head gently but finally, and I didn't say anything more. It was only as he turned away that I realized the expressionless blue of his shades was identical to the color of his eyes and exactly as revealing of the man underneath.

The next couple of weeks went pretty normally, for values of normal that included the weird world of the Free School, smuggling a talking hare into and out of the building every day, and going to all my classes—in part because I was bumping into our principal a lot more often than chance might dictate. I hadn't actually blown anything up since my mistake with the theater class, and

I was even doing a half-decent job at math now that Sparx was tutoring me there as well as in magic. The one upside of my most recent mess was that Josh Reiner treated me like I had the plague and needed to be avoided at any cost.

Then all of a sudden it was the first week of October and the weather, which had been soggy and gray for weeks, opened out into a perfect golden fall day, and I knew there was no way I was going to stay in classes and miss out on the best part of the afternoon with winter on its way. Not when I could get out, away from everyone, and especially not on a Monday.

When I told Sparx my plan to play hooky, he gave me his disapproving look but didn't actually veto the idea—mostly I think because he was sick of hiding in my bag. That was good enough for me. So, after math I slipped out to the playground, over the back railing, and then around the gym and up past the capitol.

I didn't want to get anywhere near those tunnels, so I stayed aboveground, and a lone kid out on the capitol lawn was a lot less conspicuous than one over by Regions Hospital, which was my other route for getting from school into downtown proper. The freeway cut between the capitol complex and the main part of downtown, and you could only cross it on the bridges.

Once I got into the big urban canyons where the streets ran between the concrete towers of the city, I picked up the pace. I didn't want to stay out in the open where some bored cop might pull over and ask if I was supposed to be there. I just hurried straight on South, heading for the Mississippi. Another bridge took me across the river and then I cut west along the bank, heading for the wooded area of the bluff beyond the high bridge.

It's maybe a mile and a quarter from the doors of the school to the little slice of forest, but it was also a perfect day and I walk a lot. As soon as I got to the bluff, I ducked onto one of the many footpaths that run through the woods and got up above the road. The whole area is too steep to build on, so it's basically a ribbon of wild land running through the middle of the city. I stopped once I was out of sight of the road below and opened up my backpack for Sparx.

He poked his head out. "Spirits and shadows but I'm coming to hate that bag." Then he jumped down to the trail, where he briefly stopped to sniff the west wind. "I smell change on the breeze, frost and falling leaves and the fallow Crown lying uneasy in its casket as the season closes."

"Fallow Crown?" I asked as we walked along the trail. I was good on frost and falling leaves. That was October in Minnesota, but this was the third or fourth time he'd mentioned a crown in connection with the seasons. "What are you talking about?"

"The Corona Borealis." His voice went far away, like he was reciting something from long ago—and not for the first time. He was hundreds of years old, and sometimes it came out in his speech. "Four months it rests on Winter's brow and four on Summer's. Now, with Summer faded and Winter still lurking beyond the horizon's edge, the Crown rests."

That rang a few bells. "Wait, Corona Borealis, isn't that a constellation?" We'd covered them in a mythology class I'd taken with our English teacher. I was reminded of something my mother had said, too—a rhyme maybe? "That's the Crown of the North, right?"

"That too. Seven stars set in a silver band mark the Crown of the North. Tarnished and black while Winter's Queen or King wears it, bright and shining on Summer's warm brow. During the interim the lands rest in harmony between the powers." He shook himself, visibly coming back into the moment. "At least, that's the way it's supposed to work. These last few years . . . have been more turbulent."

"Why?"

"I don't know. The Kings and Queens have all come from your people for many long years now, and the process has become opaque to those of us who wear different skins. The Crown of the North lies in humanity's hands, with all the whims and wiles that brings."

"Why is that?"

"Your kind grow ever more numerous, while the other kindreds remain static or decline. As you have so recently seen, belief is a powerful driver of magic, and your kind believe in yourselves to a terrifying degree. With so many minds dreaming the same dream, how could you not wax in power?"

"Huh." I'd have to think about that. "And the fate of the universe all turns on Minnesota?" That seemed unlikely at best.

Sparx snorted. "No, of course not. There are many crowns north and south, east and west. Some are season crowns, some represent the winds and tides. The one true Corona Borealis rides the skies untouched by any soul on this planet. The Crown that rules the headwaters of the great river"—here he jerked his chin toward the water flowing by below—"is only a reflection of that celestial power, though it's a mighty one."

"Hang on, the Mississippi starts up in Itasca."

Sparx briefly put his head in his paws. "It does that, child, but those lands are ruled from here, where the river's power truly rises. That power is part of why the matter of who wears the Crown is so important."

"And who is that?"

"That, too, is hidden from me. All I can say for certain is that it rests in human hands, as it has for many cycles. Beyond that, it's a matter of reading the signs, and those are dark and troubling." Before I could say more, Sparx rose onto his hind legs and held up one paw like a stop sign. "Tread quietly, boy. The shadows in the caves beneath us have awakened, and they are hungry. You haven't learned to mask your strength yet, and we should not have come this way."

I froze. I knew about the caves in the bluff—tunnels really, since they were all human-made. We'd taken a tour of some of the open ones as part of a Free School field trip a few years ago. The tour guides had told us about how the caves had been used over the years, including for storage and mushroom farming, and even speakeasies, which were illegal bars during Prohibition. Most of them had been sealed up years before, but I'd heard from my student mentor, Aleta, that many of them could be gotten into, and some of the older kids used them for parties.

"Should we turn back?" I asked.

Sparx shook his head. "I don't think so. The presence feels stronger behind than ahead. We should move now, but quietly. Follow me, and don't use *any* magic."

"You *know* I don't know how to use magic," I whispered angrily.

"Not well, at any rate, though it hasn't stopped you yet.

Just . . . don't DO anything, all right? I'd rather not end up on some delver's dinner plate, if it's all the same to you."

For the next fifteen minutes we moved forward in slow stops and starts, traveling steadily westward along the river. I asked about heading inland or down to the riverside at one point, but Sparx simply shook his head and made hushing motions. Finally, as the bluffs curved away south, we made our way down the slope to the edge of a big swampy area.

"Now what?" I'd never been so far west along this bank of the river before. Though we'd probably come no more than another half mile, I didn't know the area at all.

Sparx pointed to a line of small trees and scrub brush that ran along the sides of a raised causeway. "Railroad. We can use it to cross the swamp, and maybe the great river as well, though I'd hate to have so little between me and *Her.*"

I didn't like the idea of crossing the river on a railroad track, either, but there wasn't another bridge in sight, and if the things in the caves were anything like the one under the capitol, it was an easy choice in my book. So, we skirted the edge of the little swamp and climbed up onto the railroad siding before heading back toward the river.

Perhaps halfway across the little swamp we came to a wide place in the causeway where a fire pit held a couple of smoldering log ends left over from the night before. I would simply have passed on by if Sparx hadn't hopped over to the fire pit. I figured it was the remnant of some teen party, judging by the debris left around the sheltered little clearing in the brush, which included a torn but fashionable girl's jacket, some beach towels, and a lot of empty Schmitz cans.

Sparx gently kicked the nearest log. "Still alive. Not hot enough by any light, but it's been burning for hours. That'll help. Toss a couple more logs on this fire, would you."

I did as the hare asked, though I didn't know why. "What's this for?"

"Insurance. I've a bad feeling growing on me like eyes in the darkness, and living fire close at hand is the best ally the likes of you and me can have in a situation like this." After a few minutes, the fire was burning solidly and Sparx started toward the railway again.

I didn't move. "Wait, we're not just going to abandon an active fire, are we? What if a wind comes up and it gets away?"

Sparx shrugged. "That'd be all to the good for us, I think." Then, when he saw that I wasn't going to budge, he came back. "Fine. I'll bind it to the pit so there's no danger of burning down this lovely swamp."

Then he said something very fast in the language of fire. Though I still didn't understand it and Sparx had made no effort to teach me any of the words, I was beginning to feel as though it would start making sense to me at some point soon. When he finished speaking, a little wisp of smoke danced out from the center of the fire before spinning a circle around it and puffing away into nothing. I couldn't see any obvious difference in the fire, but I knew in my soul that it would not break the bounds of the fire pit—a very strange feeling.

"Satisfied?" demanded Sparx, and I nodded. "Good! Now, let's get moving again."

We continued along the railway for another hundred yards or so and had almost reached the edge of the swamp when a loud splash off to the right drew my attention. There, sitting on a small muddy hummock, was the biggest muskrat I'd ever seen.

When we made eye contact it leaned back on its haunches and waved. "Hello, boy." The voice was low and feminine and a little husky, and it sent a silvery shiver along my spine.

"Ignore her," said Sparx.

But I found that I didn't want to. "Hello, uh . . . lady?"

"She's no lady, kid." Sparx stamped the ground impatiently. "We need to be moving along right quick, not dallying with selkies."

"What's a selkie?" I asked.

"We are." This voice was higher and clearer, and it rang through me like a bell. "Obviously." A second muskrat poked her head up through the duckweed. "I'm Sylvia, and this is my sister, Samantha."

"Oh, that's fascinating." I nodded, finding myself with a strange desire to agree with whatever the creatures said. I didn't like that, and fought against it. "Uh, this may be a stupid question, but what makes you different from a muskrat?"

Samantha giggled. "Besides the talking, foolish boy?"

My cheeks burned at the scorn I heard there and I wanted to melt into a puddle, but I managed a nod instead. Out of the corner of my eye I saw Sparx looking up into the sky and shaking his head sadly.

"Why, this does, of course." A third selkie had entered the conversation, waddling up onto the causeway to stand a few feet away from me.

Her voice lay at the midpoint in range between the other two, soft and somehow furry sounding. She shook all over now, like a dog coming out of the water. Only instead of spraying me with swamp muck, she seemed to blur and grow. A moment later she had become a young woman, small and dark of hair and skin, wearing an indecently short dress of brown fur. I flushed even more and turned away, looking toward the river.

"Ah, Susan, look, Prince Charming is embarrassed, why don't you give him a—" Sylvia's voice cut off abruptly as I felt a hot flash across the backs of my knees and calves like a charcoal grill flaring when someone puts in too much lighter fluid.

"None of that!" Sparx's voice came out sharp and hot—English, but full of undertones from the language of fire.

I turned and found that the hare, now burning brightly, had placed himself between the fur-dressed girl and me. She snorted and shrugged before abruptly shrinking back into her muskrat shape. "Good-bye, Prince Charming. Were it not for your silly old rabbit we might—"

Sparx's fur flared up and the selkie staggered backward, toward the edge of the ridge. "Have it your way—" And then she said something short and fast in the language of flame.

The hare cursed fire before answering her in a swishing, fluid tongue that reminded me of waves on the beach. The selkie jumped as if someone had given her a hotfoot, then tumbled down the steep causeway to land in the swamp with a splash. The other two laughed nasty little laughs.

"Ha, he's sure got your number, Susie," said Samantha. "Better let his pet monkey alone."

"Shut it," snapped Susan. "You don't . . . oh." Abruptly, she dove under the water and vanished.

"What's she on about now?" asked Sylvia. But then she turned to look beyond us, made a little chirruping noise, and slid into the water after her compatriot.

When I looked for the third, I found that she had already gone. I began to get a very bad feeling in the pit of my stomach, one that got much worse when I heard the sound of footsteps crunching along the gravel of the railroad siding between us and the river.

"Well, well, well, if it isn't my little friend Kalvan."

I looked up to see Josh Reiner coming to a stop a few yards away.

Oh crap.

"You're not enough to send the selkies scurrying for the exits," said Sparx. "What's . . ."

The water on either side of the place where Josh stood started to roil and hump up as though something enormous was stirring in the deeps.

Sparx made a little whimpering sound. "That's not good."

"What is it?" I asked.

"Her, I think."

Josh nodded at that, a dreamy smile twisting his lips as he did so. "It is indeed Her."

Sparx gave me a sharp kick. "Run!"

8

Bad Hare Day

"I SAID *RUN!*" Sparx bolted back up the railroad siding in the direction we had come from only a few minutes before.

I ran after him.

Behind us I could hear a great sluicing, as though something huge and terrible were pushing its way up out of the swamp.

"Faster!" yelled Sparx.

"Stop!" The voice was rich and watery and feminine.

In response, my feet simply quit running. Unfortunately, the rest of me didn't. It was like tripping over a log. I managed to get an arm up to protect my face, but I felt as though someone had punched me in the lungs when I landed on my chest in the gravel lining the railway. From the crunching and skittering of the rocks ahead of me, I could tell something similar had happened to Sparx.

I wanted nothing more than to lie there hugging my ribs until

I could breathe again, but I didn't dare. Instead, I forced myself to roll over and look back along the tracks. A castle had risen from the water behind me. Or perhaps it would be better to say that it had shaped itself from the water. The battlements and towers were formed from living water, all browns and greens like the swamp or the muddy river beyond. A huge catfish swam back and forth within the confines of the nearer gate tower, occasionally disappearing into the depths beyond. It was like one of those enormous walk-through aquariums without all the glass between you and the action—simultaneously breathtaking and terrifying.

It took me several long seconds to notice the woman standing on the wall above the gate—tall and slender, with green hair and garments the color of Mississippi mud. Her expression was distant and imperial—a frozen smile on an inhumanly beautiful face. Her eyes . . . Her eyes were drowning eyes. That's the best I can do, deep and dark, as dangerous as a whirlpool.

I had never been more scared in my life.

She spoke again. "Child most mortal, why have you wronged my acolyte?" I saw Josh then, standing in the shadow of the gate, just this side of watery doom.

"I don't think—" Josh began, but the Rusalka cut him off with a gesture.

"You are mine and you have been attacked. These must answer for it."

A voice whispered in my ear, "Speak *not*, fire's child." *Sparx!*

Since I really hadn't started breathing again yet, I couldn't have said anything to her if I'd wanted to, but I was incredibly grateful to have Sparx there giving advice. Sure, he was grumpy and sarcastic, and occasionally downright mean, but in a few short weeks I'd grown to rely on him to help me navigate this new world of magic I'd found myself forced to deal with.

"In fact, speak not at all. The ground we tread here is fraught and fragile. Step but the tiniest jot in the wrong direction and the river's Rusalka will devour thee."

It was only with the *thee* that I realized Sparx was speaking to me in the tongue of fire, a much more formal-sounding language than English. Or at least that's how it seemed in those first moments of understanding it. Unfortunately, thinking about the fact that I *was* understanding it reminded me I didn't know the language, and the next few words came through as a smoky sizzle with a side of embers, making no sense to me at all.

I shook my head and tried not to think about what I was hearing, but only what it meant. That seemed to work, as Sparx cut back in suddenly. Understanding the language of fire felt more like remembering something long forgotten than learning something new.

Sparx continued, "Get thou to thy feet, boy. Bow deeply, and then start backing up. Slowly. The fire lies less than five yards hence, and it burns hot enow at last."

I did as I was told. At the bow, the woman . . . no, the *Rusalka* cocked Her head to one side as though She was waiting. One step back. Two. Sparx now stood between me and the deeping castle, his fur flaring bright and hot. He reminded me of nothing so much as an arch-backed cat. I slid my foot another step and froze when the Rusalka raised Her hands as though She were lifting a platter in front of Her. On either side I heard the water begin to gurgle and swirl.

Sparx said something long and cold in the tongue of water. It sounded angry and scared. A fiery whisper sounded in my ear. "Two steps more and then ready thyself for a turn and a jump." The flame on the hare's back humped higher still, rising a full two feet into the air above him.

Another step. I heard a rushing sound of water sliding down the sand, like a wave receding on an ocean beach. One step more. The waters roared and I saw high green walls rising on either side of the tracks.

"NOW!" shrieked Sparx. Then he leaped straight up and back, turning in the air—once again reminding me of a terrified cat.

I caught him out of the air like a football, spinning in the same moment and leaping toward the flames that suddenly raced through the undergrowth toward me—a slender line of crimson and yellow leading back to the fire pit. Green walls toppled toward me. Against all sense and reason, I dove into the fire. The world burned away in a spiral of red and green, like disaster's own Christmas, and I was certain I would be destroyed.

Then there came a flash and a snarl that made me think of a burning house falling in on itself, and I closed my eyes. When I opened them again I was . . . elsewhere. A low stone wall encircled me perhaps a yard away. Around it stood a group of people uniformly wearing office casual and horrified expressions. Several were leaping back from the edge of the wall, and one woman screamed, covering her face as she turned away. It wasn't until that moment that I realized I was standing in the middle of a bonfire with the flames leaping high around me.

"Fly, young fool!" yelled Sparx.

I ran, holding the burning rabbit in my arms as I ducked into a gap left by the woman who had turned away in horror. The men on either side of her leaped back as I passed between them trailing fire.

"Left, head thou for the brush!" Sparx's voice came out loud, but hoarse and tired.

I turned and bolted into a narrow gap between a couple of hoary old lilacs, half expecting them to catch fire as I passed. But the flames I carried on my person were already dying away as I pushed deeper into the scrub. Behind me I could hear a rising chorus of shouts. That only drove me to run faster.

A few minutes later Sparx spoke—more quietly this time, and in English. "I think we can stop now."

I slowed my pace and then slid to a halt, setting the hare down so I could put my hands on my knees and take a series of long, shuddering breaths. "Where are we?"

"Como Park, the bonfire pits." Sparx's voice was weak and thready. "Nearest unbound flame I could find."

Once he said it, I thought back and realized I should have recognized the place. I'd played in the pits often enough over the years—I lived less than a mile away, and Como was the biggest park in Saint Paul. "We must be in that little strip of woods to the west, then. Let me see if I can find the trail."

Sparx nodded but didn't say anything.

A question occurred to me. "If you could take us through the fire all along, why did you want to try for the railroad bridge?"

"Because fire's road is not as easy as it looks," replied the hare. Then he gently keeled over.

"Sparx!"

The hare didn't reply. He was barely breathing, and his fur had grayed to the color of ash.

"Sparx?" I bent and touched his shoulder, but there was no answer. He was much colder than usual and I felt a matching cold growing in my stomach as I looked around desperately for something or someone that might help him.

That's when I heard the voice of my grandmother Elise. She'd died when I was only five, but her smile and her voice would be with me forever. I remembered her as kind and strong despite an obvious fragility. She always had good advice for me and for my mother, and now I remembered a thing she'd told me that hadn't ever really made sense until this very moment.

Someday, child, you will see something go wrong and you will think: Somebody needs to do something about it! Remember then that you are somebody.

I scooped Sparx up in my arms and ran deeper into the little woods, looking for a place I had seen before but always avoided. I found it only a few moments later—a little rock-lined hollow scooped out in a tiny clearing sheltered by a low limestone ridge. It was a place where the homeless sometimes camped, and they frightened me. But this was more important than my fear.

Working fast, I set Sparx down in the hollow—he had grown noticeably colder in the time it took me to get there. There was a small pile of sticks and twigs near the hollow—saved for later need by those who camped there—and I made a mental promise to replace it when I could as I piled the wood around and atop the hare. My grandmother's influence again. She'd had opinions about people who took things without asking or replacing them—

her version of "Goldilocks" ended with the thieving girl getting eaten, *"and rightfully so."*

It wasn't until I had almost completely covered the hare that I realized I had nothing to light a fire with. I looked at Sparx and saw that he'd stopped breathing. I had to fight back tears at the thought of him dying to save me. I briefly considered trying to breathe fire again, but I was terrified instead of angry and even if I could muster up the rage I might do far more harm than good here.

I needed control, not power . . . but I hadn't really gotten much of a grip on any of the things Sparx had been trying to teach me except how NOT to start big fires with my breath or compel people to believe my lies. And he hadn't even *begun* to teach me any of the rhymes and spells he said I would need to know once I'd learned how not to muck things up.

If only I . . . Wait, what was that rhyme my mother had recited? The one my grandmother used to sing? Could that be a spell?

Right. "Ash and char, sun and star, wind and smoke, ash and oak . . ." That was all I had, and I could feel in my bones that it wasn't enough. It needed a closing rhyme. *Think!* "Fires bind for fire's kind, fires bright and fires light!"

Nothing.

Don't panic. Think!

Oh. Could it be that simple?

Forcing myself to think in meaning and not in words, I tried it again. This time I spoke in the language of fire, and when I finished, the piled wood burst into a gentle flame. Now, if only it would work . . .

Time passed without any apparent change in Sparx's condition. Hope faded in my heart and I felt tears well up at the corners of my eyes and run silently down my cheeks. I made no move to wipe them away as I stared blurrily into what I now feared was nothing more than a funeral pyre.

Then, just as I sighed and started to turn away, I heard a faint little cough. A puff of deep-green smoke curled out of Sparx's mouth and his sides began to move with his breath again. Though he made no other sign, the fire started to burn faster now, and I hurried into the nearby trees, looking for more to feed it.

I don't know how long that went on—the fire burning bright and fast, with me scurrying back and forth to add wood—but finally the flames settled down to a more normal pace and Sparx sat up in their midst.

He started to stretch and almost instantly stopped with a sharp indrawn breath. "Ow, I hurt all over. It feels like someone froze me solid and left the ice in my joints when they thawed me out."

All that was said in the language of fire, and I responded in the same way. "That's not too far from the truth. Thou wast cold and gray when I set thee there, more an ash hare than one of fire."

He reverted to English. "Then I owe you my life."

"No, we're even. I was just paying you back for saving mine from the Rusalka."

The hare nodded. "My name is *sprths*al*erarha." The word was in the language of fire, with three sharp crackles punctuating it.

"Tell me the words to free you."

The hare leaped out of the fire. "Perhaps later. First, I want to see what you become."

I had briefly considered going back to Free, but it was late in the school day, I was exhausted, and home was much closer. I checked the garage to make sure neither Oscar nor my mother was home before I crossed the yard to the back door and let myself in.

As soon as it closed behind me I released Sparx from my bag and headed for the fridge to look for a snack. I ended up digging a couple of waffles left over from Sunday breakfast out of the freezer.

"What are you doing?" Sparx demanded as I took my first bite.

"Eating a waffle . . ."

"Frozen?"

"They're homemade."

"But frozen."

"I like the way they crunch." I took another bite.

The hare shivered and made a disgusted face. "Humans!"

I ignored him and continued to eat my waffle. I'd learned to eat a lot of things cold or how to heat them up myself when I was little and mealtimes were less . . . reliable. I learned a lot of things about how to take care of myself back then. Before Mom met Oscar. Say what you would about Oscar being a big jerk, but he could really cook. Better than Mom, even. A lot of things had gotten more regular, too, though they could still go a little weird when he was traveling for work, or deep in a project and holed up in the basement. Oscar's basement, hmmm . . .

"Kalvan?"

"Yeah," I mumbled.

"Have you come to your senses?"

I blinked. "What do you mean?"

"You stopped eating that horrible waffle and started staring at it instead about three minutes ago."

"I did?" I realized the waffle was starting to go floppy on me and quickly took another bite. Frozen is fine and hot is fine. Cold and soggy, not so much. Once I finished it, I immediately began to feel a bit better and started in on the second. Maybe Sparx wasn't the only one who needed fuel for the fires. "I just had a thought."

"What a novel experience that must be for you. No wonder you were rendered immobile." Though his words had lost none of their typical bite, I noticed a softening of his tone—less acid, more exasperation.

I stuck my tongue out at him. "Oscar made the waffles."

"I'm very happy for him, and with the simple application of a toaster they could be rendered edible once again. Your point?"

"That they made me think of him, and I realized this is the first time since school started when I've really been home alone, and we've got at least two hours." My mom usually arranged her freelance work so she got home within a few minutes of me.

"Annnnnd . . ."

I ducked into the back hall and looked at the big antique door that led to the basement. I hated going down there under the best of circumstances, but I found myself checking the handle anyway. Locked, of course. I turned to Sparx, who had followed me into the hall.

"How are you with locks?"

"Picking them?" He rocked back onto his haunches and crossed his front legs across his chest. "No thumbs. Why do you ask?"

I had just remembered that connection I'd sensed between the model and the thing under the capitol. Add that to Sparx talking about hungry shadows in the tunnels below the bluff, and I found myself wondering about exactly why my stepfather might have something like that in his workshop. Oscar as Oscar was plenty bad enough to make my life miserable, but more to be endured than fought *because my mother*. But Oscar as dark sorcerer . . . that was something else entirely. But I didn't say any of that in case it turned out I was wrong about a connection and was just freaking out over nothing. No one wants to look dumb in front of their magic rabbit.

"Just come on," I said.

Sparx rolled his eyes but followed me as I went back through the kitchen, grabbed the LED flashlight out of my backpack, and went into the dining room. There was a weird little closet there under the front stairs. As some point, a previous owner had put shelves in, and now we used the upper ones for towels and linens.

When I was little it had been one of my favorite places to hide. The second shelf up was so deep we never filled it all the way back. So, I would crawl in behind the stacked towels, pull the door shut behind me, and read Mask comics on the old tablet computer my mom handed down to me when she got a new one.

This time, I wormed my way through boxes full of various holiday decorations and odds and ends that filled the bottom of the closet, making my way to the very back. There, under the landing at the bend in the stairs, I pushed aside a small trunk to expose a trapdoor in the floor. When I pulled on the ring, it moved slowly and reluctantly.

Sparx flattened his ears at the noise and frowned. "Squeals like a banshee with one ear caught in a bicycle chain." I looked a question at him and he shrugged. "Once heard, never forgotten. Also, you'd think she'd have learned her lesson the first time, but no."

I finally got the door up, exposing a dark void—the crawl space under the house. I leaned into the hole and shone my flashlight around. There was a concrete floor about two and a half feet down and cobwebs everywhere. Pipes and wires ran through and between the floor joists. Ducts hung beneath them, all leading toward the back of the house, where a narrow hole in the concrete passed through to the furnace in the ancient cellar some yards below.

An old broomstick handle lay on the floor about a foot away, and I used it to clear cobwebs as I crawled toward the back. Two big sheets of plywood marked what I was looking for. Pulling the nearer one aside with an effort, I exposed a sort of round well in the concrete. It was six feet deep and six across, its sides walled in with rough limestone blocks. The bottom was covered with an old rag rug.

Now, how to get down there . . . I could easily have jumped, but I'd never have gotten back up if I did so. I flashed the light into the joists above. These were arranged differently than in the rest of the house, with a rough square of two-by-sixes set into steel cradles so they could be lifted out. I knew that the floor above them was removable as well, though it involved moving the dining room table, taking up the Oriental rug it sat on, and maybe some other steps—it had been years since it was last opened.

That was how Oscar got some of the bigger stuff for new models down into the basement, through the well where the beer kegs used to come up. A vague memory from one of my previous explorations returned to me then and I pointed my light toward the edge of the square overhead. Yes! There on the far side of the well, beside a duct where someone had screwed a big stainless-steel eyebolt into one of the wooden joists, a few inches of heavy rope were visible going from the bolt up onto the top of the duct.

Reaching into the space above, I could feel more rope coiled there—thick and pliable, like the kind used by mountain climbers. When I pulled, it came free with a heavy slithering noise, followed by a thump as considerably more than six feet of it bounced off the edge and landed in the bottom of the little well. Someone had tied big knots into the line fifteen inches or so apart, making it super easy to climb. Jackpot!

"This has to be the weirdest house I've seen in the last hundred years," said Sparx as I started to climb down into the well.

"Built on the ruins of an old brewery," I replied. "The cellar's original to the previous construction." The rag rug was square, so the corners were rucked up. Grabbing one and pulling it aside revealed thick oak planks.

Before I could do anything further, Sparx, who had been looking down over the edge of the wall, gave out a sharp hiss. "Don't touch those planks!"

"What? Why?" I glanced up at him.

"Without touching the wood underneath it, can you pull the rug back a little more?"

"Sure." When I did as he asked, Sparx let out a low whistle, but I couldn't see any reason for it even though I'd exposed more than half the planks. "What?"

"Turn out your light for a second, and it may become clearer to you."

"All right, but I don't . . . oh." With my light off everything should have gone pitch-black, and it did, except . . .

So, magic is weird stuff. A rough brown line traced its way along the edge of the plank floor just within the circle of the stone wall around the well. A second line was inscribed about a foot in from the first, and a series of wavery symbols had been drawn in between the two. I shouldn't have been able to see them in the dark, but . . . well, they all glowed. Only, *glowed* isn't the right word because they didn't add any light to the well.

Try this: imagine something drawn with a rich brown earth tone on bright-white paper. You're looking at it in bright sunlight so you can really see the richness of the color. It practically shouts. Now take away the light and the paper and fill it all in with black, except you can still see the brown. Like that.

"What is it?" I asked.

"Earth-sign, a warding, and powerful. I can't say much more than that. I speak the tongue of earth, but I don't feel it in my marrow. That's a very dangerous piece of magic."

9

Mischief's Child

I STUDIED THE spell for several long seconds. "How do we get past it?"

"I'm not sure we can. I don't like finding it here in a house of fire, but I'm reluctant to try to break or bypass it if we don't have to. It could have been here for a hundred years without causing any problems. Why do you suddenly want to get past it now?"

I turned my light back on so I could see him. "The basement is Oscar's domain."

"Your stepfather, right? The one you've been making very sure to keep away from me and vice versa."

"Yeah, I don't think he'd be happy to see you even if he thought you were a regular rabbit. Oscar's the reason we don't have any pets. He says it's because he's allergic to everything, but I've never seen him have any kind of reaction. I think he just doesn't like animals."

"Which I'm not."

"I know, but I'm pretty sure he'd like elemental spirits even less. I don't think he really likes anybody except *maybe* my mom. Also, he says you shouldn't believe in anything you can't see and touch. I remember when I was little my mom and I used to go to this church or temple or something—I don't know which; it was almost as hippie as the Free School. But as soon as she started dating Oscar, that stopped cold. He says any time you hear a priest clear their throat you should get a tight hold on your wallet."

"He's not wrong. But you still haven't explained what that has to do with why we're down here."

"Sorry. Oscar . . . well. Let me tell you about Oscar and what's under this." I pointed at the hatch. I'd already long ago related my experience under the capitol to Sparx, and now I told him how the model in the basement echoed that terrible feeling of presence. And because talking about it reminded me of the morning I'd seen Oscar as a man of stone, I mentioned that, too.

Sparx leaned back on his haunches. "That does put a different spin on things." He peered down at the planks again. "I don't like this at all, but after what you've told me, I like not knowing what's on the other side of that ward even less. Can you roll the rug back farther without touching the wood?"

"No problem." I was soon standing on a little mound of rug against one wall of the well. "I'm going to turn the light out again, so I can see the lines."

But I still didn't actually know anything about spell casting, and the dark kind of started to freak me out after a little while, so I turned it back on. Meanwhile, Sparx simply sat on the edge of the well and stared down at the drawing.

"Do you want me to lift you down?" I asked after maybe ten minutes. "So you can get a closer view?"

He shook his head. "That's not going to help, and I'd rather not get too close. There might be something in there that would notice."

I glanced at the planks with fresh alarm. "What about me? I'm already here."

"Too late to worry about that now. I'm pretty sure you didn't trigger anything when you first went down there." He flicked his ears forward and back. "From what I can tell, I don't think it's all that sensitive, but it's very powerful. I'm really not seeing any way to crack it. I think we're going to have to let it go and find another way in."

"No." I didn't mean to say anything; the word just sort of welled up from somewhere down deep in my heart, a reflexive denial.

Sparx cocked his head to one side. "No what? Do you have some idea for breaking the ward without setting it off?"

"Not at all, but there's got to be a way." I thought about something I'd learned at Free. "If you can't see a solution to a problem, there's a good chance you're looking at it the wrong way."

"I'm listening."

"Look at Alexander the Great."

Sparx raised an eyebrow. "Still listening, but very confused."

"The Gordian knot." Another one from my mythology class. "It was this big thing back in ancient days—a knot no one could untie because it was impossible to find the ends. Alexander just took out his sword and cut the knot, *making* the ends he needed. He found a solution to the problem by looking at it from a different angle." That last bit was the point of the lesson, according to my English teacher.

The hare crossed his forelegs across his chest. "All right, smart boy, so what's the solution?"

I deflated a bit. "I don't know. I don't really understand the problem."

"Well, it's a nasty ward designed to prevent people from getting through the well."

"How? I mean specifically. What's it supposed to do?"

Sparx shrugged. "I don't read earth sign well enough to get into the depths of it, but if any of those boards is moved, it'll sever the circle and all sorts of hell will break loose."

"All right." I nodded. "We can't break the circle. What else?"

"If anyone touches the warded planks, that'll set it off, too. I don't know what *exactly* will happen to whoever does that, but it will be bad."

"But I was able to walk on it with the rug here, and that was all right."

"Well, yes, but standing on it won't get you into the basement."

I turned out my light and looked at the outer circle of earth magic. "It doesn't go all the way to the edge, does it . . ."

"Huh?"

"The circle, it's not actually touching the stones of the well, is it?" In the dark I couldn't be sure.

"No, it's not," said Sparx. "Does that matter?"

I flicked the light back on so I could see the hare. "What if we could lift the planks all together, like a trapdoor? Would that set off the ward?"

There was a long, thoughtful silence before he spoke again. "I wouldn't think so, but how would you do that? It's big and heavy and there's nothing holding it together."

"Yet," I replied. "Come on!"

I scrambled back up the rope and led Sparx through the house and out to the garage. Oscar was an engineer, and he kept a pretty good set of tools out there, as well as some lumber and hardware for projects around the house. He'd even installed one of those special ventilation systems for the bigger power tools, like the table saw. Sawdust was one of the main reasons it was all out in the garage instead of down in the basement with his design stuff.

I selected a couple of two-by-fours, some screws, a battery-powered drill with a screw bit, and a battery-powered jigsaw—the reciprocating saw was probably a better tool for what I wanted, but it scared me. Picking up the saw and the drill, I headed back to the house. This was going to take a couple of trips.

"You know how to use all that stuff?" Sparx sounded amazed. "I thought you were more of a book nerd."

"Free School. For graduation we have to prove we can do stuff in a bunch of areas, like life skills. We need to take at least one life skills class every semester. I've taken shop, sewing, intro to metalworking, cooking . . . At first some of it's scary, especially the stuff with power tools, but in the end it's all *applied thinking*"—my shop teacher's phrase. "Sure, it takes some coordination, but a lot less than you'd think going in. If you carefully work through the idea first, it all becomes a lot easier."

An hour later, I was sweating, and I had a giant black bruise growing under my thumbnail from where I'd slipped with the screw bit on the drill, but I had also turned the loose planks into something that looked a whole lot more like a trapdoor, and I'd done it without triggering the spell. I'd also discovered that I was going to need some more rope, a pulley, and a ring bolt . . . no, two. Oh, and time I didn't have, because my mom would be home not too long from now.

So, I finished setting things up—I found the bolts and some yellow nylon line in the garage along with a rusty old pulley. Then I put all the tools away on their little pegboard racks and closed everything, even rolling the rug out over the well cover and sliding the plywood back into place.

As long as no one went into the crawlspace and looked really closely, I'd be fine. Actually getting into the basement was going to have to wait a bit, which was super frustrating. Especially since I didn't even know if my idea would work. What if the planks were attached from the underside somehow? What if I wasn't big enough or heavy enough to pull the thing up? What if? What if? What if?

I only barely made it in time, too. The back door opened as I was crawling out of the closet for the last time.

"Kalvan, are you home?"

"Yeah, Mom, I'm in the dining room." I quietly closed the closet behind me.

A moment later, she came through from the kitchen. "Oh my, Kalvan, you're as filthy as if you'd just dug your way out of your own grave!"

"Huh?" I looked down and realized I was covered in dust and cobwebs, and the knees of my jeans were ragged from crawling across the concrete. "Oh, uh . . ." I glanced guiltily at the line of footprints leading back and forth from the closet. "I . . ."

"Take those shoes off before you move another step! Then, into the shower. You can throw your sneakers into the washing machine with the rest and start it running when you get out. In the meantime, I need to get this cleaned up before Oscar gets home." She turned her eyes on Sparx. "You too. You're *covered* in filth."

Sparx rocked back onto his haunches. "I'm kind of allergic to showers, actually."

"Then go flare it all off. But NOT in my house—I abhor the smell of burning dust. Move, both of you!"

"It still doesn't strike you as the least bit odd that he's a rabbit that talks?" I asked.

Sparx rolled his eyes. "Hare."

My mother shook her head. "Why would it? He's very articulate—and *much* more polite than the vacuum cleaner is going to be about this mess. Now, scat."

As I stuffed my dirty clothes into the washer—our laundry closet opened into the downstairs bathroom—I turned to look at Sparx. "Do you think our vacuum can talk?" I was pretty sure I knew the answer, but maybe I was wrong.

"With the right enchantment it's not impossible, I suppose. But . . . well, where do you keep it?"

"It's in the closet off Mom's office."

"Not in that basement?"

I shook my head. "No, definitely not."

Sparx sighed and looked more than a little sad. "Then, no, your vacuum doesn't talk. There is nothing in your house this

side of those wards that bears an enchantment of that magni-
tude. I'd feel it." He paused for several heartbeats before going
on. "I'm sorry. I know that you worry about her and . . ."

I felt a bit like someone had punched me in the chest. "It's not
your fault. She's always been that way. I . . . no, forget it." I didn't
want to talk to anyone about how protective I felt of my mom,
not even Sparx. "Look, you'd better get cleaned up, too." I leaned
over the counter and cranked the window open a few inches so
he could get in and out, then climbed into the shower and turned
it as high and hot as it would go.

When I was done, I found a very clean-looking hare by the
sink, sitting atop a pile of fresh clothes. After pressing start on the
washer, I got dressed. There was a plate of fruit and cheese waiting for me in the kitchen. The door to Mom's office was cracked
open, which was an invitation to stick my head in, so I picked up
the plate and stepped through the door.

Mom's office had once been the house's smallest bedroom.
Now it had two desks and six filing cabinets crammed into it.
Three computers with five monitors between them took up most
of the available desk space. My mom was staring intently at a huge
spreadsheet on the largest of the monitors.

I settled in with my back against the door as I ate a piece of
cheese. "How was your day?"

"It's very nearly there," she replied. "The 990 isn't tying out to
the audit, mainly because FASB 116 and 117 require funds to show
in the year the pledge is made, so they're reflected on the restricted
income statement but not the program income in the 990."

"You realize that makes no sense in English," I observed.

"Uh-huh. And the related costs mean the functional expenses appear overstated in management and administration, which is going to put the program expense below standard ratio."

I sighed, gave her a quick over-the-shoulders hug, and exited stage right. Mom was deep in the land of *focus*, where very little existed outside whatever problem she was working on. I didn't understand a word of it, but the few times I'd met people she worked with, I'd been assured she was absolutely brilliant at her job. I didn't doubt it. She might be kind of disconnected from reality, but I'd always known she was one of the smartest people I'd ever met.

Sparx hopped up on my bedside table. "How often does she get like that?"

"All the time. But do you know what the most frustrating part is?"

"No idea."

"If I were to go back in there and tell her all about my day, it would *seem* like she wasn't hearing a word I was saying right up until I accused her of not listening. Then she'd be able to recite back everything I said nearly word for word." We'd had a couple of screaming arguments about it over the years—well, I was screaming anyway.

"So, she is actually listening?"

"No, I don't think so. Not like you or I listen, anyway. I think it all goes in through her ears and straight into her memory without her even noticing it passing through. I'm pretty sure if no one called her on it, she'd never know it was there. It's only when you ask that she hits the mental playback button. It drives me crazy."

"Short trip."

I rolled my eyes. "Like I haven't heard that before."

The fire burned without consuming. I stood in the midst of a garden of flame, with a million candlelight flowers dancing madly around me. Reds and yellows dominated, but there were also blues and greens and brilliant purples. The cavern of the Free School's over-size theater bloomed bright and hot—Dante's inferno in a nutshell.

I stood center stage, the star of a play whose lines I couldn't remember to save my soul. And that *was* the wager: my soul against the fires. Evelyn sat in the front row, burning brightly and mouthing the words I so desperately wanted to say. But when I tried to read her lips, I realized that she was speaking English and I knew only the language of fire.

I started forward, hoping to see better, but the orchestra pit suddenly opened into a yawning void before my feet, a void filled with the same malice I had felt beneath the capitol. It hungered and it hated and it had me in its sights. Leaping back, I stumbled and fell, striking my head on the stage so that the fires spun and doubled and I thought I might throw up.

Rolling to the side, I fell out of my bed and landed hard on hands and knees. When I forced myself to my feet, I felt the harsh rutching of soot under my heels and toes. Again my dreams of fire had spilled into the waking world. A tiny hiss of indrawn breath drew my attention to the big drawers in my captain's bed. Pulling the nearer one open, I exposed the nest I had made for Sparx. In it, the hare twitched and kicked like a cat caught in a nightmare. Gently, I touched his shoulder.

Sparx woke with a sharp jerk and whipped his head up to look at me. "Your dreams are deep and dark—a snare for the unwary familiar."

It was the first time he'd used that word, though I recognized it from a hundred fantasy novels. "Is that what you are now? The familiar to my boy witch?"

"Half a familiar, at any rate, to go with being half summoned."

"So, you saw my dreams. Did you see this as well?" I raised a foot to show him the soot that covered the sole.

The hare blinked several times, then reached up and touched a paw to my big toe. "Now, isn't that interesting . . . Makes me wonder."

"Wonder what?"

"Whether you are walking in dreams or they are stalking you in our world." He sniffed at his paw and then flipped his ears backward and forward in a sort of shrug. "No answers here. Nothing of dreams, and little of magic." He rolled onto his back feet. "Hey, now that everyone's asleep, what do you say we take another crack at that basement?"

I thought about it for a while. "All right."

I'd taken to leaving a towel tucked into the dead space between Sparx's drawer and the head of the bed. It was a good place to hide things and surprisingly roomy—I used to crawl in there myself and pull the drawer in behind me when I was five or six and wanted to get away from the world—I've always needed a lot of time alone. I like people, but when my brain gets to spinning, I need to get away from everyone and everything and distract myself. Now I used the already sooty towel to clean my feet.

Dressing quickly, I brought the towel along as we slipped into the crawlspace under the house. We'd already cleared much of the filth out with our earlier comings and goings, and I used the towel to finish up the job now.

It took about ten minutes to get the plywood out of the way quietly and the ropes and pulley in place, and then it was time to—SKREEEEEEEECH! I dropped the rope like it had turned into a snake in my hands.

"Sparx, run up the stairs and listen for Oscar and Mom, quick! Warn me if you hear them coming." The hare bolted for the trapdoor while I yanked the pulley off the ring bolt I'd put in for it.

That went on top of the ductwork, and then I dropped down into the well to roll the carpet back over the hatch. I didn't know if my attempt to lift it had woken up my mom and Oscar, but I had a hard time imagining a world where anyone with a pulse could have missed it. Heck, I had a hard time imagining a world where that wouldn't wake up a few folks of the pulseless variety. Fortunately, the nearest graveyard was a couple of blocks away, so I wouldn't have troubling the dead on my conscience.

A fire flower bloomed in the air above me, and Sparx's voice spoke out of it. "There's someone moving around up here, you need to get OUT."

10

Long Day's Bunny into Night

I **CLIMBED OUT** of the well so fast I skinned my palm on the rope, and then I had to pause while I shoved the rope on top of the duct with the pulley. After that I scrambled like mad back to the closet, scuffing my injured palm painfully in the process. As I climbed out of the crawlspace, I heard heavy footsteps on the stairs overhead.

With my heart clawing its way up into my throat, I closed the trapdoor as quietly as possible and practically teleported from there to the front of the closet. But it was too late. By the time I got out into the dining room, I could already hear the doorknob between the stairs and the living room starting to turn. That's it, I was dead.

I froze, trying to decide if it would be better to pretend I was on my way back from the bathroom in jeans and a T-shirt, or if I should just sprint for my bed and hope Oscar didn't hear or see me. Dead. The knob finished turning . . . and the door clunked but didn't open. My heart started beating again.

Thank God for converted duplexes! Someone had locked the inner door—as sometimes happened. From the other side I heard Oscar curse. I didn't know if he had his keys with him or would need to go back up or around, and I didn't care. I was going to live! Tiptoeing frantically, I crossed the three yards to my bedroom door, slipped through, and then skinned out of my clothes before slipping into my bed.

The door to the living room rattled again, and then I heard Oscar stomp back up the front stairs. He crossed above the dining room like a grumpy elephant and then came down the back stairs. A minute or so later, he poked his head into my room. I held perfectly still and concentrated on breathing slowly and deeply while I ignored the pain in my hand.

After a little while, the door to my bedroom closed. Other doors opened and shut, including the living room, and I had plenty of time to pray that Oscar wouldn't look into the crawlspace and notice the plywood out of place. Then, Oscar clomped back to bed without even opening the closet.

With a little sigh of relief I peeled back the covers and found my pajamas—I'd have to wait until he was good and asleep to go clean up my skinned palm. I was just settling in again when Sparx returned, hopping up on the bed beside me where I could see him by the dim glow of the streetlight out front.

"Lucky that door was locked," I said quietly.

"Lucky like a rabbit's foot." Sparx grinned, blew on the nails of a front paw, and then buffed it on the fur of his chest. "Also that it was an easy bolt. By the way, you're welcome."

"Huh . . . oooooh. Thank you! That was too close."

"So, what now?"

I shrugged. "We'll have to wait until we can get the house to ourselves for a couple of hours. And after blowing off *all* my classes yesterday, I won't be able to manage that till next week at the earliest. If I miss too much class, I'll be in a world of hurt. Sometimes being thirteen is the absolute pits."

"Hey, Kalvan, time to get up." I felt a gentle hand on my shoulder.

"Huh?" I blinked my eyes blearily open and found my mother leaning over me. "Wazzup?"

"Sorry to wake you early, but I'm taking you in to school today."

"Okay . . ." I'd thought Oscar was doing that. "When?"

"As soon as you can get dressed. I'll probably be a little late as it is."

I felt a churning dread start up somewhere around my stomach. "Did something happen?"

"There's some problem with a big interchange Oscar helped design, and he needs to get it fixed no later than yesterday."

"Is he going to be gone?" That would be fantastic—the perfect opportunity to get into the basement!

"No, it's all design phase stuff. He said he'll be holed up in the basement and keeping weird hours for the next two to three weeks. He actually grabbed one of the cots and a sleeping bag and hauled them down there so he wouldn't be in any danger of waking me when he gets up to tinker with the models. Now, you'd better get dressed."

And then she was gone.

Sparx poked his head out of his drawer. "That's not good."

"No." Oscar might not have caught us, but he was suspicious now. There was *definitely* more to him than I'd ever expected, and I doubted any of it was good.

School can be a gigantic pain in the butt on the adventures front. Even at the Free School there's only so much class you can safely skip, and I was deep into the danger zone. I'm really, really smart. I know it's not modest or properly Minnesotan to come right out and say that, but it's true, and it's part of why I can get away with as much as I do with my teachers. They all complain about me not working up to my potential. But, because I can mostly learn the material even when I'm being a lazy jerk—and, if I'm being honest, that's way too much of the time—they cut me a lot of slack.

But that line was tight now, and I had to buckle down and actually work for a while to get back on the right side of my tests and assignments. I spent most of the three weeks that Oscar camped out in the basement going to all my classes and even doing some of the homework in my free periods, and at the end of it, I was almost back on top of things on the school side.

On the magic side of things, Sparx had me practicing firetongue using the rhyme I'd saved him with and a few others. He also began to teach me the written form of the language, which was incredibly complex, as each word had its own ideogram, like Chinese, instead of constructing words from letters.

It was slightly less boring than learning how NOT to do magic, which was the main thing he wanted me to practice. That involved a lot of sitting still and listening to my breathing and other things that gave my mind too much time and room to gnaw on itself. *Okay, Kalvan, I'm going to throw this smoke ring at you, and I want you NOT to blast it with fire. Just let it wash over you.* Okay, maybe it wasn't quite that bad, but I was terrible at that part of things.

It was all suuuuuper frustrating, and I wanted to bang my head on things and chew through the walls after a couple of weeks of it. Instead, I headed for the library after having lunch with Dave, because I had fourth period free on Tuesdays and I needed to keep on grinding. But ten minutes into my math homework, I'd had it.

"I hate this!"

Aleta was a couple of tables away, and she gave me a very stern look. "Kalvan, hush."

And that was it. I cracked. Very calmly and deliberately, I crumpled up my math worksheets and threw them out the window. Then I stuffed my books into my bag and stomped out of the library.

Aleta called after me—"Kalvin!"—but I ignored her and headed to the theater. I needed to get away from everybody and spend some time alone in my head. Well, as much as I could with a sarcastic talking bunny stuck to me with a thirty-foot invisible leash.

I didn't go to the main doors, which ran along the middle of the second-floor hall, where anyone could see you. Instead, I went around to the stage door and knocked loudly—two slow knocks followed by three fast ones and then two more slow.

About a minute later the door opened and Josh Reiner poked his head out.

"Oh, it's you." He looked like he wanted to slam the door in my face, but the theater was neutral ground for arts students since most of us got involved in the plays in one way or another. He might hate my guts, but he wasn't going to violate that truce.

So, Josh just let the door go and turned away. I caught it before it could shut and stepped through into the velvet darkness of the main stage where Morgan and Lisa—a couple of girls from Rob's advisory group—were practicing a dance piece. On my left I could see a half-dozen students of various ages scattered around in the seats on the lower floor—mostly studying or reading. A couple of seniors were quietly rehearsing some sort of scene in the balcony above them. On the right, the door that led from the stage to the scene shop was propped open, and Josh was already vanishing through it.

The Free School had inherited the building from a now-defunct but once well-funded technical high school that focused on teaching practical skills to students who weren't college bound. For reasons that never made much sense to me, the school had a huge theater/auditorium and scene shop—almost as big as the main stage and shop that Evelyn had taken us to visit at the University of Minnesota. It was my second-favorite place in the building to hang out after the gym, though mostly not as private.

Mostly. I went to the side of the stage facing the front windows and settled in with my back against the base of the low wall made by the raised thrust of the stage. On either side of me, louvered panels maybe two feet square let air flow in under the stage. After a few minutes of listening at the panel, I slid a finger through a gap where one of the slats had been broken away and unlatched the panel. It was hinged on the far side and opened like a door. It took me barely a second to slide through and close it behind me.

The space under the stage was about two feet tall at the front, and everything, including the concrete floor, was painted black, so the light from the louvers didn't penetrate very far. Various old props and piles of folding chairs stacked around the perimeter made it hard to navigate without a flashlight, and kind of claustrophobic for most—not a problem for claustrophile me. Sometimes older students would slip in there to make out, but usually I had it to myself.

Today was one of those days, so I let Sparx loose as soon as I'd gotten back to the depth where things opened up to make room for actors who needed to enter or exit through the trapdoors. It got pretty close to four feet high at the back—enough to move smaller bits of scenery in and out as well, and that's where I headed now. Bigger props were tucked against the back wall, including a ratty three-quarters-sized recliner that I liked to sit in.

As soon as I settled down, Sparx wandered off to poke around in the dark areas under the stage. Bliss! I was alone, really alone for the first time in more than a week. I pulled out a battered old science fiction novel and buried my nose in it. I only had a half hour or so, but for that long I was going to be able to pretend I didn't exist and get my brain to stop chewing on itself.

But I'd barely been reading for ten minutes when Sparx hopped up onto the arm of my chair and touched my shoulder with a paw.

"What is it?"

"I want to show you something. Quietly."

"Go away." I went back to my book.

Sparx's face appeared above the spine. "This is important."

"Fine!" I dropped my book on my pack. "What is it?"

"This way."

I followed him along the back wall to the corner where a three-foot steel mesh panel led into the ductwork. It had always been closed in the past, complete with a heavy padlock, but it was open now, the hasp burned through.

"Your work?" I asked.

He held up a shushing paw, but nodded. Then he touched the floor of the duct and made another shushing motion. The implication was clear, and I was careful about where I put my weight as I followed him into the duct. About ten feet back, another, narrower duct led upward. Sparx pointed to it and made a shushing noise again before he mimed standing up.

When I did so, I found myself looking through a floor-level grate in the wall of the scene shop. The pedestal of the table saw hid about a third of the room from my view, but I had a decent line of sight to where Josh was standing in front of an easel with a good-sized canvas on it. The easel was turned so that anyone coming through the door wouldn't be able to see what Josh was painting.

I immediately wished I hadn't seen it, either. It was a self-portrait. The Josh on the easel wore only a torn pair of blue jeans and a ragged tee as he leaned against a brick wall in the mouth of a rainy alleyway. Electric pain radiated from every inch of the painting. A deep-blue mark half closed his left eye. Blood stained the pavement beneath his bare feet. The image was rendered with a clarity and artistry I would never have expected from someone as downright nasty as Josh had always been to me.

I wanted to turn away. Initially it was because this was not a Josh I had ever wanted to see. I did not want to have sympathy for one of the few people at Free who I genuinely loathed, someone who had done his best to make my life miserable. But after the sympathy had washed through me, I found a second reason for wanting to turn away. I had no right to see this. Josh had not invited me to be a witness, and this was a violation of his privacy. But there is no unseeing what has been seen.

Sparx had somehow managed to climb up and perch on my shoulder while I was distracted. His nose touched my ear as he whispered, "Look over the shoulder of the boy in the painting."

It wasn't easy to turn my attention away from the portrait version of Josh to the background, but once I did, I had to suppress a gasp. Through the curtaining rain, a tall green tower rose from the river—the same one I had seen only a few weeks before when I faced the Rusalka's castle. The Rusalka Herself stood on the pinnacle, Her hands reaching forward in an offer of comfort. Her face seemed barely more than a dot, but with a few tiny strokes of the brush Josh had somehow managed to convey compassion and welcome in Her expression. This was not the monster who had nearly drowned me, this was a queen of faerie offering sanctuary to a child who desperately needed it.

The nose touched my ear again. "Now, look down; on the floor beyond the easel is another painting."

"It's a badger in a bandolier," I whispered back, my voice so low even I couldn't hear me.

Somehow, Sparx understood me and shook his head. "No, it's

not. No more than I am a hare. Less perhaps, since I have chosen a shape that conforms almost entirely to the original. That is a delver. Look at its hands and the way it walks on two legs."

Now that Sparx had pointed it out, I started to see the many ways in which the delver departed from the badger I'd first taken it for. To start with, it had thumbs and was ten times the size of any badger that ever lived. There was also the way it walked upright, though I suspected it could go at least as fast on all fours. It had a badger's face and heavy claws perfect for digging, but a higher forehead, and there was the bandolier. Bandoliers, really, since they crossed its chest in an X.

Before I could speak again, Sparx touched a paw to my cheek and then pointed down. Apparently I had seen what he wanted to show me.

"Why haven't I ever read about delvers before?" I asked once we had worked our way back out of the vent. "I mean, I never heard of fire hares before I met you, but I'd at least read about rusalkas and selkies."

Sparx laughed. "Well, you may have read about them, but what you've read and the ones you've met are only rudimentarily related. Unlike me, the delvers and selkies and Herself are all locally born. I came across from Europe in a ship's lantern a few hundred years back, and while I call most of the locals by the names I grew up with, they have other names among the tribes who were here before the white man came. Herself's older name is simply Mississippi."

"Oh." I was confused. "So, why did those muskrat women answer to *selkie*?"

"You'd have to ask them to know for sure, but I imagine it's because we were speaking English and that's the word for them in that tongue. Most elemental spirits aren't all that fussed about what we're called in any human language. You people change your speech so often it's hardly worth the effort, and in our own tongues it's impossible to mislabel us."

I blinked several times. "So, there's no equivalent to *delver* in English?"

"Not really, though *dwarf* gets close. There are delvers everywhere, and some of the more humanish sort look a bit like your dwarves, or trolls, or gnomes or what have you from legends, but the great bulk of them are more like our friend in the painting. More important than that, though, did you note the badge the delver wore on his chest?"

I thought back. "Some sort of crown?"

"Yes, the Corona Borealis. The delver that bitter-water boy painted serves the keeper of the Crown."

"So?"

Sparx rolled his eyes. "We know the Crown is held by humans at the moment. We also know the Crown is supposed to shift masters with the seasons. Under normal circumstances no elemental creature would bother to badge themselves with an allegiance so brief and transient. We live too long for such ephemeral fripperies."

"Okay. I'm still not getting why this is important."

"Fool boy, it means that something has gone very wrong with the movement of the Crown and the alignment of powers here."

"How bad is that?"

"It depends on what's going on, but if the magical balance goes too far awry it could mean floods, tornadoes, plagues . . ."

"Really? How soon?"

"That's hard to say. The Crown should never rest on any one brow more than once. It would only take a handful of years to badly skew things. I don't think you'd get a major disaster in three years, but I doubt you could go ten without one. The seasons are meant to turn and change and the Crown with them, repeating the cycle but never duplicating one. If one individual has come to control the process, it would not take long for things to go very badly indeed."

11

Smoke and Mirrors

IMAGINE A PIE in the face, one of those big heavy restaurant banana cream pies that's just begging to be used to smack someone. It hits with a sound like a foot going deep into mud at the edge of a lake, kind of splooshy and mooshy and schlorpy all at once. Imagine the squish as your world goes white, and thick streamers of cream shoot past your ears to splash the walls and people behind you. Imagine.

I did. I let the weight of it knock me backward so that I stumbled and went down, rolling along my back and up over my shoulder to land on my chest and stomach.

In the darkness beyond the black box's stage lights the room erupted in laughter. Pushing myself unsteadily to my feet, I scooped pie out of my eyes and blinked around wildly. That's when Dave hit me with another pie. This time, when I went down, I stayed down, TKO'd by a pie. A few moments later, the bouncy music coming from Evelyn's digital music player came to an end and Dave was there, offering me a hand.

"That was beautiful, man. I could almost see the pie!"

"Me too." I mimed wiping more imaginary cream from my eyes, and we both laughed. "It helps to have done the real thing in the play last fall." Dave and I had been the clowns in a Shakespeare-inspired piece, and I'd gotten hit with ten pies over the course of dress rehearsal and performances—all donated by a parent who owned a bakery. "There's something really satisfying about a good pieing even when it's imaginary."

"Maybe especially then? I remember you complaining about getting that stuff in your sinuses for two weeks after the show."

I snorted. "That was pretty miserable. Wish I'd known rule one of getting hit with food *before* that first pie."

Dave grinned and recited, "Close your eyes and your mouth and breathe out through your nose."

I nodded and we hopped down off the stage and took a seat on the floor while the next group of performers climbed up and got ready to improv. But now that I was offstage, I started to worry again, shifting around nervously instead of giving proper attention to the performers. That's because today was it.

Oscar had gone to work at some construction site this morning for the first time in weeks, and I was finally caught up enough that I could afford to slip off for most of a day, and I planned to do just that after improv finished. It's really hard to skip your first class when it's with your advisor and you checked in with her right before breakfast. It's especially hard when it's your favorite class and acting with Evelyn basically saved your soul.

I'll take anything she teaches that I can fit into my schedule, but I especially love group improv. I'll do straight-up acting for plays too, but there's something about the freedom of making it up as you go along that's like no other feeling in the world. It's this *amazing* mix of imagination and communication with the other players and the audience that can take you places you never would have found on your own.

One of the things I especially loved about it right then was the way it let me step outside of myself and my problems. For however long I was up there on the stage I didn't have to worry about my stepfather or my mom or the magic that had become such a big part of my life.

When you're doing it right, all that matters is the scene and how it affects the people watching it. Sometimes it's big and emotional and scary. Sometimes it's quiet and gentle and reassuring. But my favorites are the days where it's silly and funny and full of laughs.

During the craziness after the bell rang, I leaned in close and whispered in Dave's ear. "I decided today is the day we crack Oscar's basement. I know you said you wanted to help." That was important. I was pretty sure I couldn't pull the lid up all by myself—a fact I'd realized when I slipped into the crawlspace to put the plywood sheets back the afternoon after Oscar nearly caught me. "Are you still in?"

"When are you leaving?"

"I was thinking in about ten minutes."

"I've got a test next hour—can you wait till third period?"

I thought about it. "Yeah, that should still give us enough time. Meet me in the bushes on the far side of the gym."

"Done."

I was starting toward the door when Evelyn called my name. "Kalvan, come here for a moment."

"Yes?" I said as I went over to her desk.

"You seemed awfully antsy out there after you got off the stage, and you've been distracted basically since the semester started. Is anything wrong at home?"

I paused for a long second while I tried to frame an answer that didn't include my telling her that I thought my stepfather might be an evil wizard and that I might need to save my mom from him. I didn't think that would end at all well, but she'd caught me off guard and I really didn't have time to think of a good story. Stupid. I should have known Evelyn would notice any changes in her students. She might seem like she lived on a different planet some of the time, but like any good actress or director, she was a keen observer of people.

"Nothing's all that different from usual," I finally said, though I realized the silence had gone on too long already.

"Then you must have finally come into your magic," she said.

"I, uh . . . wut?" It was like getting a cream pie in the face all over again, but completely without warning.

"Then it is magic. I thought it might be. You've got the look to you, and so does your mother. Fire at a guess, though it's hard to tell for those of us who don't have any of our own." She reached out and gently touched my chin. "Close your mouth before something flies into it, Kalvan. You don't teach at someplace like Free in a world where magic runs beneath the surface without learning the signs. Honestly, I think it's one of the reasons the school exists—to provide a safe place for the sidewise thinkers: the dreamers, the artists, and the magicians."

"I really don't know what to say to that."

"Don't worry, your secret is safe with me, though if you'll take my advice, you'll have a word with Tanya about the whole thing."

"But she's a science teacher!"

"Also a very good windwalker, or so I've been told. Head in the clouds, feet on the ground. She's very sensible about the whole thing."

"I . . . all right, maybe."

"Good. I'm here for you, too, Kalvan. Come by my open hour anytime if you need to talk about it. I'll do what I can, though I don't have the practical experience Tanya does."

"That's really covered with spells?" Dave pointed at the bottom of the well.

Sparx nodded. "Some serious nasties. Hard to make them out in this light, though, even with the Sight."

I finished attaching the nylon line to the ring bolt I'd added to the plank lid, then shinnied back up to join them. "Come and give me a hand with the end of this."

I'd brought some oil down and glopped it all over the pulley, which cut down on the screeching, but even so, the planks made a frightful amount of noise as they dragged against the rough stone blocks. If anyone had been home we would have been sooooo busted. If we'd been doing it at any time other than the middle of the day, I'd have worried about the neighbors hearing.

Fortunately, everyone who lived close to our house worked during the day. It was a good thing Dave *had* volunteered to help out, too; I'd never have gotten it open without him.

As soon as we had the thing far enough out of the way to slip through, we tied off the line. Then I took my flashlight and shined it down through the gap. I couldn't see much—mostly a top view of the big model of downtown. From here it didn't even look all that scary. Still, I was super reluctant to take the next step.

"Maybe we'd better wait a few minutes to see if anything happens," I said.

Sparx snorted and Dave gave me a knowing look, but neither of them argued the point. Time passed. Nothing climbed up out of the hole and no one came down from the closet above to make us stop. Finally, I sighed and handed Dave the flashlight. Then I started lowering the knotted climbing rope into the darkness below. When it touched the model I stopped and waited a few more seconds, but nothing happened, so I finished letting it out.

Once the rope was all paid out, I slid my feet over the edge of the well. "I guess it's time. Sparx?"

The hare climbed into my backpack, and I half zipped it before sliding it over my shoulders. I took the flashlight in my mouth so I'd have both hands free, pushed off from the edge, and started down. With the knots to keep my grip from slipping, the climb was easy enough. But then I was hanging in the air over the center of the model, and I suddenly felt that terrible sense of *presence* again, though it had not yet become aware of me.

It hit me so hard I almost lost my grip on the rope, which

would have been disastrous when I crashed down and broke either the model or me into a million pieces. Terror thrilled through me and I could feel my whole body beginning to shake. The flashlight fell from my mouth, landing with a hard crack on the model below and tumbling so that the room went almost completely dark again. I didn't know how long I could hold on, and I was certain I couldn't climb back up.

If not for Sparx I'm not sure what would have happened next, but his voice spoke sharply from my bag. "Freeze, boy!"

I felt weight depart my back and heard a gentle thump as he landed on the table below. The pressure of *presence* eased immediately. I could sense that it was still there, but now I felt as though there were a curtain between me and it—a velvet shield hiding me in a limited way, at least for a time. I almost climbed right back up then. I probably would have if Dave hadn't been there to see my cowardice.

Instead, I took several calming breaths. I could do this. I *had* to do this. The next bit was tricky, as I was going to have to put at least some of my weight on the model. That was scary too. *What if I broke it?*

There'd be no hiding that we'd been there if that happened. Gently, I put a sneaker down on one of the streets to the east of the capitol—right in front of the Free School, in fact. Keeping most of my weight on the rope, I slowly tippy-toed my way to the edge of the model, dragging the rope into a seventy-or-so-degree tilt. Then I hooked an edge of the big table with my foot and pulled myself out over the floor. I even managed to do it without crushing anything on my way to the ground.

"Your turn, Dave. I'll hold the rope tight so you don't have to do what I did."

A few minutes later and we were both safely on the floor while Sparx remained near the center of the table.

"Is everything all right?" I asked.

"I'll survive, but I don't dare move right now." The hare's voice sounded sharp and strained. "This thing is too strong."

"Is there anything we can do?" asked Dave.

"I don't know. It feels like a deep power—earth and shadow. Turning on the lights might help."

"Hang on while I go get the overheads," I said. "It'll take me a minute. The switch is at the top of the stairs and I can't get at the flashlight without climbing back up onto the model."

"Which would be an *extraordinarily* bad idea," said Sparx.

Normally, I would have been delighted to be moving away from that sense of presence, but what little light came from where the flashlight had landed barely illuminated a bit of the table. And the darkness beyond its reach felt . . . well, full of potential. As though it were alive somehow, but lightly sleeping. The idea that it might suddenly wake up made my bones feel cold and hollow. I really didn't want to have anything to do with it, but I had no choice. I took a deep breath before I started to edge away from the table.

"Just a second." Dave pulled out his cell phone. "Does this help?" The light seemed unusually dim and pale, barely enough to penetrate the heavy weight of blackness, but it was the loveliest light I'd ever seen.

"You're a lifesaver, Dave. Follow me." With Dave's cell to

illuminate the way, we quickly made it to the stairs and up to the switch, flooding the basement with light. Seconds later, we had returned to the big table.

Sparx was waiting for us on the edge of the table with my flashlight. "*Much* better, though I'll have to stay close to keep it blocked. I don't know what that thing is, but it doesn't like the spots." He looked up. "There is an element almost like the sun in those lamps."

"They look like greenhouse bulbs to me," said Dave, squinting upward. "Full-spectrum and brighter than all get-out. My mom has seasonal affective disorder, and she uses them in the kitchen and living room to help her get through Minnesota winters."

I took the flashlight and turned it off. "Thanks, Sparx, I'd have been cooked without your help. What is that thing?" Though its power had faded considerably, I could still feel a dark and brooding something centered on the model of the capitol.

The hare shook his head. "I don't know, but I think we'd better find out before we do anything else. It doesn't feel all that intelligent, and I'm blocking it for the moment, but there may be more to it if it's really tied to the thing you felt in the tunnels. If it's smart enough to recognize you and tell your stepfather, then we don't dare stay here for long or let it get too close a look at you."

That thought had never occurred to me, and I swallowed hard as it sank in. Again, I wanted to bolt. "How likely is that?"

"No way to know without knowing what it is. In any case, I'm trapped up here for the duration." I looked at the model and shuddered. The last thing in the world I wanted to do was get closer to it, but I didn't have a whole lot of choice.

I was still trying to figure out how to go about that when Dave spoke from somewhere under the table. "Thought so."

"What?"

"My dad's a model-trains guy. He takes me to shows sometimes, and when they have big setups like this one, there are always trapdoors in the table to let you get at the middle bits without having to play Godzilla with the landscaping." A moment later the capitol lawn flipped upward and Dave stood up in the gap facing the dome, leaning in close. "Looks to me like the front of this building opens up."

"Don't touch it yet!" Sparx hopped over to join him. "Let me give you some cover."

"Is that safe?" I asked, worrying for my friend.

"Much more so for him than for you," replied Sparx. "If he's got any magic of his own, it's not yet bloomed. To creatures like me or the thing in the model, he's . . . well, not invisible, but much harder to identify."

"If *I've* got magic?" Dave's voice came out much more wistful than I'd have expected. "Is that possible?"

Sparx nodded. "Oh yes. Even if you're not born to it, there are many things that can awaken magic in your kind."

Sparx moved forward and touched the miniature building with both front paws, speaking swift and low in the language of fire—the sense of presence from within receded, though it simultaneously became more intense and angrier, as though it had suddenly registered our existence. I was reminded of my earlier feeling that the darkness might awaken around us, and spared a quick prayer to anyone who might be listening that the lights would stay ON.

Sparx backed up, but only a few feet. "There, that should hold it for a bit."

Dave reached around the back of one of the pillars on the capitol portico. There was a click and the left wing of the building swung aside. I had to bite my lip to keep from shrieking or swearing. Inside was a sort of manikin head wearing my mother's face.

"What the ever-loving . . ." Before I could finish, Dave swung the other side of the building open—the eastern side. Another manikin, this one with Oscar's face. "I don't understand."

Sparx held up a silencing paw. "Open the center."

The front of the miniature capitol folded down onto the steps. Inside was a slender silver crown with a single bright diamond like a high star at its peak and three smaller diamonds trailing away on each side. It sat upon a cushion of what looked like black velvet.

"Is that . . . ?" I asked.

"The Corona Borealis," breathed Sparx. Dave reached cautiously toward the Crown, only to have his hand slapped aside by the hare. "Don't touch that!"

He yanked his hand back. "Why not?"

Sparx looked around. "That's no cushion it's resting on. Kalvan, give me a pencil." I tossed one over and he took it between his front paws. "Watch."

Slowly and carefully he leaned forward until the tip of it touched the cushion under the Crown, then he leaped back, leaving the pencil behind. It didn't fall. Instead, it hung there in the air as smokelike darkness rolled up from the "cushion," quickly enveloping it completely like a pointing finger of purest night.

Then the darkness rolled back, taking the pencil—if it still existed—into the thing pretending to be a cushion.

"What *is* that thing?" I breathed.

"It has many names, though most would mean little to you. Fear of the dark hours runs deep in your people, and it is not irrational, it is a memory in the blood and bone. A memory of the time before your kind befriended fire, when that and its many siblings hunted you and yours in the deep hours between sunset and sunrise. You may think of it as a simple fear of the absence of light, but it is not that. What you fear is that which holds the Crown. What you fear is the Dark."

12

The Redcoats Are Coming

I TOOK AN alarmed step back from the table as Sparx's words sank in. "The Dark?"

He nodded. "Or Nightmare, if you prefer another common name. In any case it is ancient and deadly, a powerful enemy to your kind and mine."

"But it's so small . . ." Dave didn't look half so scared as I felt—maybe because he couldn't sense the weight of *presence* lurking there in the miniature of the capitol.

"No." The hare shook his head and his voice took on that formal tone I'd come to associate with things he had learned long ago. "It may appear that way, but only because most of it is elsewhere and what *is* here is hemmed in by light and what power of fire I have used in my warding. Had it wakened before you turned on the lights, or met you in its full strength, things would be very different."

"That's the thing I felt under the capitol," I said. "That's where the main body is."

Sparx nodded. "Very likely. The Dark has made alliances with powers of earth going back to the beginning of days. The sun is the Dark's greatest enemy. Any Nightmare that doesn't wish to run continually before her in an endless circling of the earth has little choice but to lie hidden deep and quiet when day looks down upon the earth with her great golden eye."

"So, what do we do about it?" asked Dave. "Get a bigger flashlight?"

The hare leaned back on his haunches and met Dave's eye with a grim look. "That would have much the same effect as poking a bear with a sharp stick."

"Get a big enough stick and you're talking about a spear." Dave looked ready to take on the world, and I wanted to hug him for it. "If all those shows about ancient history are right, spears have taken care of an awful lot of bears."

Sparx gently shook his head. "Disregarding how very much television gets wrong about the history I remember living through, there isn't a flashlight in all of creation that is big enough for that purpose. Not without considerable magical backing. No. And this is an especially bad time to try it. Today is October the twentieth. Tomorrow crowns the winter monarch, and the waxing power of the Corona Borealis will be very great for some days afterward—almost as strong as on the solstice."

Sparx pointed at the mask. "If your Oscar is a power of earth and the Winter King to come, as seems likely, this is not the moment to challenge him. We haven't a hope of making any necessary preparations in the next few hours, even if we knew exactly what we needed to do to oppose him. No, for now, we close up the model, remove all trace of our presence, and pray to the powers that we have not been meaningfully identified, while we figure out what steps we can take in the future."

I didn't much like the idea of walking away—not with that mask of my mom in there. And it was clear from Dave's expression that he liked it even less than I did, but Sparx was the expert. Besides, I had felt the power of the thing under the capitol, and I didn't think it was any old bear we'd be poking if we started something today. More like a dragon.

With the exception of one nasty little dent in a building on the west side of the capitol mall where the flashlight had fallen, cleanup went quickly and easily. Even there, Dave was able to make some quick fixes with Oscar's modeling supplies, which reminded me of how much time he'd spent with the people who built the sets for our school plays.

Once we had that settled, I looked sadly up at the hatch in the ceiling. "It's going to be even less fun climbing out than it was getting in." I really didn't want to spend any more time hanging over the model with the lights out.

Dave gave me a funny look at that. "Why don't we just go out through the door at the top of the stairs? I looked, and it's one of those old-style latch bolts that lock when you slam the door."

I blinked at Dave for several long seconds. "Because I'm an idiot?"

He chuckled, and the tension really broke for the first time since we'd gone through the trapdoor in the closet above. "Could be, my friend, could be."

∽

That night, after my mom had stopped by to give me a peck on the cheek and say good night, I crawled out of bed and turned my light back on. For the first time since I was really little, I was afraid to sleep in the dark. I also set my alarm extra early so Oscar wouldn't find out. My dreams were full of flame and shadow—nightmares, if not Nightmares.

Even with the early setting, I woke before the alarm. Looking around, I found Sparx perched atop the shelf by my bedroom door, watching both me and the door with an intensity I'd rarely seen from him. When he realized I was up, he looked a bit sheepish before he hopped down and hid himself in my backpack. I didn't see Oscar at all that day—a business trip, according to my mom. One that would keep him away all weekend. I was simultaneously relieved and more scared than ever. When he came back he would be the Winter King.

When night came again, I could feel it like a weight pressing against my window. I half expected to see the panes bulging and cracking. I turned on my light and didn't sleep at all. Fortunately, it was Saturday and I was able to go to sleep once I'd opened my shades to the dawn light. I slept nearly all of Sunday as well, though my mom seemed too preoccupied to notice. She was always a little spacey, but this was something more, like she'd gone through some door deep in her head that led to a room in an entirely different world.

Monday at school I was dead exhausted and cold to boot—fall had gone icy with a heavy frost Sunday night. If not for napping through my open period I don't think I'd have made it through the day upright. I took another nap when I got home, and Mom checked me for a fever. Oscar got in late, and I stayed out of his way even though he was obviously in one of his rare good moods—the kind that sometimes resulted in elaborate gifts for no apparent reason. Like the brand-new laptop he'd brought home for me the previous fall, or the game console he'd bought for me last Christmas.

A few days later we lowered Dave into the basement again—headfirst this time, with Sparx in one of those baby packs upside down on his chest—while I shined the most powerful flashlight we'd been able to buy down from above. He only went far enough to reach the doors on the capitol model, where he went straight to the center this time. That was all we needed to know about. The mask of Oscar's face had been moved into the central spot, and the Crown, black and tarnished now, rested on its brow while Darkness peered out of the empty eye sockets.

Oscar *was* the Winter King. Which meant that the terrible things Sparx had feared were happening with the succession of the Corona Borealis—whatever those might be—were happening in the heart of my family. I didn't sleep again that night.

"Hey, Kalvan, wake up." My mother's voice was gentle and a little worried.

"Huh." I rubbed my eyes and sat up in my bed. "Is it time to go to school?"

She touched my nose with a finger. "No, silly, it's almost time for Sunday dinner. And you need to change out of those wrinkled clothes and get a shower in beforehand."

"Oh, right. Sorry. I was only going to take a nap, and I must have gone down harder than I planned. I'd better get to that."

But my mother, who was sitting on the edge of my bed, didn't get out of the way. "Not quite yet. First I want to know if you're all right."

That brought me wide-awake—there was a lot of dangerous ground in that question, especially now, with Oscar being the Winter King. "Sure, of course, why do you ask?"

"Because you've been sleeping with your light on every night . . . when you've been sleeping at all. Also, tomorrow is All Hallows'"—that's what my grandmother had always called Halloween, and my mom followed her tradition—"and you haven't spoken a word about costumes or trick-or-treating."

"I'm thirteen, Mom! Don't you think I'm getting a little old for that stuff?"

She looked terribly sad for a moment. "It's hard to believe you've grown up so much so fast." Then she sighed. "You might be getting past the door-to-door stuff, at that. But I don't think you've lost your sweet tooth, and I'm sure there'll be a ton of costumed stuff happening at school tomorrow. Are you sure you don't want something special to wear for it?"

To be honest, I'd completely forgotten about Halloween with all the other weirdness going on in my life, but considering what that weirdness was, I couldn't tell *her* that. "I'll probably just wear all black and say I'm a vampire or something."

"That hardly seems like a costume, but I suppose you *are* a teenager, even if I hate to admit it. All right, it's your decision, but if you change your mind and want a better costume, there's not a lot of time left. Think about it and get back to me after dinner . . . which I need to go make. And you need to shower." She leaned forward and pressed her forehead against mine. "I love you, kiddo."

"*Mom.*"

She got up but stopped briefly in the doorway. "Oh, and don't think I've forgotten about the light you keep leaving on. We will definitely be talking about that again if it keeps up." She closed the door on her way out, and I snagged my bathrobe and started skinning out of my clothes.

As I slipped the robe on, Sparx hopped into the center of my bed and gave me a hard look. "You are most certainly *not* wearing black for All Hallows' or playing the vampire."

I stopped halfway to the door. "What? Why does it even matter?"

Sparx put his face in his paws. "I swear to all the powers, whatever I did to deserve you, I repent of it wholly and completely. Tell me that you're not that dim a light, child, please. It's bad for my heart."

"I don't understand a word you've just said, my funny bunny man."

He sighed. "Then I shall have to use short words and simple sentences. All Hallows' or, Samhain, as it's more commonly known in the magic world, is a day of great power. Black is the color of Nightmares and the Winter Crown. For a child of fire to wear it on Samhain would be an ill omen indeed. Doubly so, when you are in the midst of putting yourself in direct opposition to Winter's King. Triply so to play the vampire—an avatar and symbol of both death and winter."

"Oh. I guess that does make sense."

Sparx rolled his eyes. "And lo the light did shine down from above and strike the young knave full in the face, bringing wisdom and wit with it. If only in very small measures."

"So, what *should* I wear? A costume?"

"Yes. There is great power in symbol. You should dress as

something that opposes winter, of course, and wear flame's colors—gold, orange, red! If you could light yourself on fire for a bit, that would help enormously."

"What if I went as a Vulcan?"

Sparx blinked. "Like *Star Trek*? Because that doesn't make *any* sense at all."

"No, like the Saint Paul Winter Carnival. The Vulcans are the guys who dress in red and run around on a fire truck, the ones who chase away Boreas, King of the Winds, at the end of the carnival." Which sounded pretty darned weird as I said it—when you grow up in Saint Paul you tend to forget just how strange the whole thing is, with its ice palace and all the rest. "You've been around a long time. You must know about Vulcanus Rex, right?"

Sparx reached up with one of his paws and slapped himself sharply. "All right, that's it. I've gone senile. You should probably throw me in a pot and call me rabbit stew at this point."

"Wouldn't that be stewed *hare*?" I grinned. "Also, what *are* you talking about?"

"Very funny, boy. Your Winter Carnival, of course. I've never really thought about it before, because I usually head south once it starts snowing, but it's basically a huge ritual designed to weaken the Winter King and set him up to hand over the Crown to Summer. The *real* Winter King. Not this Boreas, but whoever holds the Corona Borealis for winter. It has to be intentional. I bet they had a bad Winter King back then, too."

"When?" I was having trouble following Sparx's conversational leaps.

"The year they created the Boreas myth. It's brilliant. Almost too brilliant for humans. I wonder if they had a fire hare advising them. . . . Makes no difference now, of course, but you have to think so. That's what I get for ignoring so many people things the last hundred years or so. We need to learn everything we can about your Winter Carnival."

"All right. We can Google it after dinner. Does this mean I *should* go as a Vulcan?"

The eye roll again. "Of course it does. What are you, boy, hard of thinking?"

My mother called out from the kitchen just then. "Kalvan, shower!"

"On my way, Mom!" I opened the door of my bedroom and continued more quietly, "Oh, and, maybe I'm not *completely* over All Hallows' costumes. Will you take me out to get a few things after dinner?"

"I'd love to."

Dave raised both eyebrows. "Weird Halloween costume, dude."

I shrugged. "I'll explain later. In the meantime, blame the bunny."

Halloween at the Free School was kind of surreal. All classes were canceled for the day, and each advisory group had its own holiday event set up. Evelyn's class had turned the black box into a sort of mini haunted house with the usual cold-noodle brains and pickled-onion eyeballs. The science room was filled with things that bubbled and burbled and glowed. Home economics and life skills had a costume contest—where I won a prize for Most Out of Place. Second was a kid who came as Rudolph the Red-Nosed Reindeer. We're kind of a weird lot at Free.

If dressing as a Vulcan had any impact beyond the little ribbon and candy bar I got as a prize, I didn't see it right away. In any case, as soon as school was done and I had some time to curl up with my laptop, I started researching the Saint Paul Winter Carnival.

Dude! That's some really crazy stuff there, with King Boreas of the Winds and Vulcanus Rex, god of fire, having a giant "war" through the streets of Saint Paul at the end of January, and the winter medallion hunt, and a ton of work going into a huge castle made of ice blocks that mostly melts away in a few weeks. Don't believe me? Go look it up for yourself; it's all online.

Back in 1986 they built a palace with a tower 127 feet tall for the carnival's centennial, using ten thousand blocks of ice. That was more than thirty years ago, and the designers of this year's ice palace were hoping to outdo it thanks to advances in computer-aided design and a major grant from an anonymous donor. They were talking 175 feet and thirteen thousand blocks.

What made reading about the carnival doubly surreal was how much Sparx loved every single bit of the lore and his amazement that mere humans could have come up with such a great ritual. Reading about it took me on to the parallels with Mardi Gras in New Orleans and all the stuff the Saint Paul festival borrowed from that, and Easter celebrations and the rebirth of spring. Talk about going down the rabbit hole . . .

I had just clicked a link to last year's medallion clues when I heard a knock on my door and my mother's voice. "Hey, Kalvan, do you want to go trick-or-treating? I know it's cold, but I could drive you over to the Summit neighborhood . . ."

That made me stop and think. Summit Hill is Saint Paul's historic mansion district, and the pickings there are really good.

Sure, I'm getting kind of old to be trick-or-treating, but Summit meant full-size candy bars and plenty of them, and we hadn't gone in years. It was always a hassle to find parking and Oscar didn't like it, so the practice was slowly phased out after he married my mom. I was still mostly in costume with my red pants and red sweatshirt. All I really needed to do was throw on my black boots and the red cape and helmety thing Mom had bought me the night before.

"Sure, give me five minutes." I could tuck that baby pack Dave had found under my cape for Sparx to hide in and . . . "Wait here," I said to Sparx as I put on the helmet. "I'll be right back. I need to hit the restroom and get a fresh pillowcase for a candy bag."

I was about halfway down the back hall when Oscar came through the basement door and we practically ran into each other. "Sorry, Oscar, I—"

"WHAT ARE YOU WEARING!?!" Oscar bellowed, his face a twisted mask.

I actually leaped back away from him. "It's a Halloween costume. Mom was going to take me trick—"

"IT'S NOTHING OF THE KIND! I KNOW A DAMNED VULCAN WHEN I SEE ONE!" His face had gone this terrible gray-brown color, like old brickwork, and he seemed to have grown suddenly larger, like an inflating frog.

Oscar and I have had any number of run-ins over the years since he and my mother got married. He's got a temper and he's not afraid of yelling, but I had *never* seen him nearly that angry or heard him get so scary loud before. Looking at his tightly clenched fists and the set of his shoulders, I more than half expected him to hit me. He might have, too, if Mom hadn't practically teleported in from the kitchen then, putting herself physically between me and him.

"Oscar!" She spoke sharply. "Stop that! You're scaring Kalvan."

For a moment things teetered there on the edge of violence, and Oscar's eyes glittered like there were obsidian spear points in their bleak depths. But then his rage visibly cooled into something icy and somehow much scarier. The red faded from his skin, leaving him once more gray and cold, like the granite monster I had seen him as the other morning.

"Did you have anything to do with this?" His voice came out sharp and deadly.

My mother nodded. "Of course. I told you last night I was taking him to the costume shop."

"But that's no Halloween costume! It's . . . pagan ritual nonsense!" He was still very cold and very angry but seemed more in control now, spitting his words like one of those weird cobras that use their fangs like water pistols.

"The cape was easy." Mom's voice started to go dreamy and faraway in a manner that made my guts churn—I'd seen it too often over the years. "It's part of a devil costume. The helmet was harder. We ended up buying a plastic Roman gladiator helmet and some red spray paint."

"You *know* how much I hate the Winter Carnival," said Oscar.

"My grandfather was a Vulcan, back in the fifties. It's how he met my grandmother." She glanced over her shoulder at me. "Did you know that, Kalvan?"

"I . . . no." We were way off the edge of the map here as far as conversations go—with Mom lost in space and Oscar still looking mad enough to kill someone.

"He was. And, later, he became Rex. Grandma kept the uniform in an old wooden box. Before she passed away, she gave it to my mother to keep as a remembrance. When *she* died, I thought it came to me, but I now can't find it *anywhere*. Maybe I should search the attic again. . . ."

With that, my mother turned and went up the stairs without another look at either Oscar or me. I started back toward the kitchen then, but Oscar caught my eyes and shook his head. When the attic door closed a moment later, he pointed at me.

"You are grounded. Two weeks. I want you to go back to your room right now. There, you will take that ridiculous garment off. And then you will put it in a bag and bring it back to me here. After that, I'm sure you have homework to deal with. Do you understand?"

I nodded. I didn't like it and I really didn't want to obey him, but there was a power in his voice and his glittering eyes that left me with no will to argue. I simply went and did as I was told, ignoring Sparx and his questions until I had returned from disposing of the costume and finished all my homework.

Hours later, when I was in control of my actions and my voice once again, I explained, ending with, "I don't know what came over me."

Sparx eyed me gravely, "Do you not? It was the power of the Winter King."

As if to punctuate his words, the window rattled suddenly in the wind, and pellets of freezing drizzle began to patter against the glass.

13

Fire Fur and Foul Weather

I WOKE UP to the radio going in the dining room—a voice was reading off a list of school closings. I blinked blearily and realized there was a LOT of light coming in through the window. Pulling aside the curtain, I found a world covered in ice and snow, with the dawn light reflecting from every surface, cold and bright and cruel.

I crawled out of bed as the radio announcer said, ". . . freak blizzard, completely unexpected. Worse than the great Halloween storm of ninety-one." A few minutes after that, the Free School closing came through, and I was off the hook. I pulled the blankets up and sagged back into my pillows.

I thought back over the previous day then—my encounter with Oscar and how he had compelled me against my will—and I shivered. In the frozen light of morning it seemed somehow even more horrible. Especially when I realized it wasn't the first time he had ordered me to do something and I had simply obeyed, though I'd never felt it so powerfully before or for so long.

I was just trying to sort that out when my mom came in with breakfast and a big smile on her face. "Good morning, Kalvan. I made waffles, and I thought I'd bring them in here so you could eat in bed." She set the tray down in my lap and settled herself on the foot of my bed, sitting cross-legged. "Your father used to bring me breakfast in bed on cold winter mornings, and it always made me smile."

If she remembered any of what had happened yesterday, she wasn't showing it. Whether that was because of something he'd done or simply because of her troubles, I couldn't say. So, for her sake, I decided I'd better do the same.

"Where's Oscar?" I asked cautiously.

"I think he's in the basement, though he might have headed in to the main office. There are tracks leading back and forth to the garage, but without going outside I can't see whether he's gone or not. Now, these are still hot and crisp."

She took a plate and served herself waffles with strawberries and whipped cream, and I did the same. There was also a small plate for Sparx, and he climbed up beside me. For a few minutes not much happened beyond chewing and swallowing.

Then Mom said, "I suppose you think that's a bit odd."

"What?" I'd learned to be cautious about questions like that, given how very many possibilities there were with my mother.

"That I don't know where Oscar is."

"Not really." *I'd* never cared where he was beyond preferring he not be where I had to see him.

Well, that's not quite true. There had been moments in my

life when he'd been a pretty decent dad substitute. Or at least he'd tried. Like the times he took me to hockey games, or showed me how to use some of his power tools. Unfortunately, we really didn't have much in common. I'd never cared for watching other people play sports, and I didn't *like* puttering in the shop even if the skills I learned there were useful. I think with a more ordinary sort of boy, he might have done all right as a dad. But . . . well, I was weird. Not my-mother weird, but certainly fit-right-in-at-Free-School weird.

Mom looked down into her lap, and what she said next came out very quietly. "That's sweet of you, Kalvan, but you don't need to pretend for me. We both know you have problems with Oscar, even if you're too kind to say it to me. We also both know I'm not always very . . . attached to the here and now."

I felt like someone had taken my heart and made a fist around it. "Mom . . ."

But she held up a hand. "I'm not finished. That's one of the reasons I married Oscar, you know. That I can't always be sure I'm going to be in the best shape to take care of you. I do love him, even if he's gruff and difficult sometimes. But also he . . . he grounds me. There's something incredibly solid to him, like bedrock. I was drifting for a long time after . . . after your father . . . left."

Which was one of those subjects I'd never been able to get her to talk about. I had a few memories of him from when I was very little—brief moments, mostly. A bearded face leaning down toward me. A dark sapphire earring the size of an almond with a star sparkling in its depths. A deep voice reading to me about a badger named Frances. Being lifted onto a shoulder. But then the memories stop. I didn't remember anything about him leaving. No fights. No difficulties at all. At some point he simply wasn't in my life anymore, and to this day I don't know why.

My mother had picked up a corner of her skirt and begun to gently wring it. "When I met Oscar, it felt like having a place to put my feet again. A safe place to stand in the whirl of the world. He's a hard man to like sometimes, a hard man in general, but he helps me to hold on even when he isn't here." She sighed and let go of the skirt. "But that's probably more than you wanted to know."

"I love you, Mom." I didn't know what else to say. "Is there anything I can do?"

"You can be you."

I blinked at that. "I don't understand."

"You're stronger than you know, Kalvan. Stronger than I am, certainly. More like your grandmother. You won't remember it, but when you were four I used to take you to this little playground where there was a big spiral slide. You were big for your age, bigger than most of the other kids, and you could have taken over. Instead, you always made sure the littlest kids got a turn."

I was lost. "Where are you going with this?"

"There was one day when three older kids, maybe six or seven, came by and started pushing the little ones around. You told them to stop, and one of them knocked you down. I got up to help you, but before I could take three steps you bounced back to your feet and punched him in the nose. You didn't hesitate for a second, and you didn't count the cost. You were ready to fight them all even though they would have mopped the floor with you."

"I don't remember this at all," I said. "What happened next?"

"I got there before it went any further, along with a couple of other parents, and we stopped it, but I had to actually carry you home at that point, because that was the *only* way I could keep you from going after the big kids. You were furious with me, and you kept saying it wasn't right. Do you know what lesson *I* took away from that day?"

I shook my head. "No idea."

"That I believe in you."

"Huh?"

"You have a true heart, Kalvan." She chuckled. "A lousy sense of self-preservation, perhaps, but a true heart. That's ultimately why I got you into the Free School."

"I'm not following you. I thought it was because I kept clashing with the teachers at the other schools you sent me to."

"That, too, but it's because of your heart. You won't bend when you know you're right. It'll serve you well when you're grown, but it's very dangerous at your age."

"What? Why?"

"Because the world isn't made to deal with a child who won't bend to the adults around them. School isn't just there to teach academics, it's there to mold children, to bend them to fit the world. But you don't bend. Most schools can't accommodate that, not without them or you breaking, and you're not strong enough to break a whole school." She chuckled again. "Not yet, anyway, though I wouldn't bet against you winning in the long run."

"Really?"

"Really." She nodded. "It's that true heart. There's nothing in the world stronger. I don't know what you're going to grow up to become, but I believe in you, and I know it will be amazing. All you have to do is listen to your heart."

I didn't know how to answer that. It made my heart hurt in a good way, and I could feel my cheeks heating. "Thanks, Mom. I . . . just thanks."

"You're welcome, Kalvan. I know that's not what you were asking when you wanted to know if you could do anything to help me, but it's important that you hear it. Now that you have, let me give you a more practical answer to the original question. You can help me look through the attic for your great-grandfather's Vulcan uniform. It was very important to my grandmother, and I really do want to find it."

She smiled dreamily then, briefly lost in some fond memory. "Grandpa was a sweetheart and not much bigger than you. I bet you'd look fantastic in his old red suit." The smile turned into a grin. "We'll have to find it and find out, won't we? We should have plenty of time, since you won't be going to school today and I'm not even trying to drive in that." She pointed out the window.

So, Mom and Sparx and I spent the next couple of hours digging through the attic. The previous owner of the house had mostly finished the space, with the intent of turning it into a separate apartment. But he'd never gotten around to the details, like putting a door on the bathroom, or trim around the skylights, or plates on the outlets and switches. So, we mostly used it for storage.

When my grandmother Elise died, they'd simply packed up her entire house and stuffed all of it into our attic. Anytime Oscar suggested that we do something with it my mother would go extra spacey and faraway and stay that way for weeks at a time, so it simply sat there and collected dust. Now we opened up everything big enough to contain the item my mom wanted—a wooden box that she described as looking like it was built by someone who'd read about one of those little shrines you see in Chinese restaurants but hadn't ever actually seen one.

It never turned up, and neither did Oscar, though we did find any number of other small treasures from my mom's childhood. At one point, Sparx whispered that we would need to look at some of this stuff again sometime, though he didn't think any of it would help us now.

Finally, at lunchtime we gave up. If Oscar was around, he still hadn't emerged from his basement, so the two of us put on heavy coats and walked a couple of blocks to my favorite little Mexican restaurant. The snow was halfway up my thighs and it was bitterly cold, but they were open. The family that ran it lived in the house across the alley.

It was the first of many cold days. Once winter got a grip, it went right on squeezing. The weather people kept saying things like *polar vortex* and *arctic outbreak* as they talked about the dark-blue spot that hovered over Saint Paul on all the weather maps while the rest of the country was having one of the warmest winters on record. And that was probably true as far as it went, but none of it spoke to what Sparx and I knew to be the real cause—the wrath of the Winter King.

The two of us spent a lot of time trying to figure out how to do something about Oscar's control of the Corona Borealis, and the thing in the basement. Dave helped when we found things he could do, which wasn't often. But over and over again we'd start looking into something only to come up cold and empty at the end of the trail. I slept better as time went by, but too often with my lights on, and we got no closer to a solution as the weeks slid icily away toward Christmas.

Portrait of a boy and his bunny. The date is Tuesday, December the twentieth. It is the last day of school before winter break. The two of us are sitting under the main stage at the Free School, surrounded by moldering theater props and worrying desperately about the next day.

"It'll be the solstice," said Sparx, "the shortest night of the year and the peak of winter's power, a very dangerous time for the fire-born like you and me under the best of circumstances. Given my druthers I'd have headed for points south weeks ago like I usually do. Since I'm stuck here with you, I'm going to suggest we simply lie low and spend a week or two pretending your stepfather isn't Winter's King until the pressure eases."

I shook my head. "It's also winter break, which means we'll have the house completely to ourselves most days. That's going to offer us opportunities like nothing we've had this year to get in and out of the basement without getting caught." I had a growing sense of urgency about the whole thing, as if there were some hidden deadline coming up. "We *need* to take advantage of that."

Sparx threw his paws in the air. "How? Nothing we've learned in the last few weeks offers us any hope that a largely untrained mage child and a fire hare missing three-quarters of his powers can take on the Winter King on his home ground at the height of his reign."

"Then we need to broaden our search."

"Again, how?"

"I don't know!" I snapped.

"I do." The voice was quiet and calm on the surface, but there was an anger underneath that I knew well.

"Josh?"

A rough foam gargoyle from some long-ago play shimmered like moonlight on water and became the older boy, sitting cross-legged. "I've been keeping a very close eye on you and the hare since that day when you spied on me while I was painting."

My stomach filled with acid shame. "I'm sorry about that. Sparx wanted me to see the magic in the paintings. I don't think it occurred to him how much of a violation of your privacy me looking at the . . . the one with the bruises would be. I should never have seen that. There's no way I can unsee it, but I am truly sorry. I had no right. If you want to beat the crap out of me, well . . ." I shrugged. I couldn't have done much to stop him under normal circumstances, but this time I wouldn't even try because I figured I'd earned it.

Josh shrugged. "It doesn't matter. When I'm old enough to walk away, I'm going to show that picture to the whole damn world. That and all the others—because they've done worse. I can't do it yet, but I *want* people to know what kind of people my parents are. And I want my parents to *know* that people know. I want them to drown in it."

His voice was still calm and quiet and oh so very angry. I didn't know what to say to that. My relationship with Oscar was bad, but . . . "I—I'm sorry, Josh. It's not right. Maybe you could—"

"Shut up!" The rage suddenly boiled over, and I half expected him to punch my face in. "I don't like you, Kalvan, not one little tiny bit. I don't want your sympathy or your stupid suggestions. Child Protection took me away from my parents for a while, and my foster home was worse. I just need to wait it out for a few more years and then I'll get out and get even. I could do it now, you know. Ms. Sippi would help me. She's offered, many times. She likes drownings, but I am *never* going back to foster care."

"I—" I began again.

"I told you to shut up, Kalvan. I didn't think she should drown you that day on the railroad, but I wouldn't have been sorry for more than five minutes if she had. Not after you nearly set the class on me with your devil's tongue."

I was simply too stunned to respond to that.

But Josh was still talking. "Ms. Sippi was surprised when you got away, and that made Her curious. So, She exerted Herself to learn more. She's ancient and very powerful. When She wants to know something She can find out a lot. That's why I'm here now. If it were up to me I'd as soon see you rot, but She thinks you have some interests in common. So, if you want to learn some things that might help you with *your* parent problems, I can take you to see Her."

Sparx shook his head firmly no, but I asked, "When?"

"Tomorrow. Noon. Meet me at the railroad bridge on this side of the river." While he was speaking Josh stood up—well, as high as the low ceiling of the stage would let him, anyway. At the end he turned away from us.

"We are *not* doing this," said Sparx.

"Makes no difference to me," Josh said over his shoulder. "Be there or don't. Honestly, though, I'd come if I were you. She wanted to see you pretty bad, and standing Her up might piss Her off enough to drown you both."

"We'll be there," I said.

"Have I told you how much I hate the idea of getting anywhere near the Rusalka?" Sparx's voice was muffled by my backpack and several layers of thermal blanket. Even at noon the temperature was down around five below zero, and the breeze coming off the river was brutal despite the bridge support I'd chosen as a windbreak.

"Only about eleven thousand times." I patted the pack gently—easy enough to do since I was wearing it on my front this time.

"Well, call this number eleven thousand and one. She's too dangerous for the likes of you and me. It's unnatural, like mice having tea and cookies with a cat."

"It sounded to me like the kind of invitation that's more dangerous to refuse than it is to accept."

Sparx sighed. "There is that to consider."

"Why do you suppose Josh called Her *Ms.* Sippi?"

The top of the backpack unzipped itself and Sparx stuck his head out, his expression indignant. "We're about to risk skin and soul to deal with the most dangerous water spirit anywhere this side of Lake Superior, and *that's* what you're wondering about?"

"Yeah. What people choose to call themselves and each other matters. It can tell you all sorts of things about respect and self-image and personal and group identity. I mean, is *She* calling Herself that? Or is it just Josh? Or what? This stuff is important."

Sparx's eyes caught fire for a second—literally—but then he took a deep breath and pushed it out. "Riiiight. I keep forgetting you've been corrupted by the crunchy-granola types who run that hippie school of yours, and that you're completely serious when you say things like that."

"Of course." I nodded. "So, back to my original question: Why *Ms.* Sippi?"

"Because She's no one's Missus," said a voice from the brush down closer to the river. Josh followed his words out into the open a moment later.

"What's that?" I pointed at the long, narrow pack he had hanging over one shoulder, its strap cutting deeply into the material of his parka.

"Door knocker."

"Huh?" I didn't get it.

"You'll see. Come on." He started out onto the bridge.

"Eleven thousand and two," grumbled Sparx. He was visibly shivering, but he didn't pull his head back into the bag.

Warily, I fell in behind Josh. My reluctance was half because of the icy winds and half sheer terror. I might not have been willing to follow Sparx's advice on this one, but that didn't mean I wasn't listening to him and scared six ways from Sunday about the whole thing. Heck, I was scared enough that I'd written a note to my mom and mailed it off to Dave to give to her if I didn't come back. Pretty soon we were out over the middle of the Mississippi. For only the second time that I could remember, it had completely frozen over all the way through downtown.

"What if someone sees us up here?" For anyone looking we'd show up pretty well as two little black specks in a sea of ice-white.

"Won't happen," replied Josh. "I've covered us in a seeming of snow."

"Seeming?" I asked.

"A type of illusion," said Sparx, taking on what I'd come to think of as his "teacher tone." "A lot of water magic plays with light and reflection."

"Here." Josh stopped walking so suddenly that I almost bumped into him.

"Why?" I couldn't see any differences in the snow blanketing the river below us.

"Weak place in the ice. Hang on." He shrugged off his pack and pulled out a half-dozen pieces of rebar that had been taped into a tight bundle that tapered to a point at one end.

My heart jumped in my chest like it was trying to get out, and I said the first thing that came into my head in hopes of putting things off a little longer. "You're not going to drop that off the bridge, are you?"

"Duh." Josh looked at me like I was some kind of idiot. "Gotta break the ice so we can talk to Herself."

"From up here?"

"Wouldn't go through if we dropped it from down there." He pointed at the ice. "And we wouldn't want to do it that way even if we could."

I shook my head. "I don't understand."

"There's plenty of spots you could break through the ice with a decent hammer, but none of them are close enough to shore or over the gentler channels. The farther you get from calm waters, the harder a time She has treating you as a person."

"As opposed to?" My voice actually squeaked a bit then, but I hardly noticed.

"A toy." Josh's words came out as flat and cold as a sheet of ice.

Sparx flicked his ears against my chin. "She's one of the great elementals, boy, and nothing like human—infinitely less so than I or even the deepest sort of delver." He pointed at Josh. "She cares for you, does She not?"

He nodded. "I believe so."

"But you would no more venture out on that thinner ice alone than you would with us along, for fear that Her nature might overcome Her urge to nurture. Am I right?"

"She's still better than my parents. She *warns* me where the ice is thin. But this is all wasting time." Without another word, he picked up the rebar bundle and dropped it off the bridge point first.

It hit with a sullen thunk and barely slowed as it punched through the ice and vanished into the darkness and the deep. As it went through, a fountain of black water shot upward. It should have stopped rising within a few feet. Instead, it kept right on climbing, taking on subtle shape and form as it did so. By the time it came level with our position on the bridge it had assumed the appearance of a beautiful woman's head and torso attached to a long and fishy tail, like the body of an enormous eel. Minnows flickered in the depths of her head and chest like silver coins amid green weeds.

She reached out and touched my cheek, my chin, my nose. Her hand burned cold where it touched my skin, and when I looked into Her eyes all I could see was a terrible, churning hunger. I tried to speak, but when I opened my mouth water filled it.

I was drowning.

14

Drowning Season

WHEN I WAS four or five—after my dad left but before Oscar—
my mother took me up north to visit my grandmother at some
family friend's lake house. I spent much of the afternoon in the
water, chasing tiny sunfish through the shallows. I was having
the time of my life until I hit the drop-off where the swift little
stream that fed the lake had gouged out a deeper channel.

One moment, I was running along in water that rarely came
up past my knees. The next, I was under it. Reflex opened my
mouth in a scream and physics filled it with water. I panicked,
thrashing wildly. I was too young for my brain to really process
the possibility that I could die, but my lungs and gut had no such
issues. My body thought I was going to go under and never come
up again. It *understood* drowning.

If the water had been deeper, I might have done just that,
because I'd been playing safely for hours, and that meant my

mother and grandmother were paying less attention than they probably should have been. In my panicked flailing, I put a foot down on the bottom. More by reflex than planning I pushed off hard and my head broke through the surface. I caught my first breath of air since going under and started coughing and shrieking . . . and kept right on shrieking and coughing as my feet touched down again in water that was barely deep enough to reach my ribs.

My grandmother was there seconds later, scooping me up onto her hip and soothing me with gentle words and gentler hands. She carried me back to where my mother stood on the shore looking utterly lost and half a scared child herself as the tears streamed down her cheeks.

I reached out toward her as we got closer. "It's all right, Mommy. I'm fine."

I wasn't. Not in my heart. I was coughing and still terrified, but she looked soooo lost, and I knew she needed to hear that I was going to be okay. That she needed *me* to reassure *her*. I lost something in that moment, something that I have a hard time talking about even now. I lost the sense of security that comes with knowing your mom can protect you from the world. Because, in that instant, I could see that the world was more than my mother could handle without help. I've been trying to protect her ever since.

It changed the way I see the world and left me with a lifelong suspicion of deep water. My grandmother paid for me to take swimming lessons after that, and my mother made me go until I was good at it. But I've still got a down-in-the-bones fear of drowning, and the Rusalka's touch brought the whole thing back in one terrifying instant.

I think I screamed. I know I wanted to, and my throat was raw afterward. But that might have come from getting a mouthful of thirty-three-degree Mississippi River water. A very brief mouthful since She pulled Her hand away in an instant, but more than enough to send me into a complete freak-out. Leaping backward, I caught my heel on one of the rails and went down hard.

The second rail caught me in the lower back and I discovered why all those characters in the books I loved made such a big deal about getting punched in the kidneys. My whole world went runny around the edges and my mouth suddenly felt like I'd been chewing on old pennies and nine-volt batteries—simultaneously metallic and fizzy.

I could hear Josh laughing, harsh and hard like a crow. That made me angry enough to want to punch his face in, but every slight movement sent spikes of pain through my lower back. *Maybe I can just lie here for a while and suffer quietly, I thought. Yeah, that's a good plan.*

Suddenly, Sparx was leaning in very close and speaking to me in the language of fire, which was losing some of that formal air as I became more used to it.

"Kid, you need to get up, right now. Actually, two minutes ago would be better."

"Hurts."

"Not half as much as drowning in ice water, which is all too likely if you don't move. You can't show weakness in front of a spirit like the Rusalka. Not if you want to walk away."

I blinked. Then, slowly and with great difficulty, I rolled onto my hands and knees. Not fun. Standing up followed, though I'm not quite sure how I managed it. When I turned back to Josh and Ms. Sippi, I could see a hungriness in the latter's eyes that underlined Sparx's warning.

Right, no weakness. I could do this. Sure. Absolutely. No time like the present. With the greatest effort of will, I painted a smile on my face and stepped in close to the Rusalka, looking deep into those hungry eyes and holding their gaze.

If this were one of my books, there would have been a long, meaningful wordless exchange between the two of us and She would have looked away first. Unfortunately, it was not one of my books and it was winter in Minnesota. So, after about fifteen seconds of trying to stare down an elemental in the face of a bitter sub-zero wind, my eyes filled with tears and I had to blink them away.

When I could see again, the Rusalka had moved back a bit and humor had joined the hunger. "You're a funny child, with your boldness and your fiery Halloween costume play. I like that. I don't think I'll kill you today. In fact, I'm going to help you. Later, if you survive everything else that's coming your way, then maybe I'll kill you. Maybe. So much depends on mood."

Yay? "That's . . . well, kind of a jerk move on your part." I felt my throat going warm and fuzzy, but I fought it down—I didn't think my power would do much more than irritate the Rusalka. I needed to convince Her the hard way. "Not the not-killing-me-now bit. That's good. But the maybe killing me later? Jerk move. I mean, I'm about to do something that you really, really want to have someone do for you, so I'd think the *least* you could do is pretend that you were going to be grateful if I can manage it."

The water that made up the body of the Rusalka seemed to become darker, full of silt and hidden hazards. On my chest, Sparx slipped farther down into his bag so that only his eyes and the top of his head were showing. Out of the corner of my eye I saw Josh move slowly back into the shadow of one of the bridge supports.

"You dare to speak to me so, boy?" Her voice sounded cold and cruel—utterly inhuman. "Why should I not kill you now?"

"Because you have a problem with the Winter King, and you want me to solve it." I had a sudden insight as I was speaking. "It blocks your power, doesn't it?"

"What?" The Rusalka actually looked startled.

"The ice. That's why Josh had to crack through from above. You couldn't do it yourself. Not when the whole surface is frozen like this. And I know it's got to be worse in your tributaries. Some of the smaller streams freeze all the way to the bottom. You don't like this weather any more than we humans do. Less even. That's why you want to help me, so I can loose you from the chains of ice."

Translucent eyelids closed, partially masking the equally translucent eyes behind them. When She opened them again they were sparkling and bright. The Rusalka threw Her head back and laughed—a sound like bright water running shallow over stones.

"Oh, child, well done. You are as clever as you are funny, though it is not nearly so simple as that. It's more the will behind the ice than it is the presence of the stuff."

I remembered then what Sparx had said about the Northern Crown and the great river back in October. "The Corona Borealis gives my stepfather power over you, and not just through the ice. It burns you."

"True enough, but not enough of the truth. I am Mississippi; a passing season is nothing to me. But your Oscar pushes for so very much more. He would make himself King of the North the whole year round. He cannot do it yet, but the longer he controls the Corona Borealis, the greater his mastery becomes and the harder it will be to stop him. He is a growing threat to me and mine. But that's a problem we share at the moment, is it not?"

"Details." I waved a hand dismissively, though the fear I felt in facing down the Rusalka had me sweating under my jacket. "What matters here is that the Winter King blocks us both, and you want me to do something about it. So, maybe you should try playing nice."

"We are fire and water, you and I, and pretending otherwise is barest farce, but all right. I shall pretend to be grateful and I shall lie prettily and tell you that this is an alliance to last the ages instead of the briefest truce between ancient foes."

Sparx vanished completely into the deeps of my bag, but I simply stuck out my hand to shake. "Deal."

The Rusalka took it in a brief soggy grip and smiled. "Done. Next time I see you, I will welcome you with open arms and you shall be as safe with me as you are in your own bed, watched over by your loving parents."

She emphasized the *s* in *parents*, and didn't that send a nice little icicle sliding along my spine—score one for the ancient elemental. "Right. So, what do you want? Or perhaps I should ask: What help are you going to give me to help you?"

She laughed again. "Little enough, truly. If I could offer you spells and charms of power, I would. But water cannot aid fire so directly. That is a marriage that must always end in quick divorce or quicker murder. So, advice will I offer and nothing more."

"Oh, *that's* going to help."

Sparx shivered in his bag but didn't say anything. I wanted to growl at him and point out that he was the one who'd told me not to show fear, but the Rusalka was already speaking. I heard the words in my heart, for She spoke in the language of fire—beautiful and burning bright—and they carried so much more weight that way, but I will try to translate them as best I can.

> *Comes now the frigid solstice night, Corona*
> > *Borealis at its height.*
> *Ice that is fresh will not shatter.*
> *He who would break Winter's power must await his*
> > *proper hour.*
> *Only then can he press the matter.*
> *But time will not win this fight alone; more is*
> > *required to seize the Throne.*
> *Long-hidden treasure he must bring.*
> *Heirlooms of ash and oak, bound in flame and*
> > *blessed with smoke,*
> *Needs he who would discrown the King.*

"I don't understand," I said.

"I have given you what *clues* I can; finding the answer is now your task." With that She let go of her demi-human form. For one brief instant more, a narrow column of black water hung in the air in front of us before bursting apart and flash-freezing into a puff of snow.

"Huh," said Josh. "I was almost hoping She'd eat you. Oh well. Later." Without another word, he turned and started walking across the bridge toward the frozen swamp.

I wanted to hate him then, but I found that I couldn't. I had some inkling of what his parents were, and while Oscar might never have hit me, I had more insight into Josh now than was entirely comfortable. What if, instead of Sparx, I'd found someone more like the Rusalka when my magic first awakened?

A swirl of wind brought more tears to my eyes. As I blinked them away I realized I was shivering, though whether that was purely the cold or a delayed reaction to my fear, I couldn't easily say. Turning in the opposite direction from Josh, I headed back to shore and then started plodding toward downtown proper, where I could catch a city bus home. It was too bad I didn't live on the light-rail line.

After a while, Sparx poked his head out of the bag. "That went as well as we could have hoped."

I raised an eyebrow skeptically. "It did? How do you figure?"

"We are still alive, and we have new information to ponder."

"Yeah, because stupid riddles are going to help us soooo much if we have to go up against Oscar and the Darkness under the capitol."

"Riddles will not, but their answers . . . well, that's another story."

"So, you know what she meant by all the gobbledygook?"

Sparx shook his head. "Not all of it, certainly, but it's clear from the first riddle that we cannot defeat the Winter King now, at the height of his power. We must lie low for a while, which gives us time to figure the rest out. Lying low as—I must note—I told you we should be doing yesterday."

"Yeah, yeah, yeah, you told me so. Nobody likes a sore winner." I sighed. "So, now what?"

"Lie low. Keep out of Oscar's sight. Perform no magic. Pretend for the week that you are an ordinary boy having a good time over winter break. Today is the solstice and the longest night, which means that the light begins its slow return tomorrow. Blow off all things serious and dark for a time. It will do your heart good, and the best way to crack a riddle is to not think about it too hard."

"All right. I guess that means I get to use the Omnitheater pass after all."

The Science Museum of Minnesota was one of the treasures of downtown Saint Paul, with all kinds of cool exhibits and a huge IMAX/Omnimax theater. Since it was walking distance from the Free School, a lot of advisory groups and classes used it as a prime field trip destination, and a fair number of older students interned there.

My family had bought a membership ages ago, which meant I could visit as often as I wanted without needing to pay to get in. It was one of the best places to slip off to if you wanted to skip out of classes in deep winter without freezing to death. The membership also came with a number of Omnitheater passes, and Mom had told me I should use the last of this year's up over winter break.

The current show was something about Iceland, and it involved a lot of aerial shots of volcanoes and flowing lava with things bursting into flame at its touch. Sparx loved every moment, so we stayed for a second showing. It was fun, and for a little while at least, I did my best to follow his advice and not think about the riddle. Which, if you've ever tried to not think about something, you know is much harder than it sounds.

Christmas came and went without any huge blowups between me and Oscar, which was a relief, though my presents were kind of disappointing. I got a lot of boring clothes, including one of those winter hats that looks like a jester's, which was very meh. Especially since they were sized for me to grow into them. I did get a really nice bike, but I wouldn't be able to use it until March at the earliest! I also got a couple of new fantasy-type games for my console, but they seemed a lot less compelling after encountering real magic.

Though I spent a lot of time practicing with firetongue and drawing the ideograms for the words I was using the most, Sparx and I didn't start batting the riddles around seriously until the day after New Year's. He felt that waiting for the returning light was for the best. But come January second, we dug in.

After perhaps half an hour he slapped an angry paw down on the grubby piece of paper I'd written the riddles on. "Two things. A) This a terrible verse structure. I have no idea why the Rusalka chose something so clunky. B) Your handwriting is abominable. Were you taught penmanship by illiterate pandas, or what?"

I gave him a hard look. "One, my hands were half frozen

when I wrote this down, and so was the ink. Two, my typing and texting are just fine, which is what matters these days. Nobody writes anything by hand anymore. You might as well criticize me for not knowing how to girdle a horse."

"Saddle!"

Gotcha. "Whatever, old man. Next thing you'll be all sad about those poor bunny-whip makers going out of business."

"That's buggy whips, you . . . Wait, you're pulling my leg, aren't you?"

I tugged on his toes. "I'm told that's supposed to be lucky."

"Harrumph, I say. Harrumph indeed! To say nothing of piffle and fiddlesticks."

I grinned. "Now that we've got that out of the way, let's get back to cracking this thing." I poked at the sheet. "The first riddle pretty clearly tells us we can't do it yet and we need to wait for the right moment, but it doesn't tell us anything about when that moment might come. Thoughts?"

Sparks rubbed his chin thoughtfully. "Well, I doubt She wanted us to wait all the way till the end of the Winter King's seasonal reign. That might buy the Rusalka something for next year, but it wouldn't help Her now, and She doesn't seem overly long on patience. No, She had something more immediate in mind, but I don't know what it is. I suspect that if we crack the second riddle, it will answer the first. What is this long-hidden treasure we're supposed to be looking for?"

"She mentioned oak and ash, which tells me it's associated with fire." I thought about my various fantasy novels and the sorts of things you might need to take down an ice king. "Maybe a flaming sword?" I paused. "That'd be pretty awesome, actually!"

I picked up an imaginary sword and held it high over my head. "By the power of my ancestors!"

Sparx chuckled. "I doubt it will be anything quite that dramatic. I don't think you're ready to take on the Winter King in a physical duel. Even without the magical skill differential, Oscar is twice your size. I suspect it will be something small but powerful, a ring, perhaps, or a pendant of some kind."

"No magic swords—where's the fun in that?" I sighed. He was probably right.

We spent another hour talking it over but didn't get any further along in figuring it out. Not then and not the next day, either. When we showed the riddle to Dave the day after that, he came up blank as well.

"I fear we're missing an important clue," Sparx growled as we reread the lines for the umpteenth time.

We were, but I didn't find it until a few weeks later. Even then, it was more by accident than intent. I'd woken up well before the rest of the house on a Sunday morning—side effect of my newfound fear of the Dark and the ensuing insomnia issues.

I was sitting in the living room quietly playing one of my games on the big TV when the paperboy bounced the *Pioneer Press* off the front door, and I figured I might as well go out and get it. It was January 22 and the opening of the Winter Carnival. The first clue for the medallion hunt was at the top of the front page, above an article about how the historic cold snap was enabling the construction of the record-breaking ice palace they'd hoped to build. I took one look at the clue and cursed when I recognized the rhyming structure.

I leaped up and ran back into the house. "SPARX!"

The hare bounced out of my room waving his front paws wildly. "Hush, boy! Or do you want to wake Oscar up and let him know you have a fire hare besides? Now, what's up?"

I showed him the newspaper and he began to swear quietly but intensely in the language of fire.

"This is exactly what we needed," I said. "Why are you so upset?"

"Because I like to believe that I am smarter than the average hare, and now that the answer is pointed out I feel like a fool for not seeing it sooner. Of course the key is the Winter Carnival. It's an entire city getting together to enact a two-week ritual designed to drive out the power of winter. We need only figure out a way to focus that power to our advantage. The question is how? We know the time, and it is now, but what does the second riddle mean?"

I tapped the paper again. "Could it be the medallion itself? You thought it would be something small. That's definitely a hidden treasure, and they've been doing it for years."

Sparx scratched his chin pensively for several long seconds and then finally shook his head. "I don't think so. It's hidden treasure, yes, but not long-hidden by any means, and not directly associated with fire. No, it will be something else."

Then it hit me. "My great-grandfather's Vulcan uniform! That's why Oscar was so upset by my costume, why he didn't want me to have anything to do with the Vulcan myth. He called it ritual nonsense. But it's not nonsense; it's real, and he saw it as a threat. My mom said her grandfather was Rex after he was a Vulcan. I thought she meant he was Vulcanus Rex in a later year, but that wasn't it at all. She meant that he took the Corona Borealis and became the Summer King."

"How do you figure that?"

"Because she only talked about his uniform, not his *uniforms*, and she mentioned how fine I'd look in my great-grandfather's red suit. Vulcans wear red. Their leader wears black."

"I think you might be onto something, Kalvan. The next question is: Where is the uniform?"

"Not in the attic. That's for sure. We spent hours up there and didn't find *anything*. Besides, he'd want to keep it someplace safe and well guarded."

We both glanced downward. It looked like I was going to have to confront my newfound fear of the Dark sooner and more directly than I wanted.

15

Fireship Down

"IT'S NOT DOWN HERE." I shone my flashlight along the underside of the model table, looking for doors that might lead to hidden compartments in one of the buildings other than the capitol—we'd started above but found nothing.

"Keep looking!" Sparx was still poking around up there while keeping one eye on the big cardboard ring we'd placed around the capitol model and the Darkness within.

Knowing what we were in for had given us a better chance to prepare this time, including making the ring—which was a sort of portable warding circle designed to keep the Dark confined to its box within the miniature building. It had taken Sparx and me a couple of days to make it, which had put off this foray until Friday.

We'd left Dave out of it this time since he was home with strep throat, and getting the hatch open had almost been more than I could manage. But even if Dave had been available, I'd have been reluctant to include him. Oscar was so much more powerful now that he had actually become the Winter King. Bad enough risking my own neck without putting my best friend's in the noose beside me.

Minutes ticked past with no sign of anything that might hold the missing Vulcan regalia. Sparx hopped down to join me as I finished up under the big model table and crawled out into the open.

"What next?" I glanced around the room. Between the tables and the various cabinets, there were a lot of places where you could hide things.

"Let me look for signs of magic. I was too busy holding the Darkness at bay last time to do that properly, but the warding circle seems to have it covered this time."

"I'll go poke around in the utility closet."

The only interior wall in the basement blocked off an area beside the stairs where the furnace and water heater lived. It was a biggish space, but searching it turned up nothing except dust and disappointed spiders, so I soon came out and started opening cabinets. Mostly what I found were the tools of Oscar's trade. That included various sorts of refills for the big 3-D printer he used to make parts for the models, tons of older-model pieces ready for reuse, and a fair pile of things like X-Acto knives, paints and paintbrushes, and sanding blocks.

While Sparx sniffed around for magic, I slowly worked my way toward the desk where Oscar's computer sat beneath an enormous wall-mounted LCD TV he used as a monitor. Next to that was an old-fashioned drafting board that I'd never seen him use.

I'd just opened a big steel cabinet full of surveying gear when Sparx rejoined me.

"Try that one."

He pointed at the next cabinet in line. The first thing I noticed was a shelf at about waist level that was covered with an array of stone knives that made me think of every story I'd ever read about ritual sacrifices. Looking at them gave me a feeling in my middle like I'd swallowed a gallon of live worms, so I shifted my gaze upward. The next shelf held dowsing rods and wands. The one above that was covered with crystals and geodes and slices of polished rock.

Sparx let out a low whistle then, and I bent to see what he was looking at. The bottom of the cabinet held dozens of roughly carved stone figures. I didn't recognize many of the forms, but right out front were several of the badgerlike delvers. Though they looked crude, the carvings conveyed an incredible sense of vitality and presence, like they might spring to life at any moment. My guts did the crawling thing again and I found myself backing away from the figures without any conscious intent.

Sparx hopped to the left and pushed one side of the cabinet shut. "Get the other door. What we're looking for isn't here, and there are things in there it would be better not to wake."

The cabinet next closest to the desk was set up like a wardrobe. It held robes and cowls in a variety of colors above and matching boots below. Sparx had me pull out one of the boots to check the sole, and I was surprised to find the bottom of the boot was *literally* made of stone—a red granite that matched the shade of the leather. I was almost disappointed to find nothing but office supplies in the cabinet after that—the one closest to the desk.

"Have you spotted any more magic?" I asked Sparx. "Besides those two cabinets, I mean?"

"There's low-level stuff in most of the models, but I don't think it's what we're looking for. It feels wrong for that. Let's try the desk." An easy bound landed him beside the computer.

The desk was huge and ultra modern, with chromed supports and a massive granite desktop. It was almost more a table than a desk, and I couldn't see anyplace to hide something as big as a Vulcan's helmet, but there was literally nowhere else left and Sparx was the expert. So, I settled into Oscar's chair and pulled myself in close. Then I reached for one of the drawers. Or, rather, I tried to reach for it, but I couldn't move my hand from where I'd grabbed the edge of the granite. In fact, I couldn't move *either* hand.

"Sparx!" I yelped. But he didn't respond, and I realized that he hadn't moved or spoken at all since he'd landed on the granite surface.

Even as that thought crossed my mind, I felt a terrible cold seeping out of the stone and into my fingers, like I'd grabbed a block of ice. The cold moved from my hands into my wrists and started working its way up my arms, seeming to go faster as it climbed toward my heart. I tried to yell again, but my mouth wouldn't obey me this time. I felt ice in my feet and calves then as well and looked down, though bending my neck seemed an almost impossible task. I'd never noticed it before, but the floor under the translucent plastic chair mat was made of the same icy-gray granite as the desk itself, rather than concrete.

The chair mat seemed to flow away like water as my feet slid through to the stone floor beneath. A moment after that, they began to actually sink into the granite, and I was slowly pulled off my chair and down into the floor. Looking up at Sparx, I saw the hare was also sinking. He was up to his midriff in the desk, though I couldn't see from where I was if the rest of him was hanging out the bottom or what. I could feel another scream growing within me, but the terrible cold reached my chest in that moment and froze the sound in my lungs. Then the ice was climbing my neck. When it touched my jaw, everything went away.

Fire ran through the endless night and I ran through the fire. I was in a dark place deep beneath the earth—a cavern of some sort. Despite the brightness of the flames I could see only an occasional glint of reflected light from the stone of the walls and ceiling. It was as though the darkness were a living thing that drank the light before it could travel more than a few inches.

That darkness felt ancient and angry and terribly heavy all at once, like an animate force that wanted desperately to crush me. But the fire that held me also held back the darkness. I sensed the dark like it was some great fist trying to close on an ember. The will was there, but the flesh could not bear the pain of burning long enough to snuff out the light within.

"Where am I?"

"*We* are in the place between." The answering voice belonged to Sparx and seemed to come from all around me.

"Between what?"

"Exactly!" He said it in what I had come to think of as his sarcastic teacher voice, and it made me want to growl at him.

Before I could formulate a more coherent reply, the darkness went away, taking the fire with it. Leaving me . . . where? The cold that had taken me earlier still pervaded my body, though it seemed to be sinking toward . . . my back? Orientation returned. I was lying flat on my back on what felt like a rough slab of rock. More rock was above me, little more than a few arm's lengths away, and there was dim gray light coming from the stone itself . . . no, from a tiny forest of upside-down mushrooms clinging there.

I tried to turn my head. It took enormous effort, but I finally managed to tilt it to the right and . . . ! If I'd had the power to move, I'd have rolled backward off the rock I lay on then. For Oscar was there. He sat on a massive stone chair, his elbow on its arm, his chin on his fist, anger on his face, and the Corona Borealis on his brow. He wore robes styled like those we had found in his cabinet. These were the yellow gold of freshly exposed sandstone.

"What am I to do with you, Kalvan?"

"Huh?" It was the wittiest thing I could think of in the moment—sue me.

"You pose a *very* difficult problem for me." He rose from the chair and came to stand and stare at me, his face as hard and cold as the stone around us—he had never looked less human. "I put as strong an influence on you Halloween night as ever I've spun, but it broke within a few hours. I felt it crack and fall away like a distant landslide. That should not have happened."

"Our boy is full of surprises." The voice came from somewhere down by my waist, and I realized then that I had a warm weight resting against my right hip.

"Sparx?" I croaked.

"I'm all right." He didn't sound it. He sounded frightened and angry. "The Winter King and I have been having a little chat while we waited for you to wake up."

Oscar spoke again. "Ever since Halloween I've been trying to sort out how you broke my spell. The influence I placed on you that night was tailored to fire, and not just any fire, but to the fires of ash and oak, the ancient flames of your house. You shouldn't have been able to break it at all, much less so quickly.

"Not while I wore the Crown of the North fresh and renewed from the fallow time." Oscar touched a finger to the white stone at the center of the Corona Borealis. "But you shook it off. That one and three more since. When I first found the hare trapped with you in my studio, I thought that perhaps he was the author of your resistance to my spellwork. But the experiments I've conducted over the past hour have dispelled the notion. There is something deep in your heart that resists the weight of stone as no flame should."

"Maybe you're just not all that and a side of fries?" I asked, and heard Sparx's sudden indrawn breath.

Oscar hissed sharply, like an angry snake. "No, the fault isn't mine. The fault lies here." A long stone knife seemed to simply appear in his hand, and he pressed its point into the flesh above my heart, which froze in response. "Should I dig out the answer?"

That's it, then, I thought with a strange sense of calm. *Last stop for the Kalvan Express.*

But then Oscar withdrew the knife and made it vanish as mysteriously as it had appeared. "If only it were so simple. No, Kalvan; two things keep you alive for the moment. The first and far more important issue is your mother. The bond of blood between you is reinforced by the bond of fire. If you die, she will know it in the same instant, and she is far too fragile to survive the experience in any shape that is useful to me."

"What is she to you?" I asked.

Oscar laughed. "Genevieve is my Summer Queen, obviously. You've known about the Crown for some time. You and your familiar were messing about with it back in October, though you covered your tracks well enough that I didn't figure out what had happened until my subtler trap caught you today."

I saw it then. "You pass the Crown to her when winter ends, and then force her to pass it back to you in an endless loop!"

He nodded. "For now. I'm close to finding a better way, but at the moment breaking her would inconvenience me. Which is the first reason I don't want to kill you. Fortunately, once I've cracked the second reason I won't need to end you."

"What's the second reason?" I asked.

Sparx sniffed, and I could imagine him rolling his eyes. "He wants to find out how you broke his influence so he can lay a better one on you and trap you the same way he has trapped your mother, of course. You would become his backup plan."

Oscar flicked his gaze toward the hare, and the knife was in his hand again. "You would do best to remember that neither of those reasons prevents me from killing *you*."

I tried to reach up and knock the knife aside, but found I still couldn't move, though the cold had mostly faded. "Leave him alone!"

The knife vanished. "I will, but only because killing the familiar can have very unpredictable effects on the master. But you, my boy, would do well to remember that your pet is a spirit of fire, with all its endless variety and vitality, and that means there is a very great deal I can do to him short of death. Cooperate, and he will be spared a theater of pain."

"Anything!" I felt sweat break out on my brow and slide down my temple—I didn't dare let Oscar know Sparx wasn't *really* my familiar. Not in the normal sense of the word. That would be the same as signing my friend's death warrant.

"I wish I could believe you mean that for the long term," said Oscar. "It would solve a number of problems. But we both know you'll be scheming to break your word the second I'm not watching you. Threats to the hare merely buy me temporary leverage while I sort out the bigger issues of your resistance to the power of stone. So, I'm going to have to tuck you away for a bit while I get that figured out."

"Tuck me away? Don't you think Mom's going to notice if I simply vanish?"

"As long as you're not dead and I give her a good story, my influence should hold there. Your mother has a wild strength of fire, but it has devoured her from within. She has no control and little enough true magic left at this point. No, she won't even worry about you. Not when she remembers that you went on the annual Free School J-term trip to Washington, DC."

"But J-term's over, and I was doing the play anyway, like I always do."

"If you really think your mother is connected enough to the world to know that, you're more foolish than I imagined."

I was still trying to think of some response when Oscar cupped the hand that had held the knife and I saw one of the stone figurines from the cabinet nestled there—a delver. "Cetius! Come to me. I have need of you!"

Setting the figurine on the slab beside me, Oscar turned away and began to pace, his stone boot soles clicking against the rock of the floor as he slowly circled me. I had time to wonder where I was, but no way of sorting it out. Still, there might be other things I could learn.

"You destroyed my great-grandfather's Vulcan regalia, didn't you?" It sure hadn't been in the basement.

Oscar turned his all-too-familiar disappointed-stepfather gaze on me. "That's the most transparent ploy I've heard in a long time. You're a very smart boy, if troublesome. I expect better of you."

"We both know you'd see through it even if I tried something much smarter than that, so why bother to play it clever?" I felt a weak heat at the back of my throat, barely more than a glow, but there nonetheless. "Either you're going to tell me where the Vulcan stuff is or you're not, so the rest is wasted effort. Yes?"

Oscar snorted. "Better. Truth with a side of sneering, and just the thinnest layer of wheedling. You're right, I'm not going to tell you where it is no matter how you ask. It's funny, really; you were so very close to it and at the very same time impossibly far." He laughed. "Not that knowing the location would do you any good. It's too well protected."

So, it did still exist! That was half of what I'd wanted to find out, and an enormous relief. I didn't think the Rusalka would have sent me after something that had already been destroyed, but the possibility had weighed on me more and more as we searched for the gear without finding it. Also, I knew now that it was someplace Oscar thought I couldn't get to. So, probably not under the house.

Before I could speculate further or pry any more information out of Oscar, a deep grinding sound came from somewhere down beyond my feet. With a supreme effort of will I raised my head. In the dim light I could just make out a place where the dark wall became even darker, suggesting the entrance of a cave. A moment later a low and hulking shape appeared from the darkness.

"Wotcher need, Majesty?" The voice was deep and growly.

"Ah, Lud d'Raven, I'm so glad you could oblige me."

"Cetius will do well enough without the ludships, Majesty. We're not so long on formalities underhill, as you well know."

Oscar nodded. "And you've no need to *Majesty* me simply because I wear a Crown for one winter."

The figure moved forward into the light and I got my first good look at a delver in the flesh. He was furred and colored like the badger he so resembled, but no badger had ever been half that big. Cetius was about four and a half feet tall and three feet wide, with no neck to speak of. Unlike a normal badger, his hips were set more like a man's and his arms were longer, ending in stubby but serviceable hands.

He snorted now. "Five winters and counting, Oz. I think that's enough to buy the occasional *Majesty* from one who has served you for many years."

"Never served, Cetius. Say rather that you are my most valued ally since boyhood and we'll be more honest about it."

The delver nodded and his expression became less grim. "Well enough." He waved a hand-paw dismissively.

The whole exchange had more of the sound of a well-rehearsed play than any normal conversation, and I wondered how many times they'd gone over this and why it needed repeating. Something to talk to Sparx about later, if we had a later.

"What do you need?" asked Cetius.

"You recognize the boy, of course." Oscar indicated me with a nod.

"Your stepson, the one what broke that influence. Yes?" Cetius tromped over and glared at me, his head barely topping the slab on which I lay. "Doesn't look like such as should be so much trouble. Not even with the k*tsathsha helping him." The firetongue word sounded wrong coming from the delver's mouth, hard and cold where it should have been hot and crackling.

"There's more to him than can be seen on first looking," replied Oscar. "Or even in second sight. I've tried several spells over the last hour, and none of them showed what I need. He has a hard core that resists a weight of earth like no fire should."

"Interesting." Cetius cocked his head to one side. "You want we should take him apart and see what his heart looks like?"

"Much as I'd like to do it the easy way, no. For his mother's sake I want him intact but immobilized, at least until I know for certain whether he can be turned to good use or not. I would prefer to own him heart and soul, but if I can't have that I'll destroy him. We might be able to make a golem from his bones."

The delver snorted. "They's powerful unreliable."

Oscar shrugged. "It wouldn't fool a normal mind for long, but with the influence I already have over my pretty Genevieve I might be able to make it serve for a few years. We should know the truth of the thing within days, I would think."

"Good enough." Cetius pointed at Sparx. "What about the

k*tsathsha? There's fine eating on 'em and they're devilishly hard to bind short of death."

Sparx replied in the tongue of fire, swearing sharply.

Oscar ignored him to answer Cetius. "Perhaps later. For the moment he's too valuable a lever for moving the boy. But you needn't worry about him escaping. I've just the thing for that problem." He set a heavy stone lantern on the table—it looked like something from the Japanese tea garden at Como Park.

"That'll do," said Cetius. "Do you want to put him in, or should I?"

"It'll be gentler my way." Oscar's next few sentences came out slow and sonorous in what I presumed was the speech of stones.

When he finished, there was a sharp *fwooshing* sound like a lit bottle rocket and Sparx was sucked into the lamp. The effect on his appearance was startling. Where he normally looked like a bright-red hare with the occasional wisp of flame curling through his fur, now he looked like a bright fire that only coincidentally resembled a hare. A moment later even that view of him was hidden as Oscar slid the stone shutters into place, cutting off the light of his internal fires.

Oscar turned back to me then, and there was a nasty smile on his face. "If anything happens to that lamp, your familiar's fires will go out forever. Any attempt on your part to do more than open the shutters will only result in his extinguishment. That wouldn't exactly break my heart, so feel free to give it a go. But understand that the consequences will be your fault alone."

16

Fireheart

CETIUS BARKED SOMETHING in earthtongue and another half-dozen delvers appeared from the cave mouth. They quickly took positions on either side of me, like pallbearers at a funeral. Thick hands reached out and took hold of the edges of the surface on which I lay—their clawed fingers sinking into the rock as easily as if it were clay. With a sharp crack like a breaking bone, the stone lurched and rose a few inches into the air.

As they carried me toward the tunnel mouth I glanced back and saw an enormous block of red granite. Whether my slab had been sitting atop it like a capstone or they'd simply split the top couple of inches off of the base I couldn't tell by looking. But I felt in my marrow that it was the latter, that these badger-men could crack stone as easily as I might snap a twig.

For another few seconds I could see Cetius deep in conversation with my stepfather, but then we made a turn and darkness hid everything. I don't know how long we moved through the eternal night that lies beneath the earth, but eventually we emerged into a series of sandstone tunnels faintly lit by more of the phosphorescent mushrooms.

After carrying me another hundred yards or so, the delvers stopped in front of an apparently blank section of wall where two more of their kind waited. There was a brief exchange in earthtongue. Then the waiting pair reached into the stone wall and silently pulled aside great sheets of it, opening a gap in the manner of theater curtains being drawn aside. Their action revealed a void in the rock like a small windowless room. My bearers carried me inside and lowered the slab to the floor before withdrawing beyond the stone curtains. A moment later the pair closed the stone behind them.

Darkness absolute descended on me, like a great velvet weight. It pressed heavily on my soul, robbing me of the will to do anything. Breathing became difficult and I opened my mouth to scream. But nothing came out. Instead, foul darkness poured into me, filling my lungs as it clogged my mouth and nose and eyes. It felt as if I were drowning in cobwebs. I lost myself then for a long time, hours at the least—possibly days—while even the memory of light fled from my heart. Ages, it seemed, ages locked in silence and deepest night.

It was the rattling that brought me back. A faint sound like a breeze gently shaking the windows of an old house. At first it seemed to come from a very great distance. But ever so slowly, it got closer. And closer still. Finally, it sounded as though it was shaking the windows beside my bed, and not so gently anymore.

I roused myself to do something about it, and only in that moment remembered that the room that held me now had no windows—and that indeed there was even an *I* to begin with.

The cold paralysis that had held me earlier was gone now, and I sat up and groped sightlessly toward the source of the noise. It was somewhere near my feet, and I rolled onto my hands and knees to better search for something that I knew I needed without knowing what it was or why. It wasn't until my outthrust fingers ran painfully into a heavy stone something that I remembered Sparx and the lantern they'd bound him in. Moving more quickly now, I slid my hands up the sides and found the knobs that opened the shutters.

Light bloomed in the darkness and flames woke in my heart, the fire within reawakening and bringing me back to myself. It felt like returning from the lands of death as bright air filled my lungs and the weight of night fell away. I was once more a living, breathing child of fire, full of light and life and a terrible burning joy like nothing I had ever known before. I recognized the power within me then in a way that I never could have without first being drowned in the dark.

I was.

No. I am.

Born of fire. Filled with fire. Fire itself.

Rising to my feet, I pointed my palms at the curtain of stone through which I had entered the room and opened my heart. Rivers of flame shot from my hands, splattering the wall and covering it in a great burning sheet of red and gold. This was not like the rage-driven dragon's fire that had destroyed my haven on the hill. This was purer and stronger, a flame that answered to my will instead of fighting it. Heartfire. Long seconds slid past as the flames poured forth.

Roaring, burning, breaking!

Falling, failing, receding.

Flame could not conquer stone. Not even the fire of the heart. Not here, at any rate, and not now. The fires within me were insufficient to the task. My heart closed and I fell to my knees, drained, but not yet beaten. I could not break the wall, but I knew now that the darkness could not break me, either. Not while the fire lived inside me. Not while I lived.

"Childe Fyre to the dark powers came." The words were spoken in the tongue of flame and drew my attention back to the lantern and the burning hare within. "You are awake. Truly awake this time. Awake to who and what you are at last. You still have much to learn about control, but that was very well done. The fire that serves rather than the fire that masters."

I grinned ruefully at my friend. "That's nice and all. Add a dollar and it might even buy me a soda. Unfortunately, it doesn't seem to do much for getting us out of here."

He shook his head and the flames danced through his whiskers. "No. The weight of stone is far too great here for brute force to free us. But there may be other ways to light our way out of this prison."

"I'm all ears."

"That's my line, boy." Sparx waggled his own then and laughed—a surprisingly happy sound.

"You seem awfully chipper for a bunny caught in the lamp of death."

"That's because I know something that the man who put me here doesn't know."

I wasn't following him at all. "What's that?"

"That I'm not really your familiar."

"And?"

Sparx chuckled. "Yet."

"Huh?"

"I'm not your familiar . . . yet?" He looked at me expectantly.

"I am so not getting it."

Sparx rolled his eyes. "I swear, just when I think you're finally turning into the bright young sorcerer you have the potential to be and I start to get excited about the prospect, you open your mouth and all my illusions melt in the mindless intensity of your jibber-jabber."

I gave him my best raised eyebrow.

"Fine," said Sparx. "I'll spell it out for you . . ." He paused, as if waiting for something.

I shook my head wordlessly.

"*Spell* it out for you . . . That's a pun, boy. *Spell*, like magic. *Spell*, like spelling . . . Oh, never mind. Look, I'm only half summoned. That means the spell that binds me to you is in a special sort of magical limbo. This lamp is a nasty piece of work. Under normal circumstances no one could get me out of here safely but Oscar. I don't have the power to do it from within, and if you tried to do it from the outside, it would destroy me."

"I got that part, and I think maybe I'm starting to see the rest of it. You're like Schrödinger's cat."

He leaned one ear forward and one back. "That weird quantum physics thing where the cat is both alive and dead inside the box because you haven't looked to find out which it is yet?"

I nodded. Finally, I was getting it!

Sparx sighed. "No. Not even a little bit. That's physics. This is magic, which is much more like mathematics. It's all symbols and proving that a thing that can happen is the same thing as the thing happening. Think of me as the variable in one of those 'where is the train' algebra problems. Until it's solved, you don't know what the value of X is, with X defining the position of the train. In this case, finishing the summoning solves for X where the value of X is out there with you."

Trying to make sense of that gave me a headache. "You know how bad I am at algebra."

"Well, I'm quite good at it, so you're just going to have to trust me on this one."

"Fine. I trust you. Now what?"

"Now, you summon me, there's a big old popping noise, I end up out there with my full powers restored, the lamp implodes, and we bust out of this joint. Duh."

"Wait, I thought you didn't want me to summon you because that would put you entirely in my power."

"That was before this lamp put me entirely in Oscar's power. Given a choice between the two of you, I'd much rather have you as my Accursed Master."

"Your Accursed Master?" That sounded awful.

He spread his ears in a sort of bunny shrug. "Yep. As in, 'What is your will, O Accursed Master?' I'm afraid that's the traditional term, and we're stuck with it."

"Not if I don't summon you, we aren't. I'm not anybody's master, accursed or otherwise." I crossed my arms.

"*That's* your sticking point? Not my being stuck? Not the summoning? Not me being bound in your power as long as you live? But *Accursed Master*?" He grabbed one ear in each paw and pulled as though he wanted to tear his head in half. "Fine, we'll negotiate on the Accursed Master thing, but will you please get me out of here?"

"You're really okay with me summoning you and you becoming my familiar?" Because I wasn't. We might not have started out that way, but Sparx and I were friends now, and I didn't like this at all. It was too much like owning him, and I said as much.

Sparx sighed. "No, truth be told, I'm not okay with it. But those are the cards we've been dealt, kid. We're in a deep, deep hole here and there's no way we get out of it with me at half power and you at half wit. Sorry, cheap shot. But seriously, this is the only way I can see to get out of this lamp soon enough to do any good. This scares the crap out of me, but we need to do it and we need to do it now. Are you with me?"

"All right, but I'm releasing you from your summoning as soon as we get loose of here." Sparx didn't answer me, and I gave him a hard look. "There's something you're not telling me. What is it?"

He shook his head very firmly. "Uh-uh. I need you focused for the summoning. It's harder and more dangerous than it looks. Especially given the circumstances. And you're not all that good with the tongue of fire yet. I don't want you thee-ing when you should be thou-ing and turning me into a hamster."

"Then I'm not playing. You can rot in there."

"You know that's not an option. If I stay in the lamp, you stay in the cell, and we're both doomed anyway. My way, we've got a chance."

I didn't move.

"Look," said Sparx, "I'll make you a deal. You summon me, and I swear on my name that I'll tell you all about it once you get me out of this box."

I sighed because I could see that was the best I was going to get. "All right, but once we're out of here I'm releasing you."

"I'd prefer you wait a bit on that, because you have some very important work to do, and me remaining in your power will make those things much easier. But if that's your choice at that point . . . well, I won't be in any position to argue with you. Now, do we have a deal?"

"Deal."

Sparx looked relieved.

I held up a finger. "But I've got one question first. Why didn't you teach me about heartfire earlier?"

"The fire of the heart cannot be taught, it can only be found by looking within. You didn't think I've been having you do all that quiet breathing and magical meditation for the fun of it, did you?"

"Maybe a little, though I can't say *I* was having any fun. I guess you were right, though."

Sparx sighed. "Of course I was. Can we move on now? I need you to listen carefully because you'll only get one chance to do this right."

A few minutes of tutoring later and I was ready to make the attempt. First, I found a sharp edge on the granite slab and used it to gash my thumb. Using my own blood, I drew a two-foot circle on the stone and roughed in a number of ideograms around the edges—Sparx explained that I needed to create a place for him to be summoned *to* or the spell wouldn't draw him out of the lamp. I'd never been gladder that I'd spent all those hours learning how to write basic firetongue. Finally, I opened my heart and traced over the whole diagram using the fire within to burn the blood into ash and bind it to the stone. It was time.

I knelt in front of the circle and began to speak in the tongue of fire. "I conjure and abjure thee, *sprths*al*erarha. By fire and smoke, by ash and oak, by the flame in the darkness and the powers it awoke. Come to me now, no matter where you are. Ash and char, sun and star, wind and smoke, ash and oak!"

As I spoke this last sentence, I felt each of the signifiers burn briefly on my tongue before it left my lips. "Ash" flew from my mouth to become a bright, candlelike flame hovering in the air on the far side of the circle—simultaneously a winking teardrop of flame and the ideogram for "ash" in the tongue of fire. "Char" followed, taking up station directly in front of me.

"Sun" moved to my left and "star" to my right, defining the four points of the compass along with the first two burning ideograms. "Wind" blew itself to the northwest, and "smoke" drifted to the northeast. "Ash" again, falling in the southwest this time, and finally, "oak" standing like a pillar to the southeast.

For a moment eight flaming symbols hung above the circle in front of me. Then, all together, they fell—dropping to land on the matching ideograms I had drawn in my own blood and bound to the stone with my heartfire—sizzling and crackling like fuses on the world's biggest firecracker or a pan of frying bacon.

SSSSS . . .

BANG.

BOOoooOOM!

A hiss. A flash. A crash.

All in an instant. The ideogram lights went out. In his stone prison, Sparx's fire flared brighter than any lightning flash. An instant later, the hare appeared in the center of the circle, leaving a hole in space in the center of the lantern, which fell in on itself with a fierce implosion. A thick haze of smoke filled the room and my lungs.

Blinded. Deafened. Choking on the dense black clouds . . . that's where I should have been. Instead, I found the smoke easier to breathe than clean air and my eyes were undazzled by the brightest of flames, though my ears were ringing like a church full of bells. And there, in the circle in front of me, stood Sparx.

I wanted to hug him, but I wasn't done yet and this could still go wrong. Squeezing my thumb to bring the blood back to the surface, I held my hand above the center of the circle and let three drops fall on Sparx's head, where they sizzled and vaporized like water spattered across a hot griddle. For the moment at least, he was still nearly as much flame as hare, looking much as he had in the lantern.

"Ash and char, sun and star, wind and smoke, ash and oak." Again, the words fell as fiery ideograms from my lips, hovering in the air above the circle that held the hare. "Heart's blood and heart's fire, bind thee now to my yoke."

I really hated that last bit about binding him to my service. Doubly so since it came after I'd already gotten him out of the lantern, but Sparx had promised me that it was critical to the success of the thing, and that leaving the ritual unfinished could have catastrophic consequences for both of us.

The words of binding rolled out of my mouth as a flaming chain. It curled and coiled in the air in front of me, extending one end forward to wrap itself around the hare's neck and the other back to twist itself around my hand. For one beat of my heart the chain stayed like that, connecting us with links of fire. Then, with a bright flare and a burning pain where it touched the flesh of my palm and fingers, it vanished.

Sparx sat up on his haunches and looked me in the eye. "Well, that's that, then. I guess I'm stuck with you."

His words sounded fuzzy through the ringing in my ears, and it took me a moment to parse them. "No you're not. I promised I'd release you from the spell as soon as I got the chance."

"I'd really rather you didn't." Sparx's words had none of their usual lightness, making me instantly suspicious.

"Why not? Is this part of what you weren't willing to tell me earlier?"

He nodded, and his flames dimmed, though they didn't fade completely. Which was a good thing, since he was providing the only light.

"Are you going to tell me now?" I asked.

"Of course, that was *my* promise, and, unlike humans, we spirits are much more tightly constrained by even our most casual oaths. Would you let me out of the circle first, though? It makes me feel like I'm trapped in a bell jar."

I drew my still bleeding thumb across the ashen circle, symbolically breaking the line. Sparx let out a long breath and visibly relaxed.

"That's sooooooo much better. Hang on a tick." Three hops took him to the nearest wall, where he gently pressed his forehead against the rock. It sank into the surface as easily as if it were water, and Sparx stood there for a couple of seconds before pulling himself out of the wall and returning. "I appear to be me again, which is an absolute delight."

I gave him my best skeptical look when he didn't say anything more right away. "And . . ."

"And you *can't* unfamiliar me because that would also unsummon me." He pointed over his shoulder to the place where the lantern had collapsed in on itself. All that was left was an egg-sized globe of shiny black stone like an obsidian ball. "Which would put me inside that."

"I don't understand. You just stuck your head through a rock wall." I bent and picked up the globe. It felt smooth and heavy and impossibly cold. "Why is this so different?"

"Because that is a collapsed spirit trap. It's specifically designed to confine creatures like me and destroy them if they attempt to escape, and setting it off, as we did with the summoning, makes it not one iota less lethal. If you release me from your service, I will return to the trap and I will die."

I squeezed the stone as hard as I could. I wanted to crush it, but that was far beyond any strength of mine. "Why didn't you tell me?"

Sparx raised one eyebrow. "If I had, would you have summoned me?"

"Of course not!" I flung the globe across the room.

"That's why." He held up a paw to forestall my speaking further. "I also didn't tell you that if you got the summoning the tiniest bit wrong I would have died. Or that I wasn't completely sure that getting it right wouldn't kill me either."

"Sparx, how could you?!?"

"Kalvan, I'm sorry. But I didn't tell you any of that because

I needed you to get me out, and I needed you calm and focused to do it. That's because there was one more thing I didn't tell you. The lantern was unmaking me, which is a fate infinitely worse than death. Death is a doorway. Not one I want to walk through anytime soon, mind, but a doorway nonetheless. It provides a path forward. Where to, I don't know, but it's not an end.

"That is." He pointed at the fallen stone globe. "I'm not sure how long the unmaking would have taken. Hours? Days? Weeks?" He shrugged. "Certainly no more than a month, and probably much less. The lantern was designed to house a powerful spirit of fire. Me, as I am now, summoned and whole. Not me as I was two minutes ago, half one thing and half another, with most of my abilities missing in action. Not me as I have been since that day when your accident with the light switch bound me into a weak shadow of myself trapped at your side."

I looked down at the ground, unable to meet his eyes. "I . . . I didn't know. That was never what I wanted. I didn't . . . I wouldn't . . ."

"I know that you had no intention of trapping me so, and I forgive you for it now, though I was angry enough to have roasted you over a slow fire in those first few days. It's not your fault that Fate or Luck decided we must become partners, and I don't blame you for it. In fact, I'm not even particularly angry at whatever power arranged it anymore. I've come to like you far too much for that."

I retrieved the ball and held it out to him, still reluctant to meet his eyes. "Is there any way we can fix this?"

"It's worth hanging on to, but I don't really know. Certainly not this side of whatever is to come between you and your stepfather. After that . . . maybe. If not, I've already had a very long run."

That made me look at him. "What do you mean?!?"

"My life is now tied to yours. I can only remain your familiar as long as you are alive to be my sorcerer, and when you are gone I will return to the stone. Now, don't give me that look. You're young yet, and that door is still some way off. Besides, the horse might learn to sing."

"What?"

The hare sighed. "It's an old story. A man was sentenced to death by an angry king. When the time came for his execution, the man cried out to the king: 'Stop! If you spare my life and give me one year, I will teach your favorite horse to sing.' The king held up a hand to halt the executioner. 'Let him go. I would like to see this singing horse. If he fails you may have his head one year from today.'"

Sparx continued. "Later, the executioner went to the prisoner in the stables and asked him how he would teach the horse to sing. The prisoner just shrugged and shook his head. Surprised, the executioner asked him why he had made the promise. The prisoner's answer: 'A year is a long time, and much can happen. I might die, in which case it won't matter to me. The king might die, and his successor might spare me. Or, you never know, the horse might learn to sing.'"

"Where there's life there's hope?"

The hare nodded. "More or less. Now, let's get out of here."

"How?"

Sparx chuckled. "No idea. The lantern was my executioner and you were the horse."

"You're not serious?" I was aghast. "You really have no idea?"

"Hey, I can only teach one horse to sing at a time."

17

Red Rabbit Rising

"WHAT HAVE I got in my pockets?"

Sparx nodded. "That's what I asked, yes."

"Not much." I pulled out my wallet, a few coins, some string, a comb, and the little LED flashlight I'd tucked in there after turning the lights on in Oscar's basement studio. "Oh, and these." My keys landed on the pile.

"Disappointing." The flames dancing through Sparx's fur dimmed slightly, making it harder to see anything.

"You were hoping for a pickax?"

"That would have been nice, yes. I guess we'll just have to make do."

"You're not seriously suggesting that I dig my way through a foot of sandstone with a plastic comb and my keys, are you?"

Sparx had scouted around and found a narrow passage through the stone that passed within a foot or so of the back wall of our little cell. One that didn't have any guards in it at the moment. He shrugged now.

"You *are* suggesting that?" I asked.

"Yes. No. Sort of."

"Oh, that's *very* clear, Sparx."

He poked at the items with a paw. "I think it can be done. It will require magic, of course, and thumbs. Which is where you come in." He held up his paws. "It's really the main thing you folks are good for."

"Why do I suspect that the digging part is going to be all on the thumb-monkey, too?"

Sparx smiled evilly. "Because you're brighter than you look? I mean, you'd have to be, right?"

"Yeah, yeah, yeah, very funny. What do I need to do first?"

"Do you think your key ring will fit over the shaft of the flashlight?"

It did, but only barely—the keys stuck out from the ring at a sharp angle. "Next?"

"You're going to take the comb in your hand and use your heart's fire to melt it around the flashlight where the key ring is and fuse the two together."

"Won't the plastic just catch fire and burn away completely? Not to mention burning me?"

Sparx shook his head. "Not if you do it right."

"So, don't screw up?"

"Exactly!" He grinned. "As I keep telling you: Control, my child; it's all about control."

"You know, you are not one bit more helpful as a true familiar than you were as a half-summoned one."

"Whatever made you think it would work any other way? The k*tsathsha"—and here Sparx pointed at his chest—"are spirits of mischief every bit as much as they are of fire. *Everyone* knows that."

"I didn't." I gave him the hairy eyeball.

"You've never heard the tale of Brer Rabbit and the briar patch?"

I blinked. "Uh . . . well, actually I have heard that one."

He nodded. "Ever seen that movie *Harvey*?"

Dim memories of watching ancient movies on cable with my mom dredged themselves up in the back of my mind. "Something about a giant invisible rabbit?"

"He was actually a fire hare pretending at being a rabbit, but yes, that's the one. My kind are tricksters. Capricious, changeable, occasionally malicious." He threw himself into my lap, landing on his back with his paws in the air. "And now, ALL YOURS. Aren't you lucky?"

"The *luckiest*." I dumped him back onto the floor.

"Was that sarcasm?" he asked. "I think that was sarcasm."

I touched the tip of his nose. "Not only mischievous, but perceptive as well. You are good. That makes me twice as lucky, right?"

"Just melt the comb, kid." So I did. "Not bad, Accursed Master mine. Not bad *at all*. Now for the tricky bit."

I resisted the urge to swear. I'd already had to blow out the burning comb twice. I was covered in sweat and soot and had a blistered thumb to match my bloody one—a bit of molten plastic had landed on the hand I wasn't using to channel fire and stuck like red-hot glue. And we hadn't even gotten to the tricky part?

"Go on," I said.

"You know how smiths use fire to harden the steel in swords and other weapons?"

"Yeah." I nodded cautiously. "Or at least I've seen it in movies and read about it. Is that what we're doing?"

"Not at all, but the end result is very similar."

This time I did swear. Some time later my improvised tool had acquired several flame-tinged ideograms and a flickering sheen visible only to those with the second sight.

I held it up. "That has to be the *ugliest* magic item I've ever seen."

"That's because you've only ever seen the kind they put in video games and movies. Bangles and baubles for the rubes. Real magic makes do with what it can get. Why, I remember one Accursed Master I had back in the eighteen hundreds who turned a washboard into an enchanted shield and a half-rotten broom into a spear."

"Really?"

"Would I lie to you?" Sparx blinked his big eyes innocently.

"I'm pretty sure the answer to that is yes, but I'm not going to press the point. So, where do I dig?"

Sparx led me to the far wall and hopped up to touch a spot about three feet off the floor. "There."

I gingerly pressed the tips of the keys against the sandstone, more than half expecting the whole thing to come apart in my hand the second I applied any pressure. Much to my surprise, the points sank easily into the stone, and when I levered back with the flashlight handle a piece of rock about the size of a plum fell free.

Sparx drew a sharp breath. "Holy crap, it works."

"You didn't think it would?"

"I hoped . . . but, well, I didn't expect results like *that*." He looked momentarily troubled, but then shook his head and waved both paws at me. "Never mind. Keep going, but put the lanyard around your wrist; you don't want to drop the digger when you break through into the passage."

It wasn't like digging through dirt—too brittle. But neither was it anything like as hard as carving sandstone should have been. More like breaking up one of those horrible little white cookie-like monstrosities that are always the last thing anyone eats at Christmas, all powdery and chalky and friable. The ones your mother only makes because *her* grandmother loved them and she thinks the holidays wouldn't be the same without them staring palely up at you from the cookie plate.

Five minutes later, my little digger broke through into . . . "Are you crazy, Sparx?!"

"What? It leads up toward the surface."

"STRAIGHT up! That's not a passage, that's . . ." I stuck my head into the hole again and looked down this time. "It's a bottomless pit, is what it is."

Sparx shook his head. "It's not bottomless. We're really close to the river here; you wouldn't fall more than forty feet before you hit water. At the most."

"Oh, good, so I'd drown after I went *splat*. That's *very* reassuring."

"You're not going to go splat or drown." Sparx rolled his eyes. "The walls of the shaft are barely more than two feet apart. Just brace your back on one side and your hands and feet on the other and climb it like you would a door frame. I've seen you do it often enough in your closet when you wanted to get something off that top shelf."

"Which is less than six feet off the ground and brightly lit!"

"The principle is exactly the same; I don't understand what you're whining about."

"The only principle that matters is that if I slip and fall in my room I'll land on my butt and be embarrassed, and if do it here, I'll fall to my death."

"Well, if you want to stay here until the delvers come in and find me loose from the lamp and you digging holes in the walls, you're the boss. But I don't think that Oscar will be nearly as gentle with us a second time around, do you? And he was already planning on feeding your flesh to the delvers and using your bones to make a golem if he couldn't simply destroy your will and take over your soul."

I winced. "There's no other way out?"

"Well, there's the way we came in, which leads past the guards and through the delver village out there. Or you could just keep digging until we're clear. I imagine that would only take a week or three. How long did Oscar say he thought it would take to figure out whether he could break you or not? A few days?"

Swearing again, I wedged myself into the hole and started worming my way into the vertical shaft. "Where does this go, anyway?"

Sparx climbed onto my shoulder, providing me with a flickering red light. "Up."

"Very helpful. I never would have figured that part out as I was climbing." I shifted my hand up to grope around for a new grip—as I got higher in the shaft, I was finding bits of other kinds of rock in the sandstone, making it an easier climb. "I mean *after* that."

"I imagine we'll find out when we get there."

I gave him a sidewise glance. "Why do I think you know exactly where it goes, and it's going to lead to another horse that needs to learn to sing?"

"Because you have a nasty and suspicious mind."

"I didn't used to. I used to be all sweetness and light. But then I met this flaming rabbit with an infectiously bad attitude and a very loose relationship with the truth."

One of my feet slipped then and I had to suppress the urge to scream as I smacked the back of my head against the wall. That helped to arrest my slide, but it hurt like nobody's business because I'd hit one of those other bits of rock pretty hard. It felt sharp against my scalp and I wanted desperately to move my head away from the pain, but I didn't dare until I got my feet properly braced again. Basically, the rock sticking into the back of my head was the only thing keeping me from falling.

"How bad is it?" I asked Sparx as I finally started to move upward again.

"You were lucky, and your hair is soaking up most of the blood."

"And *that's* lucky?"

"Less messy, anyway. But that's not what I meant. I meant you were lucky to catch that rock with your head. I'm pretty sure you'd have fallen to your doom otherwise."

"I thought you told me I wasn't going to go splat or drown," I growled.

"I also told you that I lie."

"You did no such thing! You said, quote, 'Would I lie to you?' unquote."

The hare laughed. "What do you think I meant by that?"

"That, of course, you'd lie to . . . Oh. Fine. Have it your way." I had to laugh, too.

"I usually do. By the way, it's time to teach the next horse to sing."

"Meaning what?" I asked.

"Meaning we're at the top of the shaft and there's a pretty good-sized plug of dirt overhead. You'll need to pull it down on top of you without knocking yourself loose or suffocating."

I sighed. "Good thing I left the digger hanging from my wrist, then, isn't it."

"Yep, that was the plan. Now, you start hacking away on this side, and I'm going to go up top and start digging down to meet you. Hares are excellent tunnelers, you know."

"Yeah, I read *Watership Down*."

Sparx hopped off my shoulder and vanished into the stone wall to my left. The next few minutes were hellish. With the hare gone, I was in complete darkness. My legs and arms were already sore and tired from the climb, and now I had to hold myself in place entirely with my back and feet. Wedging my toes against one of the protruding rocks helped, but my calves and thighs were burning and starting to get shaky. Once I started digging into the soft soil above me, the shaft quickly filled with a cloud of dust that choked me and got in my eyes.

It wasn't just earth plugging the shaft above, either. Rocks and sticks bounced off my head and shoulders as I pried them free. Clods of dirt did the same, or broke up to slide into my shirt along with some of the smaller stones. I was pretty sure I was collecting a few hibernating bugs and worms as well. But I did finally break through to meet Sparx coming down from the top. Five seconds later, I was climbing again when about a cubic yard of snow from the dense cover above fell in on me. That was the point where I simply had to laugh. It was that or start crying, and I didn't know if I'd stop if I started.

Sparx gave me a funny look as I pushed my way out into the bright winter sunlight. "You okay, kid?"

"Oh yeah, I'm dandy. Never better. Why do you ask?"

"Just wanted to make sure that wasn't the beginning of hysterics. I've dealt with a couple of hysterical Accursed Masters in the past, and it can be a challenge. Glad we're not going there. Speaking of going, that's what we should be doing now. We want to be far from here when the delvers find us missing. They don't much like the light, but they *can* tolerate it, and it won't last long at this time of year."

"All right." I stood up and then almost fell over again as my right calf cramped. "Ow!" Bending, I rubbed the cramp away. Walking was going to be absolute gangs of fun. "Two questions."

"Fire away." Sparx grinned. "Get it? I'm a fire hare and I said fire away. Laugh. It's a joke, kid."

I snorted. "Not a very good one. First, go where? Second, why am I not freezing to death? I'm knee-deep in snow in only a T-shirt and jeans." It was one of the first things I'd noticed once we broke through into the outdoors. In Minnesota you learn about warm clothes and not freezing to death really young if you want to get any older.

"Second question first, as it's easier to answer. That's partially from finding the fire in your heart. Now that you can tap that, you'll be much better able to stay warm even on the iciest day. The rest of it is that you now have a familiar with his full powers, which means I can help the fire in your heart fight the cold."

A long silence followed before I finally prompted, ". . . And the first question?"

"I don't know." He pointed beyond me. "The river's down that way, and this is no place to linger. I think we'll want to get over it as quickly as we can. We're not far from the swamp where we met the selkies this fall, and that means we can use the railroad bridge to cross. But after that?" He shrugged.

I wasn't sure, either, so I just started trudging. The swamp was frozen solid and covered with snow, the selkies nowhere in evidence. By the time we got across the river and into downtown, the sun was already starting to lower in the cloudy sky.

That made the fairy-tale castle on Harriet Island all the more visible. As I passed the science museum, the intense light show playing out in the clear block walls of the ice palace drew my eye. The Winter Carnival design team had gone all out this year, using lasers and a computerized control system to create armies of frost giants and other creatures of myth and legend on and within the record-setting palace. Blue warriors rode polar bear–like steeds around the outer walls, while snowflake-winged fairies flitted to and fro in the upper reaches of the central tower.

For a few brief moments the beauty of the place lifted me out of myself, but that ended when I noticed a museum security guard giving me the eyeball through a window. He wasn't the first. I'd collected plenty of hostile looks from passersby on my way here. Not that I could entirely blame them—between the dirt and my ragged clothes and the blood in my hair I must have looked like hell's own street urchin. As the guard reached for his radio, I decided it was time to get moving.

Somehow, we managed to make it all the way to the Free School building without getting arrested or otherwise picked up by the powers that be. Sparx and I had talked it out and decided the school was our best bet for the moment. Classes were over, but I waited in the hedge at the base of the parking ramp across the street until I saw the janitor leave before going around back to the playground. The doors were shut tight, but Sparx just slipped through the wall and jumped up to push open the locking bar.

I'd been in the building in the evening before for rehearsals, but there had always been other people around, and at least some lights on. The halls felt infinitely larger and lonelier now, all dark and empty. Every noise I made seemed to echo weirdly as I limped along the tile floor. But I didn't dare turn on any lights as I headed for the theater—not this late on Friday. When I got there, Sparx opened the doors once again. Back in the costume racks I found some pants and a shirt that wouldn't look too out of place in the real world. Then it was off to the gym for a shower.

My first impulse when I got there was to simply strip off my torn and filthy clothes and throw them in the trash. I got as far as peeling off my shirt and rolling it into a ball when a thought hit me and I froze mid-gesture.

Sparx gave me a funny look. "Are you okay?"

"I don't think so." I shook my head. "You remember earlier

when you asked me if I was going to have hysterics, and I said no? Well, I'm thinking about changing my mind now."

"Tell me about it."

"It was the shirt. I was going to throw it away, but then I realized I didn't know when or even *if* I could go home to pick up a replacement. I mean, as long as Oscar's there, with all the power of the Winter King and controlling my mom, I'm pretty much homeless, right?"

"I don't know that I'd go that far. I mean, when we were talking this over on the way here, we figured the next thing in the plan after you get cleaned up was to give your mom a call from one of the school phones, right?"

"Do you really think that's going to help? Really?" I felt tears starting to burn in the corners of my eyes.

Sparx sighed and shook his head. "No. I don't, but I didn't want to bring it up because of that whole hysterics thing. Which I still recommend against. I mean, you've got a ton of stuff to freak out about, but freaking out won't actually help at all. At least not yet. Look, I'll make you a deal. You're cold and filthy and starving, and that makes for really bad decisions. Once you're clean and dry and we've sorted out food and getting you set up with someplace to sleep, you can have a complete flip-out."

"What's your side of the deal?"

"I'll watch?"

I snorted through the tears that had started to leak down my cheeks. "Jerk." It really wasn't all that funny, but it was enough to help me to get it together again, at least for a little bit.

I went and turned the shower on, taking my shirt with me as I stepped into the warm water. It was easier to scrub the worst of the filth off my jeans and sneakers with them on me than otherwise, so I did that before stripping down and cleaning myself up. It wasn't until I tried to wash my hair that I remembered about the big gash in the back of my scalp. Cleaning that out used up as many swear words as I would normally go through in a year, but I knew I had to be thorough.

When I'd finished showering, Sparx made me bend down to his level, where he did something hot, magical, and extremely painful to the wound. Since it was on the back of my head I couldn't see it or what he'd done, but it involved a sizzling noise, the smell of burning hair, and promises that I'd thank him for it in the years to come. Then we raided the teachers' lounge for some granola bars and a half box of stale doughnuts—nothing ever tasted better—before calling my mom's cell.

"Helloooooo, this is . . . Genevieve."

Ugh, not a good start—she sounded like she was on another planet entirely. "Hi, Mom, it's Kalvan."

"Oh, that's nice. . . . Kalvan who?"

I wanted to scream and cry, but I'd spent a lifetime learning to be gentle with my mother, so I took a deep breath and tried to stay calm as I spoke. "Kalvan, your son."

There was a long pause, then, "Riiiiight. Sorry, Kalvan. I was having one of my headaches, so Oscar gave me my meds and I'm a little loopy now." Another pause. "How's DC?"

"I'm not in DC, Mom. I'm at school."

"Don't be ridiculous, darling. It's nearly eight o'clock on a Friday. School's been closed for hours."

Another deep breath. "Yes, it has. That's why I was hoping you could drive over and meet me here, Mom."

"I'm sorry, Kalvan, but you know I can't drive after I've taken my meds. Especially not all the way to DC. Do you want me to get Oscar to meet you?"

"NO!" I shouted, and my mother drew in a sharp breath. I kicked myself mentally. "I'm sorry, Mom. I didn't mean to be that sharp, but I really don't want to see Oscar. We . . . uh, had another one of our big fights. Better not even mention me to him."

"All right. Ohhhhh my, the room seems to be spinning a bit; I'd better go lie down again. Have a good time in DC."

It took everything I had not to yell again. "Mom, I told you I'm not in DC."

"Not in DC? . . . DC, what does that remind me of? Oh yes. Daisy . . . *Daisy, Daisy, give me your answer true. I'm half crazy over the love of you. It won't be a stylish marriage, I can't afford a carriage, but you'll look sweet upon the seat of a bicycle built for two.*"

I hung up.

Sparx put both paws on my thigh. "I'm sorry, Kalvan. Are you all right?"

"Not even a little bit." I felt sick to my stomach and clenched my jaw to keep from losing those doughnuts. "But I think I can hold off the freak-out awhile longer. The teachers' lounge isn't the place for it." I was really glad I had the weekend to be a basket case before I had to face anyone.

Once I'd settled into the easy chair under the main stage with a couple of old velvet curtains as a blanket, on the other hand, I started to sob. That's when Sparx, who had just finished setting a magic circle around the chair, climbed up onto my chest and tucked his head in underneath my chin. He normally didn't go in for a lot of touchy-feely, but he was a big, warm, comforting presence now.

I wrapped both arms around him and squeezed, speaking through my tears. "Thanks, Sparx."

"Everything is going to be all right, Kalvan. I promise." Then he began to purr.

"I didn't think rabbits purred."

"Hare. And we don't. I just speak fluent cat, and past experience suggested it might help."

"It does. Thank you."

"Any time, Accursed Master, any time."

Some time later, the tears stopped, though the purring kept on, eventually lulling me into sleep.

18

Down Deep

"URG," I MUMBLED. My face felt like someone had painted my eyes shut and then poured the rest of the can into my nose. Whoever it was had apparently followed that up by burying me to my neck in sand. ". . . the heck?"

I blearily forced my left eye open. Nothing. Absolute darkness. Terror brought me fully awake as I was briefly returned to the cell in the delver tunnels, and I jerked upright. Red light flared as Sparx fell from my chest along with the heavy velvet curtains I had perceived as the weight of sand.

The brightly burning hare landed on the floor with an audible thump. "I take it you're awake?" Then his eyes met mine and his voice softened. "It's all right, Kalvan, we're under the stage at your school and free of all chains. For the moment at least."

I rubbed my other eye open and then wiped my nose with the back of my wrist. "I feel awful."

"Crying yourself to sleep will do that."

And that brought it all back. I was homeless. My stepfather was a monster. And my mother was firmly in his power. In an instant, tears were burning at the corners of my eyes again and my throat felt like I'd swallowed a handful of broken glass.

Sparx leaped up onto the arm of my chair and put his front paws on my chest. "Kalvan . . ."

I bit back the tears, took a couple of deep breaths, and then shook my head. "'S okay. I'll be fine in a minute."

"I don't think that's true."

I snorted and then had to wipe my nose again. "It's not. But maybe if we both pretend it is, I'll be able to hold it together long enough to get cleaned up and sort out breakfast." I really needed another shower, and I was famished. "Things will look better after that, right?"

Sparx spread his ears in a bunny shrug. "They almost certainly won't be worse, and that's a start."

After my shower, searching through my locker and wallet turned up eight dollars and fifty cents. That in turn bought me ten chocolate spinners, ten strawberry bombs, eight pocket pies, and two loaves of bread out of the seconds and week-old bin at the Doughboy bakery outlet store. I'd have skipped the bread, but Sparx insisted, and the way the clerk looked at me when I shouted at the backpack I'd borrowed from the school's lost and found after he called me "Accursed Master" suggested that arguing with my bag wouldn't go over well.

I ate three pies on the two-block walk back to Free and a pair of strawberry bombs as soon as we got inside. Then Sparx made me eat a sandwich with some Cruncher's peanut butter that was in the teachers' lounge fridge.

"Better?" asked Sparx when I'd finished my sandwich.

"A little, yeah. But any time I think about what's going on with Oscar and my mom . . ." I shuddered.

Sparx nodded sympathetically. "Unfortunately, that's exactly the thing we need to be thinking about."

"I know. It's him or me now, isn't it?"

"Unless you're willing to abandon your mother and run far away from here, I'm afraid that it is."

I winced at that. "We're going to need some help. I'd better call Dave."

Veronica Harris picked up the phone on the second ring. "Hello."

"Hi, Veronica." She insisted I call her by her first name, like I did my teachers. "This is Kalvan; can I speak with Dave?"

"Sure, honey, I'm pretty sure he's awake. I'll bring him the phone. Hang on a sec."

"Kalvan?" Dave sounded like someone had kicked him in the throat. "What's up?"

"I'm kind of in a mess . . ." I had to stop and take a deep breath then, because my voice wanted to break. "I broke into Oscar's studio again yesterday morning."

"Without me? Uncool, dude. Uncool."

"If it's any consolation, Oscar caught me and I got my butt kicked nine ways from Sunday in the process." I didn't like to think about what might have happened to Dave if he'd been with us—Oscar didn't have any reason to keep my friend alive. "And I'm kind of in a mess now."

"That's what you get for cutting me out. Tell me about it."

So I did. When I finished Dave let out a low whistle that ended in a harsh cough.

When he could speak again he said, "Uuugly."

"I know, right?"

"Hang on a minute, I'm going to ask my mom if you can come stay with us for a few days."

"Wait!" It cost me to stop him, but I did it anyway.

"What? Why?"

"Dave, come on. What are you going to tell her about why I'm staying?"

"I'll tell her you're having some problems at home. She's met your mom, and she used to be married to my dad; she'll understand."

That sounded so nice, and I wanted it, but . . . "No. Look, Oscar knows you're my best friend, and he knows where you live. That's the first place he'll look."

"And he won't find you at school?"

"No. I don't think he will, and neither does Sparx." That was part of why we'd come here in the first place. "He says that all the comings and goings at the school over the years, many of them mine, makes it easier to hide me here in the magical sense."

"All right, I can buy that, but what are you going to do when classes start up again on Monday? Won't Oscar just be able to call the school and come get you?"

"I don't know. I guess I'll have to figure it out."

"Do you still have your science museum membership?"

"You know, that just might work . . ." I felt a little trickle of relief as Dave solved a problem I hadn't even thought about in almost the same instant he pointed it out to me.

"And this is why you need me. You've got brains coming out your ears, but no street smarts."

I laughed. It wasn't much, but it felt good. "Hard to argue with that."

"Don't even try, my friend. Don't even try."

"Deal. Now, you get better quick so you can do more than just offer me good advice."

"Will do. I'll bring some clothes that'll fit you, too, and leave 'em under the stage, because I bet you hadn't thought that part through, either. Talk to you soon."

Fire ran through my heart, the flames running bright and hot in my veins. I could feel the light in my chest as it pushed back against the shadows pouring in through my throat and nose, fighting the dark that slowly filled my lungs. I was drowning in darkness. No. In *Darkness*!

"That's it!" I shouted myself awake.

Sparx, who had been curled up on my chest, literally bounced off the underside of the stage above me. "I'm awake! I'm awake! The square root of negative one! 'Friends, Romans, countrymen!' Unicorn poop makes an excellent ointment for the treating of magical frostbite!"

"What?"

"Sorry." The hare shook his head. "This whole living-in-a-school thing is taking me back to my days at Blackstock College." It was Tuesday night, and we'd spent two days hiding out at the museum during the day and spending our nights at the school.

"Wait, there's a college for fire hares?"

"Of course not. That would be ridiculous. Far too specialized. Blackstock admits any of the major elemental spirits. Well, they did when I was there, anyway. It's been a few centuries since I visited. I think the alumni association still has my address in London."

I was having serious trouble with the idea. "*You* went to college?"

"Yes, at Oxford. Studied with Professor Medeous. Horrible creature, but a brilliant claw with an enchantment."

"Claw?"

"She was a raven at the time—element of shadow—though I don't know if she stayed with it."

I pushed the idea of an Oxford college for elemental animals aside. "We have more important fish to fry. So, never mind."

"Shouldn't that be 'nevermore'?" He waited a moment while I gave him the hairy eyeball. "It's another joke, kid; laugh."

"Ha. Ha. Ha. Now, can we be serious?"

"Probably not, but I can fake it if you need me to, O Accursed Master."

"What is with you today?"

"Sorry, you woke me from a pretty deep sleep. I'm not at my best first thing out of dreams. I tend to wake up odd. Wait a second." Sparx canted his head to one side quizzically. "If I'm not misremembering, you were yelling something about 'That's it.' Which is?"

"Which what is?"

"The *that* you shouted about, of course."

"Oh, *that* that. I figured out where my great-grandfather's Vulcan uniform must be. Oscar said it was someplace we could never get at, and I figured out what he meant."

Sparx suddenly looked *a lot* more awake. "That's fantastic! We can't beat Oscar without it. Where is it?"

"It's not under the model of the capitol in our basement. It's in the basement under the capitol. The real one. That's why he said we were so very close and yet impossibly far. We actually looked in exactly the right place, just in the wrong version of it. That's why he said we could never get past the guardian."

"Because the Darkness lives under the capitol—the real Darkness and not just the shadow in the model." Sparx winced. "That's going to be rough."

I bit my lip. "Do you think we should bring Dave?"

Sparx shook his head. "He's not up to it yet. Today was the first day he's been well enough to return to school, and it clearly took a lot out of him. You heard how tired he sounded on the phone when you checked in earlier."

"I promised not to cut him out of anything again."

"You can blame me."

I shook my head. "I can't do that to him."

Five minutes after we got into the capitol tunnels Dave was breathing hard and looking winded. He really hadn't recovered yet, and I wanted to tell him to go back to school. But he kept his game face on and I knew he had my back, so I swallowed my worries for the moment.

When we got to the little half-height door in the basement, it was closed and locked. Not good.

"Sparx," I whispered, "can you manage the door?"

He slid through my backpack and the door itself, poking his head out a moment later. "Not without burning the lock away completely. That's going to take some time and make a lot of smoke."

"That's not good." There weren't any capitol guards around now, but smoke would set off alarms and bring them out of the woodwork mighty quick. "What do we do?"

Dave grimaced and then sighed. "Let me take care of it."

"What? How?" I asked.

"Provide a distraction. I'm no help on the magic side of things, especially when I'm not recovered. But I *can* open up a fire door and draw the more normal sorts of guardians away from this part of the building."

"What if you get caught?"

He shrugged and looked grim. "That's my problem, but I won't get caught. Now, you find someplace close to hole up while I go buy you some freedom to work your magic."

Sparx started on the lock in the very same instant the alarm started ringing. I stayed in the niche I'd found in the shadow of some ductwork across the hall until the door, which now had a red-hot patch around the lock, suddenly popped open. Then I bolted across and yanked on the doorknob, burning my fingers a little in the process.

A moment later, I closed the half-height door behind me as well as I could and then froze when I contemplated the path ahead. The three-foot-tall tunnel with its pipes and cables seemed to extend forever. It was infinitely harder to move onward knowing what waited for me than it had been back on that day in the fall when I'd known nothing about magic or what it could do. That had been an "adventure" for a boy with no concept of what the word meant, where this was the real thing, with a monster that had stalked my kind for millennia waiting for me somewhere up ahead.

"It's not going to get any easier if you think about it." Sparx had taken up station beside me. "Quite the opposite, really."

"That's *very* helpful."

"You're welcome," replied Sparx.

"I was being sarcastic, Mr. Funny Bunny."

"I know, but you weren't doing a very good job of it."

"You are the most aggravating familiar ever!" I threw my arms up and smacked the knuckles of my right hand on a pipe. "OW! I'm . . . You . . . Argh!"

Sparx quickly hopped out of reach. "That was smart."

Anger made me scramble after him. He hopped a few feet farther down the hall and I immediately followed.

He laughed and pointed and kept just out of reach. "So, are you finally mad enough to end your little woe-is-me party and get moving again? Or are you going to let the time Dave bought you go to waste?"

"Yes! I . . . Wait, is that what that was all about? Getting me going?"

"Of course." He continued ahead and I followed along.

"You're a brat and I am totally going to get even with you for this."

"You'll try."

As we got closer to the little ladder that led down into the older tunnel, I felt the fear returning. But I kept moving. Pausing beside the little door had been a mistake. There is an inertia to fear. If you stop, it's hard to get started again. If you start running, it's hard to stop. As long as I kept moving, that tendency worked for me. Just keep moving.

If the Darkness had any awareness of our presence yet, I couldn't feel it. Which was all to the good. I don't know if I could have advanced in the face of the implacable hatred I'd found here the last time. Not knowing what I did now. Perhaps it was asleep here at the brightest part of the day. That *was* why Sparx and Dave and I had chosen noon for this foray. The hope that even there, in the deep places of the earth, the monster that lay below could feel the weight of light pressing down from the sun in the sky above; that it would somehow weaken the thing.

All too soon, we arrived at the short descent to the lower tunnel. My brain wanted to pause and think things over. Or, better yet, to turn and run for it, but my body kept right on doing the last thing I'd told it to do, and I climbed down to the lower level, where the walls changed from concrete to limestone block and the air took on a dank weight.

Fifty feet more passed in a dream, and then I stood above the big round hatch in the floor that led down into darkness. Or, more terrifyingly, into Darkness. With one hand I pulled out my little flashlight and flicked it on while I used the other to brace myself as I began my descent. As my head passed through the hatch, Sparx hopped onto my shoulder.

Simultaneously with his weight I felt another. A weight of presence, as the Darkness finally noticed me. Only it didn't push down. It pushed in. I felt it like deep water, a pressure that pressed on me from every side. I was four again, back at the lake and losing my footing as I plunged into the drop-off. But this time there would be no rescue. My grandmother was long dead and my mother . . . well, just as she had on that day at the lake, my mother remained on the shore, lost and unable to help me.

I opened my mouth to scream and the Darkness rushed in with my breath, a cold, aching poison, bitter and black, that invaded my lungs and ran from there into my veins. I almost lost the battle then, before it had truly begun, without even realizing the danger. I almost reached for my throat there on the ladder, almost let go of the rungs, almost fell. Almost.

What saved me? The same memory that nearly drowned me. The memory of my mother standing on the shore, lost and weeping. My mother unable to save me on that fateful day. Unable to even save herself. If I drowned, who would save her? It was a quiet little question there in the dark. A tiny thing for a drowning boy to cling to, but sometimes a tiny thing is all you need. A tiny thing that moves the focus from the problem to the solution. From mindless reaction to active thought. Who would save her from Oscar?

It had to be me. I squeezed the rungs tightly in my hands and forced the Darkness up and out of my lungs, making myself exhale through sheer force of will. Then, in again, breathing the Darkness in with the air that I had to have to keep from drowning. Out again. And in. I did not master the Darkness, did not tame it to my will, didn't even beat it. But I didn't let it beat me, either. And so I passed the first test: learning that I could survive the Darkness within, if only for a time.

I opened my eyes, only then realizing that I had closed them against that first icy wave of the Darkness. The pale glow from my little flashlight painted the shadow of the bars across the limestone blocks of the wall behind. I willed my right hand to let go of the rung, to move down and take the next one. Willed my left to follow. My feet to descend. On the wall the shadows moved, and I knew that my body was obeying me despite the press of the Darkness.

Time slipped past, one rung at a time. Eventually, I became used to the weight pressing on me and began to have thoughts of other things. How long had I been climbing down? It seemed like years, a feeling reinforced by the ache in my hands and arms, the numbing of my toes. Had I passed a hundred rungs? A thousand? Should I count? How far did I have to go?

They always say don't look down. Never look down. I looked down. And . . . it made no difference at all. My flashlight should have illuminated the ladder for at least a couple of yards below me. I couldn't even see my knees. The rusty steel ladder might have extended another twenty feet or two hundred or two thousand. There was no way to know until I reached the bottom. *If* I reached the bottom. If there *was* a bottom . . .

Slowly, my light began to dim. So slowly that I barely recognized it in the fading of the shadows on the wall, the blurring of those lesser darknesses into the greater Darkness all around me.

"Sparx, do you see that?"

"What?"

"The light's going out. Is the battery dying? Have we been climbing down that long?" It sure felt like it.

"The light isn't going out," said the hare. "The Darkness is deepening. Night has compressed itself into the blackness of the abyss and it is crushing the light, like the ocean crushing a swimmer who dives too deep."

The imagery made me shudder. "Oh. Thanks. Also, soooo not helping."

"You asked."

"My bad. Is it going to crush us, too? If we go deep enough?" I'd had a slowly growing sense that the pressure of the dark was increasing, but I'd figured it was just my imagination. Now . . .

"Not if we don't let it."

"Good. Good. Glad to hear it. Any idea how to do that?"

"Not a clue." Sparx sounded worried. "That's on you, I'm afraid. It's why the Accursed Master makes the big bucks and familiars always end up way down toward the bottom of the movie credits, along with special effects and incidental music."

"Right. Good to know." The light blinked out as I moved down a few more rungs, and I winced. "Was that bad? Because that feels bad."

"It's definitely bad."

I realized then that I couldn't see the dim fiery glow I'd come to associate with Sparx, either. "How about you? Can you light things up a bit? I can't even see if you're still on fire."

"I'm burning as bright as I can."

"I was afraid of that." I had a really horrible idea then. "We've been climbing down forever. I counted rungs for a while and hit a hundred and fifty before I gave up. That's way more than there should be. I think the Darkness is playing games with space and time."

"That's certainly possible. Why? Do you have an idea?"

I nodded. "A really stupid one."

"Tell me about it."

"I think I'd rather show you. Hang on tight."

"What!?! Wait!"

I let go, turning as I did, so that instead of climbing down I was now diving down into the Darkness. In that moment I passed the second test: accepting that the rules of the Darkness are not the same as the rules that prevail under the light of sun and stars. Just as letting go earlier would have left me broken and bleeding at the bottom of the ladder, now letting go freed me to push down into the heart of the Darkness.

It was like swimming through syrup, thick and slow and heavy. As I moved deeper and deeper into the Darkness, it pressed in on me, a great weight growing ever greater, until it crushed me utterly . . . or tried to, at least. There came a moment as I pushed downward where I felt the pressure grow so great that I knew I could not hope to survive it a moment longer in my present shape.

And that was the third test, if only I could find the answer to it . . .

19

A Midwinter Night's Hare

I **REFUSED TO** be crushed by the Darkness.

When Oscar had trapped me, he'd spoken of a hard core to my soul, a place that resisted all the weight of stone magic that he could bring to bear. In that moment, when the Darkness would have smashed me flat, I found the place in myself that Oscar had described. It was a hard, proud, stubborn place, the part of me that *couldn't* give up.

It was what made me climb onto the stage when I was terrified of an audience, what made me look out for my mother when she was the one who was supposed to be looking out for me, what had brought me here and now to face the Darkness without any true idea of how to defeat it. What my mother had called my *true heart*.

I shifted then, shaping myself to that core of unbreakable will, conforming my outer self to fit the inner. Before I tried it,

I would have told you it was impossible, but I was born with a heart of fire, and fire is the ever-changing element, flickering and fleeting in a constantly moving dance of form and light. In that moment, changing my shape was the most natural thing in the world.

Almost as natural was catching the dim and fading spark of flame that rode my soul like a hawk on the falconer's glove and pulling it into a shape that complemented my own. For the k*tsathsha was another form of fire, and fires merge and split almost as easily as water.

Thanks . . . Sparx's voice spoke directly . . . into my soul? No. In that time and place, there was no easy way to say where one soul ended and the other began. Say rather that he spoke from *within* my soul and you would have something more like the truth.

You're welcome.

Hang on, I wasn't done. Sparx's soul voice sounded shaky. *I wanted to say thanks . . . but please don't ever do that again. It's not at all comfortable being you. That is what we're doing right now, isn't it? Being you, I mean. Both of us. Together. In this.* I got the impression of wildly waving paws. *Whatever this is. Also, can we stop soon? Us being you, that is.*

I don't know. We're not moving anymore, but it's still dark out there and I feel like there's something else we need to do. Some final test we have to pass.

Any idea what that could be?

I don't know. We've reached the heart of the Darkness and survived. I don't . . .

Then I did. It's not something I could ever have seen on my

own, not without Sparx in my head—a much older soul sharing the same space, frightened, but also full of insight and a loving wisdom he masked with sarcasm and cynicism. *I get it! I'm not afraid of the Darkness anymore.* And I never would be again, because now I knew how to defeat it.

Shine!

I opened my heart then, not to fire but to light. The simple light of the soul. No matter how scarred, no matter how tattered and torn, no matter our element, we are, all of us, creatures of spirit as well as flesh, as much beings of light as we are of blood and bone.

That is why the Darkness hates us. That is why the Darkness fears us. That is why the Darkness will never defeat us.

Because we all shine from within, and it is a light we can share if only we are willing to let down the walls that separate us, as the walls that had separated Sparx and I had fallen. If only we are willing.

WE SHINE

There was a horrible scream, more felt than heard, and the Darkness was gone. I felt a bright sense of triumph, but only for a moment, because I realized then another truth I could only have seen through Sparx's eyes. No matter how bright the light, the Darkness can never be destroyed. It can only be driven away, and only for a time. Knowing what I did now, I could and would fight it for all the length of my days, but eventually my light would go out and then the Darkness would return.

It took me several long minutes to realize that things had changed around me as much they had changed within me. I was lying on my back on a cold concrete floor, and my whole body felt stiff and old and wrung out. The flashlight hanging from my wrist was pointed the wrong way for me to see much of anything beyond the suggestion of a curved metal ceiling. At least not without moving, and I *really* didn't want to move. I wanted nothing more than to close my eyes and take a little nap.

"Don't EVER do that again," said Sparx.

"Huh?"

I rolled my head to the side and saw Sparx flat on his back with all four legs pointing straight into the air, each tipped with a yellow flame. He looked like the world's weirdest festive Easter candle.

"You heard me, O Accursed Master." For the first time since he'd started calling me that, the *Accursed* bit had some real venom. That stung.

"I should have left you to drown in the Dark?" I grumbled back.

"Well, no, but . . ." He ran down. "All right, no buts. I just . . ." He shivered all over. "Let's say it's not my idea of a great way to spend a Wednesday afternoon, and never speak of it again. Deal?"

"It's not exactly an experience I'm dying to re-create myself. Deal. So, now what?"

He sighed. "Now we get up and find what we came here to get."

"No nap?"

"No nap."

"You're sure?"

"Starting to sound whiny there, thumb-monkey."

"So, definitely no nap." It took me three tries, but eventually I managed to roll over onto my stomach. "Ugh." From there to my feet didn't go at all well, but it did go. Eventually. With a lot of effort. "I think next time I'll let the Darkness win and destroy me. It'd be a lot less work. Probably less painful, too. Ow. Ow, ow, ow."

"Big baby. You don't see me whimpering about getting back up on my feet."

"Hey, I've got a lot more up to get than you do, Mr. Knee-High."

"Fine." Sparx clapped his paws in slow applause. "How's that? Or do you want a medal for standing up, too?"

"A medal would be perfect. Why don't you get on that?"

"Your wish is my command." The hare gave a sharp salute. "I'll take care of that the Tuesday after never. Is that good for you, O Accursed Master?" And that sounded much more like the old Sparx.

"Perfect." I flicked my little flashlight around.

The beam revealed an enormous barrel-vaulted space with a corrugated-steel ceiling like an airplane hangar. The curved surface was a uniform glossy gray about three shades lighter than the concrete floor. Something at about head height caught my eye. Something red. I directed the beam that way, catching a sign stenciled on the metal wall.

CIVIL DEFENSE SHELTER

"Bomb shelter," said Sparx.

"Uh-huh." I aimed my light along the base of the wall and picked out hundreds of waxed cardboard boxes labeled CIVIL DEFENSE SUPPLIES. "Do you suppose the case with my great-grandfather's Vulcan uniform is hiding in one of those?"

"Safe bet."

"So which one?" I didn't relish the idea of having to open all of them.

"I'll find it." Sparx hopped over to the boxes and began sniffing along their bases. After only a few minutes he reared back and put his front paws on a box in the bottom row. "This one smells like old fire."

He was right, as we saw when I cracked the box open.

"Ash and oak." Sparx touched the front of the little wooden case. "Of course that's what they made it out of."

Not counting the short legs, the case was about twenty-four inches tall by eighteen wide at the front and sixteen deep, and it reminded me of a puzzle box more than anything, as there were no obvious doors or latches. The only way I could even tell which way was the front was by the shape of the thing, which was wider on one side.

"Any idea how we get it open?" asked Sparx.

"I don't . . . wait." On a hunch, I opened my heart the tiniest bit, bringing fire to dance on my fingertips. "I hope this works."

As my hands got close to the wood, a pair of charred ideograms appeared about where you would expect handles to go. I touched them with my thumbs, and the whole front of the case split down the middle, opening on invisible hinges to reveal what lay within. The inner compartment was divided into three parts. The helmet of the Vulcan, with its high crest, rested in the top, held in place by velvet-covered rails. Below that was a shallow shelf filled tight with a thick red wool. On the bottom I could see the spine of one polished black leather boot and the toe cap of another.

Bingo. "Let's get out of here," said Sparx.

I nodded, though the thought of tackling that endless climb while lugging the wooden case made my teeth hurt. But I didn't have a whole lot of choice if I didn't want to separate costume from container, and that felt . . . wrong somehow. So I used my belt to improvise a carrying strap for the thing and followed Sparx to the base of the ladder.

Thirty rungs.

Thirty!

That was the length of the climb up out of the shelter. I remembered the hundred and fifty I'd counted as a partial tally coming down, and I felt my bones go cold within my flesh. And that was my final lesson of the day.

Darkness lies.

"Oh, the outfit, it's totally you." Dave held up his hands like a picture frame.

"Gosh, thanks." I tugged at one baggy elbow.

My great-grandfather's Vulcan uniform fit me like somebody else's glove. Somebody with much bigger hands. I might be nearly as tall as he had been, but I was half the man he'd been. At best.

"Aw, come on," said Dave. "It's not bad in a Santa-slash-homeless-dude sort of way." Even as the words left his mouth, Dave's face suddenly tightened. "Oh, man, I'm so sorry. That was a really stupid thing to say."

I shook my head and put on a smile I couldn't feel through the ice churning in my gut. "It's okay."

"No, it's not," said Dave. "I didn't think about your situation before I spoke and . . ." He looked down at his feet. "Frankly, it wouldn't be funny no matter what. Ending up on the street isn't something to joke about. I should know better, especially considering how easy it is to imagine my dad out there. I mean, I've heard teachers make that point more than once, but this brings it home. I'm sorry." He gave me a quick hug. "Forgive me?"

"Yeah, we're cool. And you're not wrong about how bad this thing fits me." I glanced at the mirror again.

It was Thursday the second and Dave had stayed after school to meet me and see the suit. He'd managed to slip away from the capitol after going through the emergency exit to supply me with a distraction and, so far at least, nothing more had come of that.

"So, now what?" asked Dave.

"I don't know. I originally wanted to finish this today, but Sparx thinks we won't be able to make this work until the last day of the Carnival, when the Vulcans overthrow King Boreas."

"Why?" Dave looked over at the fire hare.

"Belief."

"Huh?" Dave was clearly puzzled.

"The Winter Carnival is an engine for driving belief." Sparx leaned back and assumed his teacher face. "Belief can be used to amplify magic. You both saw that when Kalvan used silvertongue to amp up the *Henry V* speech."

"You know I don't remember a word of that," said Dave.

Sparx nodded. "Again, because of belief. The Carnival does something similar by getting a whole bunch of people to invest themselves in the myth of Vulcanus Rex and Boreas."

"I'll take your word for it," said Dave.

"You have more than my word to go on. Remember what the Rusalka said in Her rhyme: *He who would break Winter's power must await his proper hour.*"

That made my nerves twinge. "I really thought we were just going to get the suit and then go after Oscar right away. The only reason I didn't want to try as soon as we had it yesterday was because confronting the Darkness left me feeling like an old boot."

"You're whining again," said Sparx. "You need to have patience."

"Speaking of which," said Dave. "My mom won't have any for me if I don't get home soon. I wish I could stay, but I can't. Here." He held out a twenty-dollar bill.

"What's that for?" I asked.

"You need to get some better food into you than week-old sugar bombs. Go get a burger or three."

I felt heat pinch the corners of my eyes. "I can't take this." I knew Dave's family didn't have much money, and twenty bucks was a lot for him.

"You'd do it for me."

"Dave . . ."

"You can pay me back later, after this is all over."

I wanted to argue with him and tell him that I didn't know if I was going to have a later. Instead, I took the money. Partly because he wanted me to have it, but even more because the thought of real food practically had me drooling. I really did need it. And that was scary as hell.

"Thank you."

"Huh. Sparx, did you do something to this suit?" I'd tried the Vulcan uniform on again after dinner, and—because it was warm and clean, even if it didn't fit right—I'd ended up falling asleep in it. Now, waking up on Friday, it was . . . different.

"No, why do you ask?"

"I . . . Look!" I tugged at the elbow.

It no longer sagged. In fact, the thing practically fit me. It was still loose in a lot of places, but not like it had been yesterday. Then, I'd felt like a gazelle in an elephant suit, all bags and wrinkles. Now, it was more like one of those outfits your parents buy a little big for you so you can grow into it. It looked less shabby, too—newer somehow, though there were still several neatly sewn patches showing.

"Aha!" said Sparx.

"What's happening?"

"Belief."

"I don't understand. You said that yesterday about waiting till the end of the Carnival; what's it got to do with the suit?"

"I think the suit is telling you I'm right about our timing. If I'm wrong, we'll know for sure tomorrow, and one day more or less won't matter. But if I'm right, it could make all the difference in the world."

"Cool!" Dave picked up one of the red leather gauntlets.

It shone like polished fire here on this Sunday morning. It also fit like it had been made for me. The whole uniform did. From boots to helmet and all points in between, the outfit could have been tailored specifically for me. Thursday I'd needed to stuff paper towels into the toes of the boots to keep them from slopping around. Friday morning, the boots had fit okay, though they still rubbed me wrong, and a couple of old and carefully patched rips in the pants had vanished in the night.

Saturday, everything had been tighter and brighter and somehow newer-looking, as if it could see what was coming and was preparing itself in much the same way that I was. But the fit still wasn't quite perfect, and Sparx's insistence on waiting one more day to time the coming confrontation with the final moments of the Carnival and King Boreas's annual defeat by Vulcanus Rex made a whole lot more sense, even if I hated waiting.

This morning the transformation was complete, with the baggy old wool of the pants and jacket having become something much tougher and shinier, more like a snowmobile racing suit, and the rough cape transformed into a flowing, jagged-edged marvel that looked as if someone had stitched it from living fire. The helmet had gone from looking like a cheap theatrical prop when I'd first taken it out of the case to something a Roman centurion would have been proud to wear into battle. It had also acquired a pair of snowmobile goggles from somewhere.

I had always thought of the Vulcans as sort of ridiculous, the red-clad clowns of the Carnival, but when I looked in the mirror now, I didn't see a clown at all. I saw a figure that would have been right at home in a big-budget superhero movie, a sort of avatar of fire. Perhaps even more surprising was how well the outfit masked the terrified thirteen-year-old inside. If clothes make the person, the transformed Vulcan uniform had created a champion with some real hope of bringing down the Winter King.

If.

It is the scariest of words, and no less so for being a short one. If clothes make the person. If the outfit only concealed my weakness. If I was strong enough to face Oscar. If I had chosen a battle I couldn't win. If I could defeat him and rescue my mother. If I died trying and failed her. If. If. If.

It was Sunday and Carnival's end, and I was so terrified I was literally shaking. Dave came over and put a hand on my shoulder— he'd gotten up early and convinced his mother to let him come downtown for the unseating of Boreas so he could be with me.

"You've got this," he said.

"Do you really think so?" He didn't answer me, but the look on his face told me he was very nearly as worried as I was. Sparx didn't say anything, either, and that was even scarier—I'd never seen the hare looking so subdued.

I took the gauntlet from Dave and slipped it on. "I guess we'd better get started, huh?"

"Cue the dramatic music," said Dave. "Let's go break some heads."

Except this wasn't a movie, and one of the fundamental problems of being thirteen without anyone to drive you places was getting around. It was more than a mile to my house, and Sunday bus service is limited at best. It took us twenty minutes, and then the house was dark and empty when we got there. The thermostat was set to AWAY, and there was no note to tell me where Oscar and my mother had gone.

Worse, there was the sense that no one had been there for days, possibly since I'd escaped from the delvers over a week ago. Sparx said the house smelled long vacant. After keying myself up for a fight, the anticlimax left me feeling as cold and dark as the house.

"So, now what?" asked Dave.

I shook my head. "I don't know. This wasn't in the script."

Dave grimaced. "Who knew the biggest problem was going to be *finding* the villain?"

"Our challenges aren't always what we expect them to be," said Sparx.

"This isn't about challenges, this is about my mom." My panic was fading into a sick certainty that I was going to be too late.

"We'll find them," said Sparx, but I didn't believe him.

"I guess we try the capitol and hope it's open for the Carnival."

It wasn't, but Sparx slipped in and scouted things out, likewise finding it empty even of the Darkness. That was two strikes, and the only other place I knew to try was the caves where I had been imprisoned under the Mississippi River bluffs. That felt wrong, but none of us had any better ideas, so once more we started walking.

The Winter Carnival's final day was in full swing by then, filling downtown with thousands of revelers. Before we were halfway to the river we'd had a dozen people stop us so they could get their picture taken with a Vulcan. I wanted to scream at them to just let me pass, but I didn't think having a public meltdown would help anything. Besides, I didn't know of any law against impersonating a Vulcan, but I didn't want to find out the hard way that I was wrong.

The only good thing I could say about the whole thing was that between my uniform and the fire in my heart, I wasn't freezing

on one of the coldest days of the year. Dave, on the other hand . . .
After a while, Sparx moved over to ride on his shoulder and
keep him warm. Now that he had his full powers back, he could
make himself invisible to all but the most robust sort of magical
vision.

Rather than heading straight south toward the river, we angled
west, figuring on crossing the railroad bridge again. That was the
plan until we reached the science museum nearly an hour later
and I happened to glance out over the frozen river.

"The ice palace!" What better place to find the Winter King?
As soon as it occurred to me I felt his presence, like a frigid wind
clawing at my face. "Sparx!"

The hare nodded at me from Dave's shoulder. "I know, I can
feel him there, too."

Dave, who had settled into a subdued silence, brightened
now. "Let's do this."

We turned left, heading for the bridge that led to the island
and Oscar. The crowds grew thicker as we got closer to the palace and the heart of the celebration, and that meant more stops
for pictures. It was maddening. I'd just pasted on my fifth fake
smile in as many minutes when a woman asked me why I wasn't
already on the island.

"Huh?"

The woman gave me a "duh" look. "The big confrontation
between Vulcanus Rex and King Boreas is supposed to start in,
like, half an hour. Shouldn't you be with the rest of the Vulcan
Krewe?"

I realized then exactly what the Rusalka had meant about the proper hour, and I broke into a sort of congested jog, forcing my way through the crowd as best I could, with Dave trailing behind. I had no idea what would happen if I missed my moment, and I didn't dare find out.

It took another fifteen minutes to get to the island, a passage that actually got a lot easier when, at Sparx's suggestion, I started shouting, "Vulcan coming through!" and "Got a hot date with the Winter King!"

When we arrived on the edge of the crowd around the palace, I could see King Boreas and his court of Winds arranged on a big stage in front of the main gates. Whatever was going on up there, Vulcanus Rex hadn't arrived yet, and that gave us some breathing time. Rather than push forward to the stage, we angled along the edge of the crowd, eeling our way toward the side of the palace—I had no interest in the Carnival King; I wanted the real one, and I wouldn't find him on a stage out front. He was somewhere inside; I could feel his presence there like slivers of ice in my bones.

I more than half expected security to stop us when we reached the outer wall of ice blocks they'd constructed around the palace, but when I approached an arched side gate the woman there just smiled and waved me through. "Sending a few of you around back to come in through the palace? Smart. That'll look great, but you'd better hurry."

Dave started to follow me but she stopped him. "I'm really sorry, but if you don't have a pass you'll have to go to the main entrance."

I opened my mouth to argue with her, but Dave shook his

head. "GO! The sirens are coming and you're out of time. I'll catch up."

I hadn't noticed them until he mentioned it, but Dave was right. Vulcanus Rex and his Krewe always rode around the city on a big old antique fire engine, and the siren was unmistakable.

I didn't want to leave him, but I didn't have any choice. "Thanks!" Sparx hopped off Dave's shoulder and onto mine, as I bolted into the outer bailey of the castle and broke left, heading around the back.

Another security guard waved me in through the ice gate there—the palace had very sensibly been designed for one-way traffic, with carnival-goers coming in through the main gates out front, touring through the structure, and leaving by the back. The interior was deserted, with everyone out front to watch the big showdown between Boreas and the Vulcans. That let me speed quickly through to the inner entrance gate, where I slid to a halt.

Where was Oscar? I'd gone through the whole palace—not a big task since most of the construction was solid ice—but I hadn't seen any sign of him or my mom, and I was getting desperate. What was going on? Before I could make any sense of it, a huge roar sounded from the crowd out front as the siren wound down to silence. Vulcanus Rex had arrived.

"Now what?" I demanded of Sparx. "I can feel him, but I can't find him, and *this* is the proper hour!"

"I don't know." Sparx shook his head worriedly. "He's here somewhere. He's got to be."

Where was the Winter King? I whipped my head around madly, hoping for inspiration. And then I had it. Where do you find a king? On his throne, of course. But where was that? I looked up at the massive tower centering the castle. According to the articles I'd read about building it, the inside of the tower was completely inaccessible. Because of the height, the weight of the tower approached the limits of what ice could support, and they hadn't dared to weaken it by putting any doors or other openings in that core structure.

So, the frozen heart of the ice palace, which was the center and focus of the city's celebration of winter, was completely cut off from the outside world. But Oscar had ways of coming and going that most people could only dream of. If he could get into the tower, then what better site for Winter's Throne? I turned to scan the palace rooms looking for a place where I could access the base of the tower.

"What is it?" asked Sparx. "Do you know where Oscar is?"

"Maybe." I hadn't quite finished laying out my thinking for him when we found what I was looking for, and I knew I was right. "Look at that!" I pointed.

"What?" asked Sparx.

"The walls are clear, and in most of the palace you can see at least partway through them, but all I can see through the tower foundation is *darkness*."

"He's there." Sparx nodded. "With his ally."

"Yes." I placed both hands on the ice in front of me and opened the doors of my heart.

Where the fires touched, water began to flow. Within a minute my hands were six inches into the ice and a circular hole maybe three feet across was forming around them. The base of the tower was thicker than I was tall, and I had to scramble along on my knees as I burned my way through. I spared a moment to worry about the fact that Dave hadn't caught up with us yet, but I couldn't wait for him.

Achingly cold water quickly drenched me, running down my arms and along my sides as well as soaking through my pants and boots where I knelt in the stream. The fire in my heart fought the chill, but there was only so much it could do given the heavy flow, and my skin felt as though I'd been scraped with razors of ice.

If that wasn't bad enough, there was also the series of ominous creaks and pops sounding through the walls around me with increasing frequency as I pushed my way deeper and deeper into the ice. The construction team had feared putting doors in the tower, and here I was making a very crude one without any sort of special reinforcements.

The more I thought about that, the more it scared me, but then my hands broke through the last thin sheet of ice and I tumbled forward into the tower. For a brief moment I could see nothing as Darkness filled the space around me, but I answered it with soul light, and the Darkness vanished as I scrambled back to my feet.

The inner chamber was a square twenty feet per side with the ceiling a hundred feet above. In the corner nearest me a spiral staircase made of stone that looked as if it had grown there rather than been constructed led down into the earth. In the center of the back wall a stone dais held a pair of thrones, one of ice, the other of charred driftwood.

On the ice throne sat Oscar, dressed all in white with the Corona Borealis on his brow. He smiled at me now, cold and cruel, his gaze mocking. But I barely noticed. I was too busy looking at the other throne and my mother. Her thick, smoky hair hung wild and tangled, laced with dry leaves and crackling twigs. A mad smile touched her lips while a nimbus of fire danced among the folds of her red velvet dress and along the arms of her blackened throne.

She turned to look at me then, and there was no hint of warmth or recognition in her eyes, no welcome or relief. Nothing but the turbulent chaos of untamed fire and its endless appetite for destruction.

Here was my mother as I saw her in my nightmares, devoured from within by the fire of a spirit beyond her power to control or contain.

My heart shattered in my chest and I fell to my knees.

20

Burning the Candle at Both Ends

LAUGHTER. COLD AS ICE, hard as granite, cruel as the winter sky. Oscar's laughter.

It rolled over me as I knelt on the floor of Winter's throne room, broken in heart and sick in spirit.

He stood and walked slowly toward me. "Did you think it would be so easy, Kalvan? That all you had to do to defeat the Crown of the North was put on a fancy red snowsuit and waltz in to face me? Foolish child."

"Now would be a really good time to get up and start fighting back," Sparx said from his perch on my shoulder. "Because in about five minutes it's going to be too late."

His voice was quiet but deadly urgent. I ignored him.

Oscar was closer now. "Look at your mother, Kalvan. Meet her eyes. Understand what lies behind them. That's what she *is* without me anchoring her broken soul. I don't think you can beat me, boy. Not on your best day. Not even with the weight of all that ritual out there behind you." He waved vaguely toward the front of the tower, where the crowd was cheering the Vulcans on to victory. "I don't think you're even going to try. Because the cost is one you haven't the will to pay. Defeat the King, destroy his Queen."

Sparx slapped me lightly. "Kalvan, come on!"

Oscar's eyes flashed angrily. "Oh yes, the k*tsathsha. Cetius, deal with it!"

The delver erupted out of the earth by Oscar's feet. "With pleasure, Oz." He reached for Sparx, but the hare leaped clear of my shoulder, landing some feet away and bursting into bright flame.

The delver snarled and lunged after him, extending long stone-cutting claws in a slash the hare only barely avoided. I knew that I ought to help him, knew that I had to do something or lose any hope of victory, knew that I should care. But all I could do was look into the madness in my mother's eyes and despair. I had come to fight Oscar and rescue my mother, but he had defeated me without even lifting a finger.

It was over. I bent my head and waited for Oscar to do whatever he wanted with me.

Kalvan. My mother's voice, soft and quiet but steady and present. I looked up into her eyes, but there was no one home there.

Kalvan. Sharper this time, more insistent. Not through my ears, though. Not in my head at all. In my heart. The voice of a memory or a dream. *I believe in you.*

I blinked and thought back to the day my mother and I had

spent looking for the suit I was wearing now, to the conversation we'd had that morning. Phrases came back to me.

You have a true heart, Kalvan. There's nothing in the world stronger than that. All you have to do is listen to your heart.

I turned my gaze on Oscar, who stood above me now. What did my heart have to say about Oscar? What did it have to say about a man who would use my mother's illness as a weapon against me? I felt the fire within burst back into full flower at the thought. There were no words there, but the message was clear. What Oscar was doing was wrong. It was wrong, and he had to be stopped. Right here, right now, and there was only one person who had any chance of doing that.

That was another lesson I had learned at the Free School. How many times had I heard that the answer to "If not me, then who?" was almost always *me*. But at what cost? I didn't look at my mother, but I knew what she would have said on the subject.

Listen to your heart.

"Oscar?" I looked up at my stepfather.

"Yes, Kalvan?"

I lurched to my feet and pressed my palms flat against his chest. "Go to hell!"

Then I opened my heart. I wanted Oscar to hear *exactly* what the fires had to say to him.

Ash and char, sun and star, wind and smoke, ash and oak.

A river of flame poured out of my hands and engulfed my stepfather. If he had been a normal man he would have died then, but if he had been a normal man I never would have unleashed the fires on him.

He was a hard man. Stone hard. A cold man. The Winter

King. A man of enormous power. The fires roared over him and he staggered back, throwing up arms suddenly sheathed in stone to shield his face and chest. It saved his life, though his hair burned away in an instant and the fur of his robes flared and charred.

I felt the ground twist and buck beneath my feet—Oscar's element acting to protect its master. I should have been thrown to the ground then, but somehow I held my feet through all the tremors. Held them and kept pouring forth the fires of my heart until the entire central column of the great tower filled with flames.

I could feel the space through the medium of fire, the hard cold walls towering above and around me. The knot of human stone that was Oscar, like a rock in the corner of the fireplace. Sparx, a distinct flame within the greater flames—hotter and brighter and filled with light. My mother, another twist of flame, part and yet apart—cooler, smoky and swirling and somehow infinitely sad. The deep, unclosed hole where Cetius had plunged into the earth in his rush to escape. Dave, kneeling in the opening I had cut, one hand across his face, unable to advance into the fires, but ready to help in any way he could.

I felt Oscar's will pushing back against my own. Hard. Cold. Powerful. Yet overmatched. In any other time and place, I could not have defeated him. Here, now, with the weight of the Carnival's ritual battle between winter's Boreas and summer's Vulcans only a few thin spans of ice away? The power of the crowd and its belief in winter's ultimate demise was fuel for the fire of my soul. I didn't know if it would be enough, but I burned it all now, pressing down on Oscar with the full weight of my will and my heart.

With a sudden cry of rage and anguish, Oscar ripped the Crown from his head and threw it at my face. I don't think any talisman less powerful could have passed through the fires I commanded then, but he had chosen his weapon well. The Crown struck me above the left eye, a sharp, burning blow that had blood sheeting down to blind me on that side in an instant. While I was distracted, Oscar turned and threw himself down the spiral stairs, burning as he went.

In that same instant, as the fires fell, Dave leaped out and ran pell-mell for the throne and my mother. He caught her arm and pulled her toward the entrance. He might not have been able to fight someone like Oscar, but he understood why I was here. I reopened the gates of my heart and sent fire roaring down the stairs after Oscar while Dave dragged my mother back to the hole I'd made. I started after Oscar.

Dave pushed my mother through the gap behind me. From the top of the stairs, I saw Oscar lying halfway down, a shield of stone held between us. It wasn't enough; I would end this now.

But then, before I could do anything more, he chanted, "Earth and stone, blood and bone, beat the drum, darkness come."

Then he closed his fist and the earth pulled him under. The steps collapsed in on themselves, closing the hole in the ground and blocking my path. Whether it was Oscar's physical withdrawal, his release of the Crown, or something else entirely, his tower ended with his reign. In a single instant the thirteen thousand blocks of the ice palace melted and fell, taking me with them.

Black water, colder than death and heavier than stone. It pressed on me from every side. I knew that I was drowning and that this time there was no one to save me. This time would be my end. I wanted to fight it, but I had nothing left. I surrendered to the waters and drowned.

Not this time.

What? That was not my mother's voice speaking into my heart, though it sounded familiar. Again, I thought, *What?*

Perhaps later, but not today.

Not today, what?

There was no immediate answer, but the pressure eased and I saw a bright spot approaching me like a thrown torch. Or, rather, I was approaching it. As became clear a moment later when the Mississippi spat me out through a hole in the ice. I rocketed upward, riding a geyser of dark water that set me on my feet on the railroad bridge as neatly as a child putting away a doll.

For one brief instant I saw the Rusalka's face in the tower of water. "Today, I owe you a favor. Tomorrow . . ." A laugh, and then She was gone and I was alone.

Though not for long. I hadn't gone ten paces before a streamer of fire dropped out of the sky to land beside me. Sparx gave me a very hard look as he shaped himself out of the flames. "Don't EVER do that again."

"You got it."

"What?" He looked nonplussed.

"I said, you got it. I will never, ever do that again. What did you think I said?"

"I don't know. I just expected you to argue with me."

"I really don't like drowning, and not doing it again seems like a good idea," I said. "So why would I do that?"

Sparx looked at me crossly. "Because you're very difficult,

and trying, and hard on my heart. Getting washed away when the tower fell and leaving Dave and me to rescue your mother while you pretended to drown. It's inconsiderate."

"*I'm* difficult?" I snorted.

"That's what I said, yes." Sparx nodded.

"Well, it *must* be true, then."

"Obviously."

"Silly rabbit."

"That's silly *hare*."

"Fine, silly hare."

"Accursed Master."

"Where's my mom?"

"Dave got her clear before the tower went down. I'll take you to them."

"She's all right?"

"As all right as ever, yes."

A horrible thought occurred to me. "What about the crowd?"

"Cold and wet, but otherwise all right. As far as I can tell, you're the only one who decided to go for a swim."

"Kalvan?" Genevieve Monroe stuck her head out of her office as I dashed for the front door and the bus.

"Yes, Mom."

"I made you lunch."

"Thanks! Where is it?"

"It was your favorite, a bacon, bacon, bacon, lettuce, and tomato sandwich. I made it around midnight."

"And?" Somehow I didn't think this was going to end with me eating a sandwich.

"I got to repotting the spider plants—always best done by moonlight."

I nodded. "You've said that before."

"Anyway, when I got done, I was hungry. So I ate your sandwich."

"That's great, Mom. Why are you telling me all this?"

"I'm not entirely sure."

"All right. Love you, Mom. Gotta go catch my bus now. Bye." I gave her a quick peck on the cheek.

"Kalvan?"

"Yes?" I forced myself not to sound as aggravated as I felt.

"I really do believe in you."

"I know, Mom. I know."

I turned away so she wouldn't see the tears blurring my eyes and headed for the bus and school. Because that's what you do when you're thirteen.

Oscar was gone and the Corona Borealis was tucked neatly away with my great-grandfather's Vulcan uniform. No, that's not quite right. The uniform was mine now, and the transformation it had undergone was a permanent one as far as I could tell. My mother was . . . well, my mother, and as all right as ever thanks to a little help from my friends.

I had made common cause with the Mississippi and burned down the ice palace and found the fire in my heart. And none of that got me out of school. But that was okay, because it was a pretty darn amazing school, one where the principal was willing to let me get away with skipping classes from time to time as long as the school board didn't hear about it, where my advisor let me park a magic rabbit in her office and the science teacher had started instructing me in magic, and where my best friend would be waiting to meet me when I got in.

"Sparx, come on, we have a bus to catch!"

There was a flash and a bang and I felt a sudden weight on my shoulder. "Your wish is my command, O Accursed Master."

Author's Note

The Free School of Saint Paul as depicted in this book is not the Saint Paul Open School. Though my time at the latter certainly informed my creation of the former, all the characters and situations in this volume are fictitious and creations of my imagination rather than reconstructions from memory. That said, my eleven years at the Open School are fundamental to my life and to my work as an artist, and I would be a very different person without them. I owe so much to the school, its teachers, founders, and my fellow students. Thank you all. The me that I am today wouldn't be possible without you.

It is also worth noting that the downtown Saint Paul of this book differs in some significant ways from Saint Paul as it is now. It's been thirty-five years since I used to sneak off to play hooky downtown, and the version of the city I describe in this book is a mixture of Saint Paul as it was then, as it is today, and of pure fancy that serves the purpose of my story.

On the subject of mental illness and its treatment within the book, there are things I can't say without violating the privacy of people I love, but I will note that I occasionally take anxiety medications and also that I grew up in a house with people who had significant neurochemical issues, including paranoid schizophrenia and major depression. To this day, I have people I love who have mental health issues. I come at the subject very much from the inside.

Acknowledgments

Extra-special thanks are owed to Laura McCullough, Jack Byrne, Holly West, Jean Feiwel, and Sean Murphy.

Many thanks also to: my web guru, Ben; my family: Carol, Paul and Jane, Lockwood and Darlene, Judy, Kat, Sean, and all the rest; my extended support structure: Matt, Mandy, Mike, Sandy, Kim, Jonny, Lynne, Michael, Steph, Tom, Ann . . . and so many more. With big thanks to my "twin," Bethany, for the accounting garble.

Feiwel and Macmillan folks past and present who have been instrumental in making my books here the best they can be and helping me to succeed: Ilana Worrell, Bethany Reis, Kim Waymer, Liz Szabla, Rich Deas, Liz Dresner, Dave Barrett, Nicole Liebowitz Moulaison, Lauren Burniac, Anna Roberto, Christine Barcellona, Ashley Woodfolk, Morgan Dubin, Jeremy Ross, and Ksenia Winnicki.

GO FISH

KELLY MCCULLOUGH

What was your inspiration for Sparx?
I'm not sure, really. When I started thinking about writing this book, I knew that I wanted Kalvan to have a familiar, but I wasn't sure what kind. I love the whole idea of familiars and have for practically forever. Who wouldn't want a magical friend who loves you and helps keep you sane even on your worst days? In Kalvan's case, I knew that I wanted him to be a power of fire and a child of fire because fire under control is one of our greatest tools and fire out of control is one of the worst dangers we can face. From there, I decided that Kalvan needed a creature of fire that was both friend and semi-adversary, a trickster. A fox seemed too easy, and a salamander wouldn't have been huggable enough. So, I started looking around in my head, and suddenly there was Sparx, red and rough and full of sass.

Kalvan was inspired by his drama teacher, Evelyn. Did you have someone you looked up to as a kid?
I had a number of important mentors and role models as a kid, but the one with the strongest parallels to Evelyn was my drama teacher, Vaughn Koenig. In my eleven and a half years at the Saint Paul Open School, she was my teacher for at least twenty classes and had the biggest impact on me of all my teachers there.

When did you start doing theater? What was your favorite role?

I started performing in various sorts of theater at the age of eleven and it was the main focus of my life until my early twenties, when I shifted to writing after I got my degree in theater. In terms of formal roles, the favorite part I ever played was Reverend Samuel Parris in *The Crucible*, but my main thrust as a performer was always in improv theater and comedy where I didn't ever have a formal character. I loved improv and the constant shifting and adapting to keep the audience focused and laughing.

What book is on your nightstand now?

There are about a hundred, which is pretty typical for me. These days they're all on my phone because I do most of my reading electronically, but even back when I was a kid and almost nobody even had a computer, I always kept a lot of books on my nightstand. Which can have its downsides. When I was twelve or thirteen, I accidentally started a book-a-lanche one night that dropped forty or fifty novels onto my head and face. Fortunately they were all paperbacks, but even so, it hurt. The books I'm reading right now are *Last Song Before Night* (Ilana C. Myer), *Arcanos Unraveled* (Jonna Gjevre), *The Desert of Souls* (Howard Andrew Jones), *Grit* (Angela Duckworth), and *All Systems Red* (Martha Wells). Oh, and *Genghis Khan and the Making of the Modern World* (Jack Weatherford).

If you could travel in time, where would you go and what would you do?

I refuse to answer the question on the grounds that it might tend to incriminate me . . . Uh, I mean I would go to ancient Rome and walk the streets of the last days of the republic. That's my story and I'm sticking to it.

What was your favorite thing about school?
Skipping classes! Just kidding. I went to a really awesome school that has a lot in common with the school in this book. I liked a lot of things about school. I enjoyed most of my classes and I still love learning. I had great teachers and I made friends that I still get along with forty-five years later.

If you could have a familiar, what form would you like it to take?
Mine would be a cat. A magic cat, of course, that could fly, and teleport, and take me with it all over the world.

What's the best thing about being an author?
I love it all! I get to play make-believe for a living and tell stories that make people laugh and cry and sometimes I even change how they see the world. I get to choose my own hours and work when it suits me. I can sleep in if I'm tired or wake up in the middle of the night and work then. I'm part of a community of writers who live all over the world, and I have made so many new and amazing friends in this life that it's hard to believe. If I want to know more about something and I tell experts what I do, they will make time to talk to me about the cool things they do or take me on tours through the parts of their facilities that most people never see. I have marvelous readers whom I love to meet and interact with. It's really all good. It was hard to get here, and it's not the world's most secure job, but there's nothing I'd rather be doing.

Do you have any writing habits?
Not really in the sense the question is asking. I have work habits, like writing a minimum number of words every day and starting my morning with caffeine, but nothing like always wearing the same hat or only using a certain type of pen.

What advice do you wish someone had given you when you were younger?

I can't think of much advice that I didn't get that would have been useful. I was told to always try to be kind. I was told to find something to do that I could love. I was told that I could be anything I wanted if I tried hard enough. I was told to follow my dreams. I was told to be myself. Basically, I got a ton of good advice, and I followed a lot of it and I'm pretty happy where I ended up. Most of the dumb things I did and dead-end paths I followed were despite advice telling me not to do those things. I mean, *follow the good advice* would have been great advice, but I don't think I'd have done anything useful with it.

**KALVAN'S POWERS AREN'T
DONE WITH HIM YET . . .**

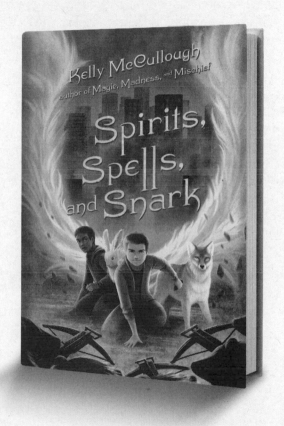

Keep reading for an excerpt.

1

When Trouble Knocks

"**ARE YOU SURE** this thing is magical?" Dave slowly turned the Crown of the North under the bright basement lights. The seven diamonds adorning the simple silver circlet barely flickered. "It doesn't look it."

"I'm sure." I touched a finger to the place above my left eye where I carried a mirrored imprint of the Crown's peak—a metallic silver triangle perhaps an inch across with a circle in the middle, like the eye in the pyramid on the back of a dollar bill.

"Have I mentioned how much I dislike that mark, Kalvan?" The rangy fire hare was stretched out on the thick green carpet my erstwhile stepfather had used to mimic the lawns in his model of the Minnesota state capitol. Sparx's fur burned a merry sort of red, though the flames never ignited anything he didn't want them to.

"Only about a million times, familiar mine, but most people

can't even see it." The scar was invisible to most everyone who didn't have magic—Dave being a notable exception.

"That's a good part of why it makes me nervous," grumbled Sparx. "I've never seen a mark like it before, and I'm old enough to find strange magic alarming."

I leaned over and poked his belly, sending the flames dancing through the red fur. "You sound more like a mother hen than a magic bunny."

Sparx gave me his best disappointed-teacher stare—it was a shame he didn't have glasses to peer over. "That's *fire hare*, as you well know, noxious child."

I was thirteen, but I let the *child* thing pass. Sparx is an elemental spirit and old enough that my *mom* probably counts as a child for him. Or my great-grandfather, for that matter. Instead of arguing with Sparx, I ran a finger around the edges of the silver scar again. I'd gotten it when my stepfather, Oscar, threw the Crown at me during our duel at the Winter Carnival a month and a half ago, and I was kind of disappointed so few people could see it. I thought it made me look more adult, not to mention mysterious and even a little heroic, the way a pirate's patch or a mystical tattoo might.

"Do you think it'll do anything special today?" Dave turned the Crown so it framed his dark face—like some antique portrait. "Because it's the equinox and all? Sundown's only moments away."

"I hope not." I shrugged. "What do you think, fuzzball?"

Sparx snorted grumpily. "Given the Crown remains fallow until Summer's reign begins in a month, it seems unlikely, O Accursed Master."

And *that* told me I'd been riding him a little too hard. Technically, Sparx *is* my familiar, but he only calls me Accursed Master when he's teasing or really irritated, and this didn't sound like teasing. "Sorry, Sparx, I'm kind of flipped out about the whole thing. I know Oscar's not the Winter King anymore and we warded the house nine ways from Sunday, but I keep expecting my earth power step-father to come back up through the floor like something out of a horror film."

Sparx shook his head. "The wards will hold and they run very deep, and I doubt he'd come at you openly even when you are beyond their protection. You beat him at a symbolic level as well as a sor-cerous one. That puts a great weight of magic on your side in any future conflict."

I was letting out a little sigh of relief when—

THUMP! THUMP! THUMP!

"Is that someone knocking on your front door?" Dave's voice came out tight and strained. I couldn't blame him—there was six feet of dirt between the roof of the ancient cellar and the much newer house above.

"There's no way we could hear it throu—"

THUMP! THUMP! THUMP!

I felt a fresh touch of winter run icy-footed down my spine. "Sparx!"

The hare vanished in a puff of flame, leaving an arcing trail of smoke that ran from the table where he'd been sitting to the lime-stone barrel vault above. Several seconds flickered past.

THUMP! THUMP! THUMP!

Sparx returned with a flash, his expression simultaneously seri-ous and bemused. "Sunset has brought you an interesting visitor. You'd better answer that door before your mother thinks to."

I doubted there was much risk of that. Not with my mother . . .

the way she was now. Her mental health issues had gotten considerably worse since the Crown went fallow, but I pushed that thought aside. Something about Sparx's tone made me dash for the spiral stairs leading up to the house proper. Dave dropped the Crown back into the warded circle on the table and ran after me.

I half expected to find a splintered ruin when I got to the front door, but the wood looked fine. The knock came again, only . . .

rap rap rap

The taps sounded so gently this time I could barely hear them.

What the . . . I yanked the door open and found myself facing a tall, slender, professionally dressed woman with sooty-black hair in a pixie cut and the amber eyes I'd only ever seen on my mother and in the mirror.

"Hello?"

"You must be Kalvan." Her voice was rich and full, yet somehow colder than it had any right to be. "I've *so* been looking forward to finally getting the chance to meet you. I can see a lot of Genevieve in your face."

Okay, that's a little weird—Genevieve is my mother's name. "Got it in one. But I'm afraid I don't recognize you . . ."

She extended her hand and I shook it bemusedly. Her fingers were icy—literally, like a steel handrail in the winter cold.

She smiled, and the expression set a weird combination of concern and anticipation dancing along my nerves. "Don't you, then? I'm your aunt Noelle."

Memories of old conversations and older pictures shocked through me and I suddenly had trouble breathing. Now she'd said it, there was no doubt this was my mother's older sister. Noelle looked exactly as she had in the picture on my mother's dresser. A picture that had been taken three years before I was born and a few weeks before Noelle died.

"Don't look so surprised, nephew. I can see from your heart and your familiar you've learned how magic runs in our family." She nodded at Sparx, who had taken up a perch on the railing of the stairs to the upper level. "I've known Genevieve needed me for some time, but the bonds of the grave are horribly strong, and I hadn't the power to burn them away. Not till tonight's turn of the fallow months severed the last vestiges of Winter's hold on both power and my sister. Now, how are we going to break it to her?"

My dead aunt stepped past me, and I started to turn to follow her. "I, uh . . . huh, oooooof." But then—as my back touched the wall—I found myself gently sliding to the floor when my knees turned to butter.

"Are you all right?" Noelle stopped midstride.

"I . . . maybe?" I felt awfully light-headed.

Dave pushed past her and squatted in front of me. "You don't look so hot."

Sparx nodded. "Try putting your head between your knees."

Something about the hare's voice made me suspicious. "You knew!"

Sparx blinked innocently and his eyes seemed to grow to three times their normal size—like a cartoon rabbit's. "Knew what, O Accursed Master?"

"That it was my aunt at the door!"

Sparx shrugged. "There's a strong family resemblance in the hair and eyes, even if your coloring is more like your father's." I was much darker than either my mother or my aunt. "What's your point?"

"I . . . but she's, uh . . ." I trailed off as I caught an amused twinkle in my aunt's eyes.

"Dead?" she asked gently.

"Yeah, that."

Now she laughed. "He's a fire hare; he couldn't possibly have missed it."

Dave abruptly sat down beside me. "Wait, you mean that thing she said about the *bonds of the grave* . . ."

Noelle nodded. "A major difficulty, but not impossible given the proper circumstances and sufficient motivation." She canted her head to one side. "Right; I'm guessing neither of you is a tea drinker, so it had best be hot chocolate." Without another word, she turned and headed deeper into the house with Sparx trailing along behind.

Dave reached over and pinched me viciously.

"Ouch! What's that for?"

"I wanted to make sure you weren't dreaming."

I blinked. "Aren't you supposed to ask someone else to pinch *you*?"

He shook his head. "When *I* dream about zombies they look like zombies, not like some lady who could be a partner at the law firm where my mom works. If it's a dream, it's all you, buddy. Mine are nothing like this crazy."

I glanced at the red spot on my forearm. "I don't think it's a dream."

"Then we'd better go after her."

We found Noelle in the kitchen with the teakettle held between her hands like a basketball. Even as we entered, steam began to pour from the spout. "Now, where are the mugs?"

"Left of the fink, fecond felf up." Sparx dropped onto the table and let a pair of hot-chocolate envelopes fall out of his mouth.

Within a few moments, Noelle had offered us each a neatly stirred mug, though she didn't take any herself. "My sister is above." It wasn't a question, and she turned toward the back stairs as she spoke—the house was a duplex my stepfather had converted to single-family living. "Come on, you can drink on the way."

I looked at Sparx, hoping for some clue. I mean, the script for pretty much every vampire or zombie movie ever said I should be trying to put her back in the grave. Like, yesterday. But movies about the undead didn't normally start anything like the way the last ten minutes had unfolded. Add in that Sparx didn't seem alarmed . . . In fact, he just smiled and jerked his chin toward the stairs my aunt had already started climbing.

So, taking a huge slug of hot chocolate, I followed her. "Aunt Noelle?"

"Yes, dear?"

"Mom's not really herself." *Understatement of the year!* She's never been all that tightly moored to reality's shore, and now that I'd driven my stepfather away, she seemed to be drifting slowly but steadily farther and farther out to sea. "In fact, she's pretty fragile."

"I know. It's not the first time. I'll see what I can do."

Riiiiight. The dead lady was going to bring my mom back to reality. This was *so* not going to end well.

My mother was sitting cross-legged on the floor of what had been the upstairs dining room, with all the lights out. Her back was to us and she didn't turn. Her long black hair hung in thick tangles, and the red velvet dress she wore had broad tears along the hem.

She'd arranged the full skirt around her in a loose circle and the rips showed dark in the moonlight.

I turned on the kitchen lights and a bright rectangle reached across the floor, stopping just short of the edge of her skirt. "Mom?"

"What is it, Kalvan?" She still didn't turn around. "I'm trying to find the place where flint meets steel."

"Uh . . ."

"It's important because steel and flint are earth, but together they beget spark, and spark becomes fire."

As with so many things my mother said these days, I didn't know how to answer. "We've got a visitor."

Noelle walked around in front of my mother. "Genevieve?" Her voice came out as gentle as if she were trying to soothe a fussy baby.

"There you are." My mother sounded relieved. "How was the drive-in? I'll never understand what you see in those awful spy movies."

Noelle blinked once, then smiled. "It was all right. Not my favorite by a long shot, but not bad. The popcorn was terrible."

My mother laughed. "It always is."

Dave poked me in the ribs and mouthed, *What the heck?*

I shook my head. One of my mother's more bizarre habits is restarting a conversation in the middle, days or even weeks after you thought it was over. I couldn't tell whether this was that or something else related to her current condition.

My mother leaned back and put her hands on the floor behind her. "Have you changed your mind about Nix? You know how much I hate to fight with you about anything important."

I twitched. *Nix* was my long-absent father's name, and it almost never passed my mother's lips. Or mine, for that matter. I knew so little about my father, but asking Mom to tell me more was pretty much the same thing as asking for a fight or a flip-out, so I'd learned to avoid the subject.

But Noelle made a noncommittal gesture with her hands, and went on as if it was nothing important. "I'm still not sure I think Nix is the best idea you've ever had, but I'm no longer convinced he's the worst."

"I said he'd grow on you."

I held my breath as I waited to hear more, but Noelle caught my eye, lifted her chin, and flicked her gaze beyond me, suggesting without saying a word that I find something else to do. I didn't want to go, but her expression told me I'd better. I nodded and caught Dave by the wrist before heading back down the stairs. Sparx seemed to think it would be all right, and I didn't know what else to do.

I dropped into a chair at the kitchen table and glared at my familiar. "I want some answers, bunny boy."

He responded rapid-fire style. "Yes. No. I don't know. Maybe. It wouldn't surprise me. And, I think she's going to do more good than harm for your mother."

"Huh?" This came from Dave, behind me.

Sparx rolled his eyes. "*Yes*, she really is dead. *No*, it's not the first time I've seen something like this. *I don't know* how it works, but sometimes the door to death swings the other way. *Maybe* it has something to do with Oscar's scheme to keep the Crown going back and forth between him and your mother. It certainly *wouldn't surprise me* if that was the case. As I mentioned when we first found out about Oscar, the Crown is supposed to pass to a new head with each turn of the seasons. Interfering with that was bound to have some very unpredictable and nasty effects."

"You are the most frustrating creature I have ever met." I glowered at Sparx.

"Hey, I live to serve."

"Sure you do." I sighed. "Do you really believe she'll do more good than harm?" I'd cheerfully invite a dozen zombies into the house if they could help my mom.

Sparx flicked his ears back and forth in the rabbit version of a shrug. "Your mother's reaction gives me hope. Sometimes the ties of the past can shift things magic dare not touch."

I winced. While my mother's problems were mostly brain chemistry, the fire in her nature only made them worse. When her condition first started deteriorating I'd asked if we could use magic to help, but Sparx felt it would do little more than add fuel to the flames already consuming her.

Sparx put a paw on my wrist. "Why don't I stay home and keep an eye on things while you're at school tomorrow."

I nodded. "That'd make me feel better."

Dave punched my shoulder. "Come on, let's watch a movie and pretend we're normal teenagers with normal problems."